DEATH OF
A CRITIC

By Dean Fuller

DEATH OF A CRITIC

An Alex Grismolet Mystery

DEAN FULLER

LITTLE, BROWN AND COMPANY
Boston   New York   Toronto   London

First Edition

The author is grateful for permission to include
the following previously copyrighted material:
Excerpt from *Intermezzo* by Jean Giraudoux.
By permission of International Creative Management, Inc.

Library of Congress Cataloging-in-Publication Data
Fuller, Dean.
    Death of a critic : an Alex Grismolet mystery / Dean Fuller. —
1st ed.
        p.   cm.
    ISBN 0-316-29601-5
    I. Title.
PS3556.U38D433   1995
813'.54 — dc20   95-11766

            10 9 8 7 6 5 4 3 2 1

                    MV - NY

        *Published simultaneously in Canada
    by Little, Brown & Company (Canada) Limited*

        Printed in the United States of America

For Loilly

DEATH OF
A CRITIC

Prologue

The Apparition

IN THE HAUT LANGUEDOC, April brings early frost to the high pasture land. Outside the mountain village of Le Pré, the slanting fields belonging to Pierre Fournier, the stone mason, remain congealed in semidarkness until the sun rises sufficiently above the Pic de Nore to evaporate the dew, chase the fog and spectres from the glens, and warm the young shepherdess minding Fournier's sheep.

This mid-April morning, the young shepherdess is Marie-Rose, age ten, Fournier's daughter by his first wife, who died bearing the child, her last of twelve. The girl, whose brothers and sisters and a favorite aunt left the village after her father remarried, has now but two friends: the sheepdog, Vercingétorix, and the Blessed Virgin, who appeared to her two weeks ago, on Friday 5 April 1985 at noon, just as the bell in the dilapidated chapel rang the Angelus.

The Virgin, dressed in white, appeared in a blaze of light with the moon at her feet and a crown of stars on her head. And where the apparition took place — in a pasture hollow a stone's throw from where Marie-Rose stood watching the sheep — there appeared a spring that now supplies fifty litres of pure mountain water per minute.

Had it not been for the spring, Marie-Rose would never have dared tell her father and stepmother about the miracle. They would've beaten her for fabricating such a story, and for daydreaming on the job. But Marie-Rose knew her father to be a practical, if not particularly spiritual, man. The spring supplied more potable water than his old well. Moreover, apart from the odd repair job to a few walls and foundations around the village, there had been no masonry work for him in nearly a year. It was, therefore, no surprise to Marie-Rose when her father, with uncharacteristic humility and piety, approached Père Labatt, the old priest in charge of the rundown chapel, described the miracle, and repeated the words the Virgin had spoken to his daughter: The people of Le Pré must do penance, say the rosary, and build a new stone church.

Part One
THE OPENING

1

Gus

WHEN SEPTEMBER CAME to Paris that year, it tantalized. The sky over the city showed signs of alarm one day, and purest beneficence the next. The Seine darkened and lightened. Still sun-burnished schoolchildren in unfamiliar new clothes, constrained by the threatening scent of chalk and book bindings, by the drone of knowledge or the flickering green screens of computers programmed to replicate the ionization equation, gazed out of lycée windows at the last golden lights of summer, fading, returning, tantalizing. Early September would not make up its mind.

This meteorologic ambivalence received scant attention from Monsieur Auguste Pezon-Schwartz. He had spent the first three days of the month sleepless, inside the Théâtre Bakoledis on Rue de Caumartin. Auguste Pezon-Schwartz, "Gus" to his colleagues, was, at age fifty, the producer-directeur of the first play of the season, a new revival of *Eurydice* by Jean Anouilh. Gus had been in rehearsal for eight weeks, during which time he had not noticed the weather. He had to replace an actor. His Eurydice and Orpheus were having an affair. The scenery, delivered late, had been loaded into the theatre and hung in an all-night session on the first of September due to a miscalculation by the scene shop, which had cost Gus double overtime because it was Sunday. The lights were hung and focused all day and night on Monday, the second. The tech rehearsal, with the entire company cutting to cues, took all day Tuesday, followed, after an hour for dinner, by the dress rehearsal, an emotional and exhausting experience, fraught with recriminations and tears, that lasted until three o'clock Wednesday morning.

Up to this point, it would have been a matter of complete indifference to Gus if it had snowed or rained chocolate kisses. But Wednesday 4 September was opening night. When he awoke at noon, Gus cocked a weather eye at the sky through his bedroom window. He switched on the TV: clear to partly cloudy, the girl in aquamarine said. Wind west at dum-dum, temperature dum-de-dum. Another beautiful day somewhere between summer and autumn. Gus normally associated beautiful weather with bad matinées. But for opening night, he'd take what they were offering.

He slowly rolled his ample flesh out of bed and padded, naked, to the bathroom with a knock-kneed, high-hipped, slightly pigeon-toed walk that was, nevertheless, surprisingly graceful for such a big man. Indeed, this walk retained vestiges of the walk he'd taught show girls and strippers thirty years before, when he worked for his uncle in Toulouse.

Gus entered the bathroom, where there was a phone next to the toilet. He sat, peed, and simultaneously called the box office.

The house was clean for tonight. House seats and critics' passes had been picked up, except for de la Pagerie's companion's, whose ticket was at the box office. Gus told the box office manager to tell Jérôme, the stage manager, to run light cue eighty twice before opening the house.

He hung up, showered, and washed his thick, wavy hair, now coloured a sort of distinguished-looking chrome. He stepped, dripping, from the shower, toweled his multiple folds with an enormous beach towel, a souvenir of a production of *The Visit* in St-Jean-de-Luz, and peered into the long mirror that stretched over the twin sinks. The mirror was opaque with steam. He seized the hair dryer and directed the hot air at the glass. As the steam evaporated, he began to see himself.

"Fade in, Gussy," he murmured, as his round, smooth-cheeked, fat kid's face emerged. While his body had changed over the years, his face had not. He still had the same fat kid's face he'd taken to boarding school at the age of eight, where he wet the bed and was the only kid that flunked recess.

It was the same face his mother covered with kisses at his bar mitzvah before she disappeared forever with a professional ballroom dancer; the same pudgy, smooth-cheeked, fat kid's face that, at eighteen, helped keep him out of the army and away from Diên Biên Phu, when his uncle (who needed him to train the girls in Toulouse) wrote the Conscription Board that Gus had flat feet and was sexually ambiguous. His uncle saved his life, gave him his start, and defended him against his furiously virile father, a lawyer, who believed there was nothing wrong with the boy that a hitch in the Foreign Legion wouldn't cure.

Gus studied the face. Why couldn't he have the face of Samuel Beckett, or Charles Aznavour, instead of this vanilla blanc-mange, Cuddles Sakall nothing? Where were the wonderful character lines? Gus deserved character lines. He'd paid his dues. He'd done stagehand, prop man, light man, scene painter, actor, writer, choreographer, box office manager, stage manager, assistant directeur, directeur, assistant to the producer, and now producer-directeur. So where was the face? He couldn't have the face of Orson Welles at least? God knows, he had the body. He even had the voice. The deeply resonant voice so essential to the directeur who, as he sits in the back of a cold, dark theatre at 3 A.M., with his overcoat draped over his shoulders, finally clears his throat and brings the eight weeks of rehearsal to an end with a solemn, reverberant "Thank you, ladies and gentlemen. Half hour is at seven-thirty."

The Théâtre Bakoledis, a block from the older Théâtre Caumartin, was built as a musical house. But, sometime in the '50s, when Paris became the graveyard of musicals, the orchestra pit was covered, four rows of seats were added, and the Théâtre Bakoledis became a straight playhouse. Because of its relatively small size, it was booked to repertory companies, short-run revivals, and mime groups. Gus had an open-ended lease on the house but had to give a two-week guarantee at three-quarter capacity.

The place had seen better days, so the exterior was painted pearl gray for the opening. There was no marquee, but new, illuminated, glass-covered sign boards, framed in delicate, rococo ironwork, had been installed on both sides of the entrance. Curtain was scheduled for 8 P.M.

At 7:15, Gus stood across the street in evening clothes, smoked, and watched the early arrivals move slowly out of the still, blue September darkness of Rue de Caumartin into the warm amber wash of the theatre lobby. The sign boards read easily from where he stood:

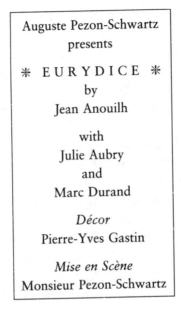

Auguste Pezon-Schwartz
presents

✳ E U R Y D I C E ✳
by
Jean Anouilh

with
Julie Aubry
and
Marc Durand

Décor
Pierre-Yves Gastin

Mise en Scène
Monsieur Pezon-Schwartz

Gus never tired of this ritual. He loved theatres: the exteriors, the interiors, the auditoriums, lobbies, backstage, fly galleries, basements. He loved the stage door alleys and tattered posters and three-sheets that hung there. Gus's dream, inherited from his uncle, was to own his own theatre someday. Théâtre Auguste.

At ten minutes past half hour, he went backstage to check on the gifts and flowers for the principals, the mementos for the bit players, stagehands, and the doorman, and the bottle of Courvoisier for the fire inspecteur.

At 7:50, he assembled the cast onstage, told them they were the most talented, the most professional, group of actors it had been his honour to know in his entire career. He then slipped through the door leading to the lower stage-left proscenium box, entered the auditorium, and joined his designer, Pierre-Yves, at the back of the house. The theatre was virtually full. The handsome, young scene designer, wearing an old smoking jacket but no tie, smiled wearily. The two men whispered the ritual word for good luck, which, in the French theatre, is shorter than the usual phrase exchanged backstage in England and America. "Shit," they said, and embraced.

At 7:55, the house manager worked his way across a column of late arrivals and told Gus the critics were all in place except de la Pagerie. Gus moved to the right center aisle, gazed down front and saw that seat 101, the aisle seat in row E, and 102 next to it, were vacant.

Virgile de la Pagerie, or "Delap" as he was known in the business, was the critic for the weekly *La Revue Endimanchée*. He was probably the most disliked as well as the most influential and widely read critic in Paris. "We'll wait for him," Gus said.

At 7:58, with nearly all the patrons seated, a stunning young woman in a minimum black silk sheath, black hose, and black pumps with sequined buckles, moved down the aisle and took seat 102 in row E. At first, Gus thought she might be Sylvie Guillem, the dancer. But Guillem was out of the country. He didn't know who this girl was. However, judging by her carriage, her walk, and astonishing legs, he guessed her to be one of Delap's new ballet babes.

Eight o'clock came and went. Gus held the curtain. The audience became restive. There were a few whistles from the balcony. Finally, at 8:08, Gus turned to the house manager and said, "Fuck him! Tell Jérôme to take his house to half."

Barely a second later, the familiar figure of Virgile de la Pagerie appeared at the top of the aisle. He was tall, slim, and elegant, the copper-coloured skin and dark, reddish hair and beard of the Martinique-born critic contrasting markedly, under the fading house lights, with the gleaming white linen suit and trademark lambskin shoulder bag. He waved airily to Gus and Pierre-Yves and quickly made his way down the aisle, where he took his seat next to the young woman. The house went to black.

In the darkness, the sound of an accordion was heard. The audience buzz faded away, and the curtain rose on Pierre-Yves Gastin's charming set of a provincial railroad station refreshment room.

There was a collective sigh from the audience as it embraced this delicious first moment of illusion in Anouilh's small masterpiece. They applauded.

Onstage, the Father finished his sums on the back of a napkin and turned to Orpheus. But before he could speak his opening line, there was a disturbance in the audience down front. A patron in the fourth or fifth row stood, his figure silhouetted against the stage picture. He stepped into the aisle and dropped to his knees.

Gus, standing in the back next to Pierre-Yves, and alert to anything that might harm his opening, hesitated for only an instant before he started down the aisle. He hadn't gone five paces, however, when the patron down front turned to the back of the house and shouted, "A doctor! Get a doctor!"

Gus reached the patron in another ten paces and saw that the figure in the white suit, collapsed on the floor, was de la Pagerie. The patron had raised the stricken man's head and was about to attempt mouth-to-mouth resuscitation.

Gus dropped to his knees. "Thank you, monsieur," he said. "Please take your seat."

"He just keeled over," the patron said. "Must've had a heart attack!" The action onstage stopped.

"A doctor is coming," Gus said and fumbled with the victim's tie. After a few moments, the house manager and house physician appeared. The curtain fell and the house lights came on.

People began to rubberneck. The audience, uninformed and annoyed, began to make a wild roaring noise.

Emergency medical personnel, in blue coveralls, arrived. After a brief attempt to revive the victim, they placed him on a stretcher, and, while he was being rolled up the aisle, removed the arm of his jacket and shirt and administered an intravenous solution. Gus, looking ashen, and carrying the victim's shoulder bag, accompanied the stretcher outside to the ambulance.

Meanwhile, the house manager appeared onstage before the curtain. He announced that a patron had been stricken but that the performance would resume immediately.

For a few minutes, an audiotape of Poulenc's *Sonata for Two Pianos* was piped into the auditorium in an attempt to divert the audience. During this, the young woman in seat 102 got up and left.

Presently, the music was discontinued, the house lights dimmed and went out, the accordion was heard again, and the performance started over.

Despite some ragged patches early on, due, no doubt, to the interruption, the audience response to the first act was extremely enthusiastic. Indeed, by the interval, the word was that Gus had himself a hit.

2

Hôpital St-Lazare

VIRGILE DE LA PAGERIE was pronounced DOA. The emergency squad had done all it could: endotracheal tube, intravenous lactate Ringers, bolus of sodium bicarbonate. The EMU had already performed CPR without success. The Paris Medical Examiner was called. He carefully scrutinized the victim. He sniffed him. He checked that all procedures had been correct. Finally he agreed to the diagnosis of cardiac arrest.

Description of the victim's clothing and personal effects was duly recorded. The white linen suit, made without pockets except for a breast pocket in the jacket which contained a handkerchief that matched the shirt, had been custom made by Delors & Fils. The pink shirt and handkerchief came from the Rue St-Honoré Chemisier, T. Barton. Leather sandals, worn without socks, were from I. Castiglione, Rome. Personal effects contained in a lambskin shoulder bag included: one lined writing pad clamped to an 8- x 13-cm clipboard, two Mont Blanc pencils, one pocket thesaurus, one miniature tape recorder, one comb, one small tube moustache wax, one tweezers, one (half) eye glasses, one address book, one wallet containing credit cards and 1002 francs in cash, keys on a sterling silver ring to which a cameo with a woman's profile was attached, one packet chlorophyll lozenges; and, in a mother-of-pearl Lalique cigarette case, decorated with gold butterflies, three condoms. All this, plus the victim's underwear, shirt, tie, jacket, trousers, and watch were placed under lock and key to await next of kin. The body was removed to the hospital morgue.

The Medical Examiner authorized the hospital to release a statement that Virgile de la Pagerie, critic-at-large for *La Revue Endimanchée,* died of an apparent heart attack at approximately 8:10 Wednesday evening, 4 September 1985.

However, mindful of the deceased's comparative youth and robust physique, and inquisitive about a faint odour of almonds that he detected around the cheeks and neck, the Medical Examiner walked upstairs to the hospital office, phoned the forensic Institut Médico-Légal, in Quai de la Rapée, and ordered an autopsy for 10 A.M.

Narcisse

The opening night party for the cast of *Eurydice* was held at a popular theatre oasis in Avenue Mogador. Red leather banquettes lined both walls of the large, rectangular space, while a double rank of white-clothed tables filled the centre. Unlike most theatre restaurants in major world cities, the walls of Narcisse were not covered with framed photographs or caricatures of well-known actors but with precisely angled mirrors, so that wherever one looked, there one was. The ceiling was similarly embellished, except for the addition of a fine line of small crystal chandeliers.

The unwritten law at Narcisse was that the most desirable

table was the first banquette to the left as one entered the restaurant from the foyer, the next most desirable the first to the right, and so on. The tables in the centre were acceptable. But a table at the very back was Dieppe, and one upstairs, Ho Chi Minh City. Tonight, however, this parochialism was suspended as Gus had reserved the entire place for his cast, crew, investors, and friends.

The reviews came in a little after 11 and were unanimous in their praise of the physical production, the mise en scène, the cast in general, and, in particular, the young actress Julie Aubry, whose performance as Eurydice was variously described as "luminous," "lapidary," and "pellucid."

No one needed to mention that this unanimity of critical opinion might not have occurred had de la Pagerie been present. Indeed, an arts and entertainment commentator for TV Antenne 2 speculated that the producer-directeur Pezon-Schwartz had taken a calculated risk in reviving *Eurydice,* a play written in 1952 by an author for whom Delap had never shown much enthusiasm. Of an earlier revival in the '70's, the critic wrote, "Eurydice (or 'Legend of Lovers,' as it is called abroad) is an overwrought fantasy by a minor playwright frequently given to saccharinalia and written in a style one might call neo–high school gymnauseum."

This reminder of Delap's acidulous pen failed to dampen the spirits of the present company. On the contrary, their initial disbelief, as the reviews were read, was now transformed into euphoria.

Gus, however, remained at the party for less than an hour. When the news of Delap's death was received around midnight, Gus seemed deeply shocked. He mumbled his apologies and was driven home by Pierre-Yves. Later, Pierre-Yves returned and told Jérôme, the stage manager, that Gus had a conviction that *Eurydice* was a success only by default.

As for the rest of the Paris theatre community, the news of Virgile de la Pagerie's death was an occasion for universal rejoicing. There was not a working actor or, for that matter, a theatre usher, theatre concessionnaire, or theatre cleaning person who, at some point, had not had the bread snatched from his mouth by a devastating notice from de la Pagerie. The fact that a single critic, on a weekly, seemed to hold the power of life or death over the theatre in a city of such diverse cultural opinion, in a country of such rich theatrical history, was a subject only the critic's victims seemed willing to debate. It was a subject on which the Académie was silent, except to suggest that newspaper critics, as a group, were a subordinate, frequently vindictive, phenomenon of the media imperium and beyond the pale of scholarly inquiry.

Consequently, when dawn arrived on Thursday 5 September (windy, chance of showers before nightfall), certain blissful individuals, some of whom had heard the news on TV or heard it from someone who'd heard it, all of whom had been up all night and still couldn't believe it, gathered in small knots of anticipation outside newspaper kiosks in the Sixth, Seventh, and Ninth Arrondissements, waiting for the early edition of *Le Matin*. When it came, when they saw it with their own eyes on page one, streets and sidewalks became littered with scattered pages that had been hurled skyward with cries of joy, and, carried by the fresh westerly now blowing in from La Manche, sailed up the avenues like warrior kites, executing loops and Immelmanns, snatching at lampposts and traffic lights and shredding themselves triumphantly on the fanciful iron grillwork surrounding the Hôtel des Invalides.

Some celebrants tried to extend this rapturous sense of occasion until lunchtime. But most went home to bed. In any case, none of them was aware of what occurred next because it was not immediately made public.

At 9 A.M., an anonymous telephone call was received at the office of Judge Jean-Paul Ariel Céstac, France's Senior Terrorist Investigator. In the toneless cadence of a robotic artificial intelligence, the caller spoke these words: "The Front Patriotique has executed Virgile Philadelphie, the mulatto mongrel of Martinique, for blasphemy and crimes against the République. Long live France for the French."

The fact that the call was made to the judge's office instead of to the wire service, Agence France Presse, or to a newspaper was later considered extremely arrogant or extremely stupid, as all calls to the Senior Terrorist Investigator's office were known to be taped.

However, this morning's message did not immediately engage the judge's attention; not until TV Antenne 2 interrupted its noon telecast for a special bulletin: A toxicology report issued by the Paris Medical Examiner following an autopsy showed that the critic Virgile de la Pagerie had died of sodium cyanide poisoning.

3

Alex

SIX HUNDRED KILOMETRES to the south, the wife of the owner of the canal-side restaurant on the Grand Bassin at Castelnaudary opened the pantry window, rested her elbows on the sill, and listened to the haunting melody drifting up from the small motor cruiser moored below. A very tall, slim man, with hair and beard the colour of marigolds, sat on one side of the cockpit of the little cruiser, propped his feet on the other, and played a soft, delicate tune on his big horn, a tune as plaintive as the sound of the morning breeze caressing the marsh grass bordering the bassin. She listened to the melody rising and falling, and permitted herself to imagine that he was playing just for her.

She'd waited on him in the dining room at lunch. He selected the cassoulet, a green salade, and a demi of red Corbières. While he was ordering, he asked her name. She was astonished. No patron had ever troubled to ask her name.

"Thérèse," she said, overcome by shyness.

"Alex," he replied and shook her hand. "Are you native to this area?"

"No, monsieur. I'm originally from Mazamet, in the Haut Languedoc." She took a breath and made a stab at sounding casual. "Euh . . . monsieur is on vacation?"

"Yes."

"All alone, then?"

"No. I'm expecting my crew this evening. We'll be on our way tomorrow." He told her he was a policeman, a Chef-Inspecteur or something, in Paris. He hoped it was not inconvenient that he'd left the number of the restaurant pay phone with his office, in case they had to reach him. She said it was not inconvenient. And that was the end of their conversation.

She'd never heard the big horn played so sweetly. The big horn in the band of Mazamet, her place of origin, made oom-pah for the polkas, oom-pah-pah for the Jadas, and OOM-oom-OOM-oom on the Fourteenth of July, when the band of Mazamet became the Military Band of Mazamet. Moreover, most players of the big horn were short and fat and filled with red-faced self-importance as they endeavored to force the air into the great round funnel of a mouthpiece. Not like this man, who made the horn seem to sigh in his embrace like a lover.

She felt the blood rise to her face. Stupid woman, she thought, what do you know about these things? She was immediately ashamed of herself. She closed the window and turned her back to the bassin. If your marriage was arranged and your husband is twice your age, you still have nothing to complain about. Your husband is good to you. He asks nothing, only that you warm his backside at night, keep his accounts, and serve his tables. Nevertheless, after this self-reproach, she turned to gaze down once more on the little cruiser and listen. As she did this, the phone rang below. Her punishment: the greengrocer wanting payment.

She hurried downstairs and answered. The call was for Monsieur Grismolet.

"Monsieur who?"

"Chef-Inspecteur Grismolet. He's on the hire-cruiser *Sirocco*."

"Ah! One moment, please!" She smoothed her apron, tucked her hair behind her ears, and ran out onto the quai. "Monsieur Alex! Monsieur! Telephone!"

Alex put down his tuba and climbed ashore. "Thank you, Thérèse."

"It is nothing, monsieur." She remained on the quai, blushing slightly, and watched him as he hurried inside.

Alex fumbled for the dangling receiver in the dark hallway. "Allô. Grismolet."

"Sûreté," said the voice at the other end. "Inspecteur-trainee Biramoule here. How's the Canal du Midi, Chef?"

"A monument to seventeenth-century engineering. Charming, restful, full of locks. What's up?"

"Hold on for Commissaire Demonet."

The boss. Instinct told Alex that his and Philippa's exploratory fortnight cruise on the Canal du Midi was slipping away.

"Alex." The Commissaire's civilized voice, the perfectly placed, perfectly authoritative light baritone, perfectly suited to patient dealings with the Ministry of the Interior, Case Judges, the Palais de Justice, even the Élysée Palace, resonated in the homely wall phone receiver. "Alex, are you there?"

"I'm listening, Commissaire."

"Have you heard about the death of Virgile de la Pagerie?"

"Read about it this morning in *La Dépêche du Midi*. Heart attack."

"He was murdered, Alex," the Commissaire said evenly. "Cyanide poisoning."

"In the orchestra of the Théâtre Bakoledis?"

"Apparently."

"How?"

"We don't know. The Toxicologist's report draws no conclusion."

"Who's handling it for the Préfecture?"

"No one, Alex. Which is why I'm calling. A political group has claimed responsibility. That takes it out of the Préfecture's jurisdiction. In any case, the Senior Terrorist Investigator wants us; and I want you and Varnas."

Alex was not obliged to accept the assignment. The Maison owed him weeks of vacation. He and Philippa had decided to devote their free time together to exploring as many canals as possible in rented motor cruisers against the day they would finally cast off *Le Yacht Club*, their barge home in Paris, and do the entire canal system of France in search of perpetual sunshine. With virtually no enthusiasm, he asked, "Do you . . . we . . . have anything to go on?"

"We have the anonymous phone call to the judge's office on tape, we have the theatre itself, which I have ordered closed, we have the producer-directeur, the designer, the stage manager, cast, and so on, and we have the man who was sitting behind the victim when he collapsed. And we have de la Pagerie's flat, which I ordered sealed off ten minutes ago." The Commissaire cleared his throat discreetly. "We also have some indication that your ward may be involved."

Alex felt his scalp crawl. "Philippa?"

"Yes. Inspecteur Varnas is with her on your barge, taking her testimony."

"Her what?"

"Alex, she was de la Pagerie's date at the opening."

Alex canceled his charter. The boat-hire firm would hold his deposit. From their office, he telephoned the lockmaster at the village of Bram, gave his name, and explained that two older gentlemen would appear below the lock tomorrow, midday, expecting lunch aboard the hire-cruiser *Sirocco*. Would the lockmaster have the goodness to explain to them that, as the captain and crew had been recalled to Paris, lunch would not take place as planned?

He returned to the restaurant and gave the few galley stores he'd accumulated to Thérèse. "I save them for your return," she said, cradling the carton to her bosom.

He stowed his sea bag and tuba into the rental car, drove to Toulouse, and boarded the afternoon Air Inter flight to Orly.

Settling into the upholstered no-man's-land of the airbus, he tried to make sense of the Commissaire's call.

Philippa de la Pagerie's date? Well, the Commissaire couldn't have made that one up. Not Commissaire Demonet, a meticulous man of traditional values who still referred to Philippa as Alex's "ward," presumably to satisfy himself that there was nothing improper about his thirty-seven-year-old Chef-Inspecteur living on a former coal barge with a radiantly beautiful twenty-one-year-old ballet dancer.

The Commissaire chose not to acknowledge that Philippa had ceased to be Alex's legal responsibility when she reached age eighteen; or that she still lived on the barge because she never considered moving away from the home she helped to build, paint, and varnish; the only home she'd ever known, apart from Wold Manor, the Methodist residence for indi-

gent children in England, where her mother repeatedly
dumped her — until Alex.

He closed his eyes.

Philippa, waif, age eight, left in Alex's care one rainy afternoon by Angela, her dissolute English beauty of a mother,
while Alex, then twenty-four, was instructing at a sailing
school in Brittany; Angela disappearing, Philippa begging
Alex to keep her (tears ... "Buy me, Alex!"); interminable
red tape establishing that the child, born out of wedlock, had
no family, father killed at an IRA roadblock, mother a tramp
and disowned by her icy, upper-class, lord-and-ladyship parents; Philippa placing her tiny hand in his as the court finally
granted him custody and guardianship. And then Paris, ex-
ams for the Sûreté, *Le Yacht Club,* the barge they'd bought
for nearly nothing and restored together, and the Opéra Ballet. And Varnas, beloved partner, surrogate father and men-
tor ...

Varnas on *Le Yacht Club* with Philippa, taking her testimony in a murder case? Unimaginable.

Le Yacht Club

Inspecteur Varnas, always correct in his black, vested business suit and homburg, carefully stepped aboard the barge,
hung his jacket and hat on the brass coat hook by the companion ladder, removed the gold watch and chain from his
vest, took off his black shoes, and prepared to undergo his
first ballet lesson. He wished to skip the basics, he said. He
knew he could never master the fifth position at his age. What
he had always wanted to know was how a dancer could turn
onstage at such a dizzying rate and not get dizzy.

"We spot," said Philippa.

"Well, that is what I wish to learn, my darling. To spot."

So, between approximately 2 P.M. and 3:30, at which time Varnas was scheduled to meet the Forensics people at the Théâtre Bakoledis, Philippa, in violet tights and a white, silk camisole, taught Varnas, in black trousers, vest, and rib-stocking feet, to spot.

Earlier, at the Maison, Varnas had intervened in the Commissaire's decision to send young Inspecteur Brieuc to *Le Yacht Club* to take Philippa's testimony. He said, "Commissaire, if you send César Brieuc, he does not concentrate. He is already in love. He is dazzled by such beauty."

The Commissaire lit the giant meerschaum on his desk, a formidable pipe carved to represent Joan of Arc in full armor. Between puffs, he eyed Varnas. "And if I send you, you won't be dazzled?"

"I am dazzled out, Commissaire," Varnas replied. "I know Philippa since little girl. I am safe with her."

Actually, Varnas had no intention of interrogating Philippa or of allowing anyone but Alex to do so. Varnas's reason was practical as well as protective. If César, or any other well-meaning foot soldier in the Maison operational bureaucracy, himself included, officially took Philippa's testimony, he would be compelled to initiate a dossier that would inevitably find its way, whether she was guilty or not, to the Palais de Justice. And dossiers that found their way to the Palais had a way of turning up when you wished to apply for a credit card, a mortgage, or a fishing license. Varnas did not want Philippa's name in the random-access memory at the Palais de Justice. Consequently, he spent his time with her, this afternoon, doing piqué turns across the barge's saloon floor while spotting the barometer on the midships bulkhead. He did this very slowly, and flat-footed.

For her part, Philippa was dying to talk.

"No. You talk only to Alex," Varnas said as he climbed back into his shoes after the lesson.

"But aren't you mad to hear about 'The woman in black?' " She was referring to a phrase used to describe her in one of the afternoon tabloids. "Besides, I've already talked to Stéphane."

"Who is Stéphane? No. Don't tell me. Tell Alex." He got up. "So, what about new car? Does it work?"

"For the moment." Philippa had recently acquired a fourth-hand Volkswagen Bug of questionable lineage, whose air-cooled, rear-mounted engine was a source of mystery.

"Good. You can pick up Alex at Orly. Bring him from airport to theatre."

"But aren't I confined to the city, or something?"

He retrieved his jacket and hat from the brass hook. "Depends on testimony which Alex takes from you on way home." He smiled. "Thanks for lesson. If today does not cripple me, I come back in two years." He stood on tiptoe, kissed her on each cheek, put on his hat, and left.

Varnas

Varnas's height of 1 metre, 62.5 centimetres, made him slightly shorter than Philippa. When placed next to Alex, who stood at nearly two metres, he barely came to the second button down from Alex's collar. This height difference, and the fact that Alex dressed casually in jeans, anorak, and running shoes while Varnas was always impeccably turned out in one of his conservative, three-piece, black suits, led to the inevitable jokes about who was the comic and who the straight man. But this jollity was muted by respect and real affection, never more so than when, two years earlier, everyone at the Maison feared Varnas would not survive the terrible wounds he'd suffered while pursuing a suspect in the Wilson case. If he had not survived, it is certain Alex would have resigned from the Sûreté. Varnas, though he denied it, saved Alex's life.

Alphonsas Varnas. His colleagues either never knew his Christian name, or thought it was Varnas, for that was what everyone called him. Varnas, Lithuanian national, twenty years Alex's senior, born in the wrong place at the wrong time; prisoner of the Soviets in 1940, deported by the Germans in '43 to the town of Dinkelsbuhl, near Stuttgart, where he laboured as a pig farmer ("on German map, Alex, Lithuania is pink. Pink means dairy products, hogs, livestock. So everyone they deport from Lithuania — poets, artists, scientists — becomes farmer in Germany. Nazi mind is wonderful thing").

Varnas spoke fluent Litvak, Russian, German, and Polish. He also spoke a sort of French and English, without articles or with articles placed where they were not needed ("So, Alex, how are the things?"). He said he was obliged to learn French and English in a rush. ("I learn French on VE Day when I walk through French sector of Germany. English I learn in American sector next day.")

That Alex was younger than Varnas but outranked him was no problem for Varnas. He'd seen enough of rank. What mattered was that both he and Alex understood they were fundamental extensions of each other.

During his long convalescence after the Wilson case, Varnas moved into a very small flat at Rue Georges-Berger, in the Seventeenth Arrondissement. This was the same address where Wilson's widow, Millicent, maintained a very large flat from April to October. It was an address that would normally be beyond the aspirations of a Sûreté Inspecteur. That Varnas made the move at all, and lived there still, was entirely due to the propriétaire of the building, Madame Clothilde Roget.

Varnas had extensively interviewed Mme Roget during the Wilson investigation. It was Varnas who discovered that this slim, grave, middle-aged war widow harbored a secret, Catholic, altogether immaculate passion for the eighty-four-year-old Andrew Wilson while he was alive. It was Varnas who anticipated that Mme Roget would remove Wilson's diary from police scrutiny in the misguided belief that Wilson might have confessed his feelings for her in its pages. What he did not anticipate, when he returned to Paris by ambulance plane with at least a year of recuperative therapy to look forward to, was that this same Mme Roget would transfer her secret infatuation for Andrew Wilson directly to him. It was she who made the flat (a former storage area under the tin roof) available, and she who nursed him back to health.

Thus did Varnas become a slave to nuance. To shield her secret affection for him from public scrutiny, he did not allow himself to acknowledge her feelings directly, which would not have been difficult, for she was pleasant company, still had the trim figure of a country girl, an abundance of thick, black hair, brushed straight back into a tight chignon ("Perhaps she takes it down at night, Alex, I'll never know"), and clear, wide eyes, the colour of the gray Jura sky in winter. But if he did not acknowledge her feelings directly, he could acknowledge them indirectly, since it helped preserve her secret. It was entirely a question of nuance.

He could thank her for doing his laundry, which she did once a week, but must not thank her immediately, and not face-to-face. Nothing face-to-face. And, of course, no touching. Indeed, the closest they came to each other physically was at mass on Sunday and when they did the dishes together. The dishes occurred on Wednesday evenings, when he dined with her in her loge on the first floor, five floors away from his flat under the roof. She cooked, he set the table. She washed, he dried. At first, she would not permit him to raise a finger to help her. She thought it beneath the dignity of a Sûreté Inspecteur. But he invented an allegory about the division of labour among songbirds that sufficiently diverted her so that she relented. Conspicuously absent from this allegory was any mention of the mating ritual or eggs.

They did not use the familiar "you." When he once called her "Clothilde," she quietly corrected him and, to this day, it is "Madame Roget" and "Inspecteur Varnas," although once, at Christmas, after eggnog, she slipped and called him "my little Inspecteur Varnas."

Her passion for him was only true and good as long as it remained secret and immaculate, her invisible talisman, to which he learned to respond by appearing not to respond.

Nevertheless, he knew that she kept her eye on him. He knew she knew when he came and went, and depended on him to report the highlights of his days, what he'd had for lunch, and so on. Therefore, after he left Philippa on *Le Yacht Club* and entered the Porte de la Villette métro station, he fished in his pocket for his telephone card, called her, and told her he would be home late.

4

Philippa

PHILIPPA BATHED, put on jeans and an old sweater of Alex's that came to her knees, and went on deck. There, she hung out her tights and replaced some of the coloured ribbons tied to a line stretched fore and aft, which discouraged seagulls and pigeons from using the barge as a public toilet. She locked the companion hatch, checked the mooring lines for chafe, and went ashore to where the Bug was parked.

The Bug, painted a sort of cream, had one purple fender. She climbed into the front seat, said a short prayer, and hit the ignition switch. The starter turned over but the engine wouldn't fire. She reached under the seat for the tire iron, got out, opened the rear hatch, and delivered the carburetor a sharp blow. The engine started immediately on the next try.

She'd bought the car for 900 francs from the bassoon player in the Paris Opéra orchestra, an older, intellectual sort who somewhat resembled his instrument. He pointed to the tire iron after the sale was consummated, and said, "Endure no Teutonic intransigence from this vehicle."

Philippa eased the Bug into the Boulevard Périphérique.

Because of the rush hour traffic she got off at Ivry and eventually picked up the A6 in Gentilly.

The A6 was no speedway either. As she rumbled slowly
south toward Orly, she thought about the circumstances that
had placed her in the seat next to Virgile de la Pagerie at last
night's opening; this, inevitably, led back to Stéphane.

Stéphane's holiday had ended yesterday, the day Philippa's
vacation was to begin. Philippa had planned to join Alex on
the canal at Castelnaudary immediately but postponed when
Stéphane implored Philippa to go to the opening of *Eurydice*
with Virgile. "Listen, it'll be a gala. It's the first opening of the
season. It's a freebie. You get to go gorgeous. And you'll be
saving my life because he refuses to go anywhere alone."

Stéphane was Delap's current trick. Stéphane, going on
twenty-six — and still in the corps de ballet — had been the
current trick of several fairly prominent men in Paris. "I'm
old-fashioned," she said. "I smoke. I'll never be Pavlova. But
I aim to please. And I'm decorative." She was. She was Greek,
blonde, long-legged, and the only dancer in the company who
needed a D-cup.

Philippa guessed it was only a matter of time before Stéphane would be forced to hang up her toe shoes and face the
harsh, non-moonlit reality beyond the Palais Garnier. In the
meantime, despite the fact that their devotion to ballet was
markedly different in intensity — Philippa was younger and a
soloist — they were good friends.

A truck driver drew alongside the Bug, yelled at her to
switch on her lights, took a second look and proposed marriage.

She turned off at Orly and experienced the tiny frisson of
anticipation she always felt before a rendezvous with Alex.
"My God," she whispered, as the skin on her forearm tingled,

"will this never end?" She saw him standing at the Air Inter exit ramp. He wasn't smiling; but he wasn't scowling either.

They stowed the sea bag under the hood and the tuba in back. "You drive," she said. "I can't talk and drive at the same time." He pushed the seat back as far as it would go, and they rolled away from the terminal.

He said, "I'm a little surprised to see you out here. Didn't Varnas put you under a restraining order?"

"Are you joking? He wouldn't listen to my story; didn't even take my name and address — saved me for you." When this comeback elicited no response, she poked him and said, "Cheer up! I'll tell you what happened."

"Good. Begin at the beginning."

"I will. My friend Stéphane and Delap went on holiday together in Spain, or Italy — I don't know which — someplace where he has a beach house. They were gone about two weeks. He had to come back to review the opening. She thought she had another day of vacation and planned to go to the theatre with him. But she screwed up her dates and found she was expected to dance Wednesday. I'm out of the corps, so I couldn't fill in for her in *Sleeping Beauty*. But when she asked me to fill in for her at *Eurydice,* I agreed. It sounded like fun. So I called you and went."

"I know that part."

"I'm beginning at the beginning."

"Okay."

"I picked up my ticket a couple of minutes before eight. Delap was late. I took my seat, fifth row center, second seat in from the aisle."

"Did that put him on your right or left?"

"His seat was on my right."

"Who was on your left?"

"A lady, gray-haired wife type."

"Go ahead."

"They held the curtain. After nearly ten minutes, people were getting pissed. Finally, just when the house lights started down, he appeared. He sat, put his shoulder bag in his lap, smiled, and said, 'Sorry I'm late.' The house lights went out.

"In the dark, while an accordion was playing onstage, I heard him take a couple of deep breaths, as if he were hyperventilating. Next thing I knew, he was leaning against me. I mean full press. Knowing his reputation as a seducer of innocent young girls, I figured he was trying to get it on with me right there in the fifth row. Since I didn't have a hat pin, I gave him a shove. At that moment, the curtain rose. The last I saw of him, he was rolling out of his seat into the aisle, shoulder bag and all.

"A man in the row behind us got up, stepped into the aisle, knelt down, and, I guess, tried to revive him. A moment later, the man turned and yelled 'Get a doctor!' That was it. Just that fast. I don't see how anyone could have murdered him. No one touched him, except me, and all I did was push him. I mean, I don't normally respond to an unwanted pass with a hypodermic filled with cyanide."

"And then?"

"Another man, I think it was the producer, rushed down the aisle and took over. He got down next to Delap, loosened his tie, tried to rub his hands, things like that. The first man sat down. Finally a doctor arrived and, soon after, a team of medics. By now the curtain was down and the house lights were back in. The medics did some stuff, then put Delap on a stretcher and took him away.

"I think the lady on my left thought I killed him. Anyway, she changed seats with her husband.

"Someone made a speech from the stage about a patron being taken ill, and that the performance would resume momentarily. While I wondered whether to stay or get in touch with Stéphane, this woman in harlequin glasses trots down the aisle and takes Delap's seat. She winks at me and says 'Better than standing room.' Right there I decided to leave and stood up. When she saw this, she turns and goes 'Yoo-hoo' to the back of the house, where another woman, an exact copy of her — same hairdo, same glasses — runs down the aisle and takes my seat. They must've been twins. The last thing I heard was 'This is our lucky night, Yvonne.'

"I left the theatre, walked across Rue Boudreau to the Palais Garnier and waited out front for Stéphane to finish. I didn't want to give her the news until the performance was over. God, I never realized how long *Sleeping Beauty* is — especially with a Russian conductor.

"I went backstage just before the finale. When Stéphane finally dragged herself into the dressing room, she looked like she needed oxygen. But she brightened when she saw me. How did I like the play? How did I get on with Virgile? She calls him Virgile. But I guess something in my expression must've telegraphed. She sat down.

"I told her he'd collapsed in the theatre and was rushed to the hospital. I didn't know which hospital, or how serious it was, but that it may have been a heart attack. She didn't say anything. She took off her ballet shoes and stuck a foot in my lap. 'Rub,' she said. So I massaged her arch and instep. Finally she said she thought it weird that a thirtyish-year-old man who jogged on the beach all day and fucked his brains out all night would have a heart condition.

"After a while she pulled her foot away, hung up her tutu, and started taking off her makeup. She dished the perfor-

mance, complained about the tempos, and said she'd better
be getting home in case Virgile called."

Alex glanced over. "That's it?"

"That's it."

"Is she always that composed?"

"No. But I had the feeling she either didn't believe me or
didn't believe his condition was serious."

"Did she love him?"

Philippa shrugged. "Love is her hobby. She has this oversize lemon-yellow rehearsal shirt with a portrait of Oscar
Wilde on it. Across Wilde's face, in puce letters, is 'One
should always be in love. That's the reason one should never
marry.'" Philippa glanced at Alex. "She cared for him. I
don't know about love."

"Where's home?"

"Excuse me?"

"You said she wanted to go home in case Virgile called.
Where's home?"

"Home is his place. Or was. She says he has the whole top
floor in a fancy building on Rue de Tournon, near the Luxembourg Gardens." Philippa turned away and peered at the
road ahead. "Which brings up a decision I undertook uni-
laterally. I hope you won't be annoyed."

"Try me."

"A couple of hours ago, when Stéphane finally learned
that Delap had been murdered, she called and told me the
police had sealed off his apartment. That leaves her without a
place to live."

"So you invited her to stay with us aboard *Le Yacht
Club*."

"Only until she finds a place."

"When does this start?"

"Tonight."

"All right. Except it's a little unusual for a suspect in a murder case to be living with her chief investigator."

"Suspect? Stéphane a suspect? Are you mad? A radical political group killed him —"

"May have killed him. Meanwhile, Stéphane is the last person who had access to him."

"I'm the last person who had access to him. He sat down next to me, smiled, said 'Sorry I'm late,' and croaked. If she's a suspect, I'm a suspect."

"Did you know him?"

"No."

"Then you're not a suspect."

"Why?"

"Because you'd never kill anyone you didn't know."

Philippa poked him again and whooped, "You're right!" She patted the spot she'd poked, and gazed through the windscreen. They were entering the Porte de la Villette. Alex was heading for *Le Yacht Club*. "Alex, you're supposed to go to the theatre."

"I know. I'll stow my gear and take the métro. I don't trust this thing."

They pulled up opposite the barge. Philippa studied his profile as he shut down the Bug.

"So . . . if she's a suspect, I suppose you'll have to interrogate her?"

"Certainly."

"I'd like to be there, if you don't mind."

"Why?"

"So she doesn't end up in your lap."

5

Théâtre Bakoledis

A POLICE BARRICADE had been placed at the front of the darkened theatre entrance on Rue de Caumartin and another at the stage entrance. Indignant ticket-holders for this evening's canceled performance waited for refunds in a line that stretched down the street as far as Rue Auber.

As he crossed the police line and passed through the lobby to the entrance to the foyer, Alex was confronted in the doorway by an outraged Auguste Pezon-Schwartz, waving a sheaf of crumpled computer printouts.

"What's this?" Gus cried, eyeing Alex from top to toe. "The second assistant janitor?"

Alex bowed slightly. "Chef-Inspecteur Grismolet, at your service."

"Enchanted. I am suing you for tonight's loss of ninety thousand francs, plus tax!" he shouted, shaking his face. "I am suing you for my daily payroll of sixty thousand francs and for aggravation and emotional distress in the amount of fifty thousand francs! So far, that's two hundred thousand francs you owe me! There's more. I have to guarantee the house for two weeks. I will therefore sue you for sixty thousand francs, plus tax for every night I'm closed, plus payroll, plus aggravation, plus tax!"

Alex smiled. "You have my sympathies, monsieur. I suggest you submit your requirements to the Ministry of the Interior."

"Ministry of the Interior?" he raged. "I've got the PLO in the lobby and you give me the Ministry of goddam Interior!" He pointed at the line of patrons. "Look at them! Every one of them wants a hundred and fifty francs and one of my gonads! Get me the Minister of Defense! Get me a tank!" He slumped. "Get me a drink!" He peered up at Alex. "Sorry. I know you're only doing your shtik. What'd you say your name was?"

"Alex Grismolet."

"Pezon-Schwartz. Call me Gus." He was about to reenter the foyer but stopped again and glared at Alex. "Just a minute! The house is already crawling with flics! We got flics taking mug shots of the cast! We got flics in the dressing rooms checking the cold cream and false eyelashes! We got flics in the flies checking the bat shit! There's even a midget flic running around in a black suit, loading trash into plastic bags! What do you do?"

"I'm the head flic," Alex said quietly, "and your theatre, Monsieur Gus, is a murder site."

"Oh, sorry. I thought you were here to audition for the road company." Gus leaned against a ticket box and rubbed his eyes. "Jesus, what a nightmare!" he moaned. Finally, with exaggerated patience, he asked, "So, head flic, what can I do to be of service?"

"Answer a few questions."

"A few questions." He shook his head. "Given the circumstances, this entire episode would be hilarious, if it weren't so sad. Answer a few questions. I already did that. What kind of questions? More questions about Delap? Okay. Nobody liked him. I loathed him. He was a destructive, unprincipled shit! If I weren't such a coward, I would've killed him myself, years ago. He could destroy a good production of a popular play because it lacked ... say ... subtext and rave about some incomprehensible piece of minimalist crap by an un-produced Romanian deconstructionist lately into semiotics. He was an intellectual bully." Gus paused and surveyed the line of patrons standing in the semidark. "But you know something? Now that he's gone, I almost miss the bastard. Life is suddenly less dangerous, less challenging. Isn't it hilarious that I can even think such a thing? No. It's not. It's sad. Sad for everybody. Sad for the audience, sad for Julie because she's suddenly a star with no place to shine, sad for the company because they'll have to block this sinister event and re-create gossamer all over again, and sad for me because" — now he was shouting — "because it's costing me one hundred and fifty thousand francs for every night I'm dark! What do you think? Sad or hilarious?"

Alex ignored the question. Pezon-Schwartz, projecting outraged helplessness, could probably hypothesize the night away, if allowed. It was time for a diversion. Underneath the easy flamboyance, Alex had detected a regional accent. He asked Gus if he was Parisien.

"Well, inevitably. I am Parisien the way Picasso and Diaghilev were Parisien, though born elsewhere through no fault of their own. I was whelped in the Midi, in St-Jean-de-Luz."

"So you're Basque?"

"No, dear. Daddy was a Sephardic jock from Bordeaux

and Mummy a lapsed Ashkenazim from St-Jean. He found her at the casino, eating a prune danish."

"Have you been in the theatre long?"

"I fucked Aeschylus on the beach at Samothrace."

Alex waited a long beat to break the straight line joke pattern he'd allowed himself to fall into. "How well did you know de la Pagerie?"

"Not at all well. No one in the theatre wanted to know him, apart from a few misguided ingenues he screwed and were never heard of again."

"Did you know him well enough to know if he owned a beach house in Spain or Italy?"

"No."

"Or if he ever used the name 'Virgile Philadelphie'?"

Gus sagged. "Really, this *is* tiresome. If some off-the-wall political group is actually claiming credit for this crime, why do you harass us? These are hoodlums. Their reality is brutality and death. We don't traffic in that kind of reality. Theatre reality is heightened reality, the reality of the imagination, reality created by analogy, by juxtaposition, by dramatic circumstance, character, language, and music. We produce a world that is more real than real. Your reality is a bore to us. Your neighborhood mechanic loves your neighborhood seamstress, but their love pales beside the love of Orpheus for Eurydice. Put another way, I can kill the Prince of Denmark eight times a week, but I wouldn't lay a finger on Delap."

"Well, somebody did, in about ten seconds, between the time the house lights went out and the curtain rose."

"Tell me. It happened in my theatre during my show. Does that make me responsible? Listen, if I'd opened in October he would've plotzed in somebody else's fifth row. No. Neither I nor anybody in my company had anything to do with his death. Now, if it doesn't inconvenience you, I'll change the subject. Wait for it. Ready? When can I reopen?"

"Probably tomorrow."

"You're divine!"

"Thanks. What can you tell me about the Front Patriotique?"

"Crazies in the south. Beat up Jews and gays, break heads and eardrums, defile mosques and temples, scare the shit out of male hairdressers."

"Why would a group operating in the south want to wax a critic in Paris?"

"Maybe because he was foreign. I hear they don't like foreigners."

"He wasn't a foreigner. He was a French citizen from Martinique."

"Maybe he gave them a bad notice." Gus shrugged. "Actually I don't give a flying fuck." He gave Alex a pat. "Call me if you need tickets." He nodded and did his high-hipped walk across the lobby to the box office. Alex watched him go, then entered the foyer.

Inside the empty theatre, the house curtain was up. The only illumination came from a single work light on the stage, which imparted a pale, monochromatic shadow over the dark flats and cutouts representing a dimly recalled railroad station. It was a drab scene, but one full of promise, like a slumbering lover, or a carousel in winter with the enameled horses waiting.

The same work light cast an eerie opacity over a dozen refuse bags and a blue fibre box that had been assembled in the centre aisle of the auditorium. Alex moved down toward a black-hatted figure seated in silhouette.

"Enjoying the show?"

Varnas looked up and beamed. "Ah! Sailor home from sea. Good. How is my Philippa?"

"Fine."

"Of course not guilty?"

"Doing a friend a favour."

"Good. You are nicely in time, Alex. We are just finished here." Varnas handed Alex his notes for the Investigation Report and a pencil flashlight. Alex sat on the arm of a seat opposite and studied the items listed.

Photolab had taken names, addresses, and Polaroids of cast and crew, after which Varnas placed them under a restraining order to remain in Paris until further notice. He dismissed them at 7:40.

Depositions were obtained from the house manager, house physician, and the critic of *Le Télégraph* (see attached).

"Who's the critic of *Le Télégraph*?" Alex asked.

"Man who sits behind victim."

"Did he tell you anything?"

"Maybe. Finish notes first, Alex."

Depositions were taken, as well, from the producer-directeur, Auguste Pezon-Schwartz, and scene designer, Pierre-Yves Gastin (see attached).

Alex looked up. "What did you get from Gus?"

"I ask him if it is true very many people in theatre business are happy that de la Pagerie is gone, and, if so, can we compile list of those who are happiest? He says probably, but if by 'we' I mean him, he is not willing to compile such list. He says theatre is small community, very competitive, very bitchy, but very loyal. Gus is sharp, elusive, spoiled, and, I think, little bit nervous. His hands sweat. Scene designer, Pierre-Yves Gastin, does not impress me. He is handsome, blond, but unassertive. Probably Gus's boyfriend. When I

interview him, he looks always to Gus before answering. I
have feeling he cannot dress himself or tie shoes without Gus.
Strange they don't live together. Gus lives alone in two-
bedroom flat in unremarkable Thirteenth, while Pierre-Yves
lives alone in secluded seven-bedroom house in affluent Sixteenth."

"Maybe they need their space."

"Maybe." Varnas pointed to the notes again. "Please to
check Forensics, Alex."

An analyst from the lab had found two poison samples,
fifty centimetres apart, on the aisle carpet where the victim
fell. Alex read: "1840 05SEP85. Detected faint trace NaCn
plus unidentifiable acid and fluoride compound. Very rough
samples due to foot traffic. Await spectrometre analysis; expect sample on victim's clothing."

"Where is his clothing?"

"Clothing and shoulder bag removed from Hôpital St-
Lazare to Forensic Lab this afternoon."

The last item in Varnas's report dealt with the crime site
cleanup. Refuse (candy wrappers, programs, etc.) had been
sorted, indexed, and stored in plastic bags. Recovered personal items from the auditorium had been indexed as well
and stored in a No. 2 police fibre case. They included ear-
rings, gloves, loose change, eyeglass case, black plastic cap,
probably from a large felt marker with stenciled legend, "Remove before Use," silver penknife, velvet bow, and several
umbrellas.

Alex asked, "Find anything near row E, seat 101?"

"No way to know. Cleaning ladies go through theatre last
night, top to bottom, before we learn critic is murder victim.
It is routine for them. Unless they find something valuable,
everything is vacuumed into dust bins. All this we index for

Forensics. We check even vacuum cleaner bags to make sure nothing leaves theatre."

They watched as a handful of Inspecteur-trainees gathered down front and began to move the collected refuse back to the stage door, where a Forensics van was parked.

Alex walked to row E, Varnas following. He sat in seat 101 and shone the light at the approximate place on the carpet where the analyst had taken the sample. He turned to Varnas. "When did the cleaning ladies start?"

"According to house manager, sometime after midnight."

"That's over an hour after the show broke. Are we satisfied the cleaning ladies turn in everything they find?"

"Cleaning ladies, from Ménage Hausmann-Auber, are bonded, Alex."

Alex got up, turned his back to the stage, and surveyed the house. After a moment, he said, "I have no idea what we're looking for. We have a telephone call from an electronic voice crediting a right-wing political group that operates in the south, not in Paris. There's no murder weapon, no ballistics profile to study, no wound, no prints. Just cyanide on the carpet. I have no idea how it got there. He was alive when he sat next to Philippa. Ten seconds later he was dead." Alex turned back to Varnas. "What about the man in the seat behind him?"

"Critic of *Le Télégraph*. When I question him, Alex, I learn that when he is not being critic, he is enthusiastic outdoorsman, very skilled in wilderness technique and first aid. Last night, when he kneels here and calls for doctor, he believes Delap is victim of heart attack. Without hesitation, he prepares to perform CPR procedure of mouth-to-mouth resuscitation. But, in that moment, Gus runs down theatre aisle and stops him. Abruptly. 'Monsieur, please take your seat,' and so on. Now, can you tell me why Gus suddenly stops this man from performing possible life-saving procedure?"

Alex answered without hesitation. "Because Gus, quite understandably, didn't know the critic of *Le Télégraph* was skilled in first aid; but, more to the point, Gus had the house physician on his way and didn't want a nonprofessional treating a heart attack victim in case the victim died and his family sued."

"Maybe. What else?"

"What else? I don't think there's anything else." Alex studied Varnas's impassive countenance. "You're not suggesting that Gus stopped the critic of *Le Télégraph* because he wanted Delap to die?"

"Maybe."

Alex frowned. Varnas was serious. Alex reversed himself and deliberately took the devil's tack. "Why did Gus stop the critic of *Le Télégraph* from possibly saving Delap's life? Because . . . because . . . Gus knew that Delap was *not* a heart attack victim . . ."

Varnas waited.

". . . was not a heart attack victim, but the victim of a lethal dose of sodium cyanide . . . which, if taken orally, would have put the life of the critic of *Le Télégraph* at risk had he performed mouth-to-mouth."

"Yes."

"No. Gus started down the aisle in response to a commotion, and because he saw the figure of a man in silhouette get up from his seat. This occurred when the house was still dark, except for perhaps the first row or two. He couldn't have seen what the critic of *Le Télégraph* was doing until he was practically on top of him. With the doctor coming, Gus simply wanted this helpful but interfering patron out of the way."

"Maybe."

"Incidentally, didn't the house physician perform CPR?"

"Yes."

"Why didn't Gus stop him?"

"Because house physician uses device called resuscitube, where there is no mouth-to-mouth contact."

"Hmm. I still think Gus was afraid of being sued. But, in the unlikely event you're onto something, we'll call up Research and ask Isabelle to do us a little dossier on Auguste Pezon-Schwartz of St-Jean-de-Luz." Alex checked his watch. "In the meantime, I have the victim's girlfriend to interview."

"Mademoiselle Stéphane?"

"Yes."

"Okeh. But before you go, Alex . . ." Varnas smiled enigmatically, moved to the right stage proscenium, and climbed the temporary wooden steps over the old orchestra pit onto the stage. He turned front, opened his arms, and said, "Watch this."

Focusing on the work light, he slowly, carefully, piquéd across the stage, holding his homburg in place, and whispering, "Turn . . . spot . . . turn . . . spot . . ."

6

Stéphane

THE MAPLE BUTTS Alex had cadged from the wrecking crew at Porte de la Villette crackled in *Le Yacht Club*'s old cast-iron stove, providing a rising column of air that caused the hanging oil lamps to flicker momentarily. Philippa got up, opened a porthole, and returned to her place on the saloon settee where she and Stéphane performed the dancer's weekly ritual of breaking in and sewing ribbons and elastic on new toe shoes.

The toe shoes were Stéphane's, not Philippa's, and the settee was a settee in the marine sense, not in the traditional. That is, it was not a small, upholstered couch but two small upholstered couches that faced each other across an adjustable table supported by a post. When the post was removed and the table lowered and covered with cushions, the settee became a double berth, suitable for the occasional overnight guest — usually Varnas. The guest tonight was Stéphane. She and Philippa had already effected the transformation, so that when Alex climbed through the companion hatch a little after 9, he was treated to the agreeable, but not nautical, spectacle of two stunning dancers stretched out on a quilted double bed covered with white toe shoes, satin ribbon, and elastic.

Philippa rose to meet him. After they embraced at the base of the ladder and Alex hung up his anorak, she turned and introduced Stéphane.

While Philippa's features were a distillation of the classic Irish beauty — fair skin, high cheekbones, masses of black hair, tangled eyelashes over blue eyes — Stéphane was a daughter of Diana: wide face, olive skin, dark green elongated eyes under thick brows, a multitude of taffy-blond hair, swept back and braided in a long pigtail that she brought forward over her shoulder and into her lap. Her mouth was large and smiling with full, rather rude lips. Philippa, dancer-strong but reed-slim, was dressed in tight jeans and a baggy, red flannel shirt. Stéphane, zaftig by comparison, wore tan nylon tights under an oversize green, V neck, wool sweater that more or less came to mid-thigh. Stretched out on the settee, her long legs seemed to go on forever in a series of remarkable compound curves that ended in feet so arched they could've been disjointed.

When she was introduced to Alex, Stéphane stared for an instant with a mildly stunned expression. She did her wide smile then, and quickly rearranged herself on the bed, tucking her legs under her and pulling the sweater down over her knees. This gesture was not lost on Philippa, who wondered if it was a good or bad sign; it was not like Stéphane to go modest in front of an attractive man.

Alex poured fingers of Courvoisier into three small snifters, distributed the drinks, and placed a canvas captain's chair opposite the settee. Stéphane put aside the toe shoe she was working on and lit a cigarette. Philippa sewed and watched.

"How many pointe shoes do you go through in a week?" Alex asked.

Stéphane shrugged. "Depends on the ballets. About ten pairs as a rule." She glanced at Philippa. "Of course, if I danced like our jewel here — at or beyond the speed of light — I'd probably go through twice that number. I'd also be in intensive care or a nursing home. I mean, she's so fabulous."

Stéphane spoke very slowly and lingered on words like "fab-u-lous." Alex noticed, as well, that she rarely blinked and, when she did, her eyelids moved as deliberately as a camera shutter set on a long time exposure. Whether this occurred as a result of a laggard metabolism or feline affectation, he couldn't say, but the effect was curiously sensual.

Philippa said, "Don't listen to her. She has perfect placement and marvelous line. Maurice Béjart offered to make her a featured dancer but she refused because she wouldn't move to Belgium."

"Greeks *die* in Belgium," Stéphane said. "Besides, I was in love at the time." With that she smiled her wide smile, gazed sideways at Alex for a moment, then looked away.

Alex said, "I need to ask you about Virgile de la Pagerie."

"I know."

"Shall we talk now? Here? Or would you prefer to come down to the Maison tomorrow?"

"Maison?"

"Sûreté headquarters."

"Do you serve Courvoisier at Sûreté headquarters?"

"Not as a rule."

"Well then, let's talk here." She took a sip and put her cigarette out in the scallop shell she carried in her dance bag for that purpose.

Alex said, "I am obliged to advise you that you're entitled to an advocate."

"Because I might say something that could be held against me?"

"Technically."

"I don't need an advocate when I go to the dentist, and I say plenty there that could be held against me. So I don't see why I need one here. Anyway, I didn't kill Virgile. I liked him and he liked me."

Alex nodded. He went to the companion ladder and withdrew a small cassette recorder from the pocket of his jacket. He placed it on the edge of the settee, switched it on and sat down.

"This is Grismolet and Mademoiselle Stéphane . . ."

"Nikolaides."

"Stéphane Nikolaides, Thursday five September 1985" — he checked his watch — "2120."

The preliminaries were dispensed with. Stéphane stated the date and place of her birth (6 May 1960, in Antibes, of Greek parents), present address (*Le Yacht Club,* moored at No. 12, Quai de la Charente), and present employer (Paris Opéra Ballet, Palais Garnier). She added that she had voluntarily waived legal counsel.

Alex leaned back and placed his hands behind his head. "Why don't you just talk and I'll listen?"

"About Virgile?"

"Yes. Anything and everything you can think of, no matter how insignificant. The more we know about him, the sooner we'll understand why someone wanted to kill him."

Stéphane suddenly exhaled and, without warning, fanned her face with her hand. "Whew," she whispered and fanned her face again. "My word! Sorry, hot flash." Her cheeks were

scarlet. "When you said what you said, the way you said it —
so unambiguously — it triggered something."

"Triggered what?"

"I'm not sure. Not the menopause, I hope. I don't know.
Reality perhaps."

Philippa, who had stopped, resumed sewing.

"Maybe it hadn't occurred to my defective brain that
someone actually meant to murder Virgile," Stéphane said.
She felt her cheeks with the back of her hand. "Sorry."
She shifted her position on the settee. "So. Tell you all I can
about Virgile, no matter how insignificant? Actually, what I
know is very insignificant, apart from what I've learned from
Délice."

"Délice?"

"His mother."

"And where is she?"

"Martinique. We met last Christmas, by phone. She's an
artist; a very good artist. We corresponded more or less regularly by mail, especially when she wanted news of Virgile. It
wasn't all that easy because Virgile didn't confide. I was his
. . . um . . . roommate for almost a year, but he didn't have
much to say to me. Actually, everything was more or less . . .
prescribed. I think that's the word. He had his room and I
had mine, both here and on the beach."

"On the beach where?"

"Marbella."

"Where is that exactly?"

"On the Spanish Costa del Sol, between Málaga and Gi-
braltar. It's heaven. In the morning, when the air is clear, you
can see across the straits to Morocco."

"Did you go there often?"

"Twice. Once last January for a week, before the winter

season, and again two weeks ago, for my vacation. But Virgile went down about once a month."

"And left you in Paris?"

"Well, naturally. I have a job."

"Where did you stay in Paris?"

"At his apartment in Rue de Tournon."

"And when he made this monthly trip to the beach without you, did he go alone?"

She tilted her head slightly. "As far as I know, he went alone. I never asked. And he didn't say."

"You trusted him."

She seemed puzzled by the remark. "Trusted him? Trust never came up between us. I never questioned what he did." She paused. "However, having said that, I do remember, on one occasion, that he didn't go to the beach house when he said he was going. I discovered this without meaning to. By that I mean I wasn't checking up on him. Three or four days after he left Paris, something came in the mail that I thought might be important."

Alex interrupted. "What was it that came in the mail?"

"Something from a veterans organization . . . Fédération des Anciens Combattants, I think."

"Was he a veteran?"

"Not that I know of."

"Did you open it?"

"Certainly not."

"Go on."

"Well, when this envelope arrived, I thought it might be important, so I phoned Marbella. The housekeeper answered. She said he hadn't been there at all."

"Can you name the housekeeper?"

"Corazón."

"Last name?"

"Don't know."

"Has she been with him long?"

"Since he's owned the house, I think."

"How long is that?"

"About five years."

"Did Corazón know where he was?"

"No."

"Did you?"

"No."

"And you didn't ask?"

"No. That would have been crossing the privacy line. As I said before, we were separate. We had separate rooms and separate baths. I mean, I never saw him brush his teeth. We ate together, played on the beach together, and swam together. But we rarely communicated verbally, apart from 'Good morning, Stéphane, shall we go to Fuengirola for dinner, shall we run or swim to the breakwater?' I won't say there weren't moments of gregariousness — after a meal, or after he'd written something he liked. But those moments were separated by long periods of silence, solitary reading and reflection."

"What did you do during those periods?"

"Swam, stretched, dealt with the guilt every dancer feels when she's not dancing."

"Then you were frequently alone. Was there ever any real intimacy?"

"What intimacy we had was ... physical; physical, but, like everything else, prescribed."

"Not spontaneous."

"Not spontaneous." She suddenly looked at Philippa. "Jesus, this is embarrassing!" She passed a hand over her face. "Um . . . when we made love, it was in the morning, and in my room. Always. I never went near his room either here or in Marbella. That would have been crossing the privacy line."

"Was that privacy or concealment?"

"What's the difference, if he didn't want me to know he snored or kept his teeth in a glass? Anyway, we never spent the night together."

Alex glanced at Philippa. Stéphane picked up her snifter and, barely rotating it, watched, unblinking, as the amber liquid clung to its concave inner surface. "He did say, once, that he felt safe with me. I realize that was not exactly a compliment. I'm sure what he meant was that I was no threat to him intellectually." She took a sip. "He was right. I mean, I know when to come in out of the rain, but Simone de Beauvoir and Marguerite Duras don't have to worry." She smiled and did a little pose. "I'm easy, I photograph well — and I have to pee."

She swiveled on one knee, stepped off the settee, and floated into the forecabin. Alex switched off the cassette.

Philippa said, "She's telling the truth. I've heard most of this before."

"Really? You said he jogged on the beach all day and fucked his brains out all night."

"So?"

"Now she says they never spent the night together."

"Alex, don't be so literal. What difference does it make when he fucked his brains out?"

"It makes no difference. But if the details of her testimony are inconsistent, it'll make a big difference how we rate her credibility."

Philippa lowered her sewing into her lap. "Maybe I exaggerated. She's as straight as an arrow ... except when it comes to men. Which reminds me: Do me a favour. Ugly up a little. Black out a tooth. Develop psoriasis. She's half in love with you already."

"Don't be ridiculous."

"Listen, I know my Stéphane. That hot flash had nothing to do with reality. It had to do with hormones. Last year, Baryshnikov came to a rehearsal and she had hot flashes for a week. I want you to sit up straight, cross your legs, and wear a prayer shawl."

"How is it she's not dancing tonight?"

"Rudy let her off, and without a fuss, which is not like him. He never lets anyone off. If you're breathing, you dance; especially if you're a girl."

"Why are you sewing toe shoes? You're on vacation."

"They're hers. But if she gets another hot flash around you, I'm filling them with broken glass."

Alex peered into the forecabin. "She doesn't seem exactly grief-stricken over the death of her lover."

Philippa snipped off a thread with her teeth. "I'm not sure she was totally committed to him; any more than he was to her."

"But you said love was her hobby."

"It is. Or was, until Délice started pushing for grand-children."

"His mother wanted Delap to marry Stéphane?"

"Not to marry. To make babies; 'beautiful Franco-Afro-Greek babies,' she said, 'with genes strong as pot warp.' The idea did not excite Stéphane. Delap either. What they had, and wanted to keep, was an agreeable ménage. They were essentially playmates. He fed and sheltered her in style, in return for which she provided cheerful company and certain adult divertissements. So to speak." Philippa poured another finger of cognac for herself and Stéphane. Alex had not touched his. She emptied Stéphane's scallop shell ashtray, returned it to the dance bag, and reinstalled herself on the settee. "It will probably come as no surprise to you to learn that both of them were casualties of earlier emotional skirmishes. Stéphane fell disastrously in love with her gynecologist when she was nineteen. He was fifty and married. It could not have been worse." Philippa did not elaborate.

"And he?"

"The gynecologist?"

"No, Delap."

"He was engaged to a young actress who died."

"Which young actress who died?"

"Angélique Églantine."

Alex had heard of her. She was a quirky, unconventional actress of promise who seemed to have faded away.

"Hmm," Philippa suddenly hummed, got to her feet and, without bending her knees, touched the floor with the flats of her hands. She'd anticipated Stéphane's noiseless reappearance.

Stéphane had unbraided her pigtail and brushed out her hair so that her face was framed on each side by a glistening mane that reached nearly to her waist. Philippa straightened up and held out the snifter. Stéphane took it and glided to the settee where she sat, cross-legged in front of Alex. She smiled slightly.

"While I was reading the instructions on how to flush the commode, I suddenly remembered that my clothes are still at Virgile's. Will I be allowed to pick them up?"

Alex switched on the tape recorder. "Certainly. After the lab people have completed their inspection. By the way, do you have a key to the flat?"

"Yes." She reached down, rummaged through her dance

bag, and extracted a leather purse. She opened the purse and produced a delicate key chain to which two keys and a small, oval cameo were attached. She handed it to Alex.

He examined the cameo. It was of intricately carved green jasper with a raised white decoration in the centre that, upon close inspection, revealed the elegant, pearl-white, swan-necked profile of a woman.

"Very nice," Alex said. "Who's the lady?"

"Marie-Joseph Rose Tascher de la Pagerie."

"De la Pagerie —"

"Who became Marie-Joséphine, Vicomtesse de Beauharnais, who became Joséphine Bonaparte."

"The Empress Joséphine?"

"The Empress Joséphine. She was Virgile's great-great-great-great-aunt." She counted the "greats" on her fingers.

"Well! And you said he never confided in you."

"He didn't. I got it from Délice."

"I see."

"It's true!"

"That Delap was related to the Empress Joséphine?"

"Absolutely!"

"But that's impossible!"

"Why? Because Virgile was technically black? I'm surprised you're surprised. The truth is that the Empress Joséphine and Virgile's great-great-great-grandmother had the same papa."

Alex looked at Philippa. She frowned and continued sewing. He turned back to Stéphane. "You're serious, aren't you?" Stéphane lit a cigarette and fished her scallop shell out of the dance bag. Alex asked, "What was Virgile's great-et cetera-grandmother's name?"

"Euphémie."

"And you say she and Joséphine had the same papa?"

"Yes."

"But not the same mama."

"No, indeed. Joséphine's mama was white, Creole French. Euphémie's mama was a slave."

Alex nodded. He took his first sip of cognac. "So, at some point, Virgile appropriated the name of his eighteenth-century, slave-owning paterfamilias."

"Yes, if what you just said means ancestor."

"When did he change his name?"

"To de la Pagerie? When he came to France."

"That was sometime in the seventies. What was his name before he came to France?"

"Virgile Bloch."

"Bloch."

"His stepfather's name is Honoré Bloch."

"And what was his name before his stepfather married his mother?"

"Géronte. Délice's maiden name."

"But Virgile Géronte Bloch de la Pagerie must've had a real father who had a name."

"Yes. He had a real father." Stéphane stroked her hair. "Délice said Virgile was a love child. He was born when Délice was fifteen. She never knew his father's name; only that he was a sailor on a banana schooner bound for Philadelphia."

Alex sighed. "So. Virgile Philadelphie."

Stéphane blinked. "Well, yes."

Alex got up, walked to the companion ladder, and turned back to Stéphane. "This is important. It doesn't matter now whether the story is true or not. What matters now is, Who else knows it besides you?"

"Knows what? That his birth name was Virgile Phila-delphie?"

"Yes."

"Does it matter?"

Alex studied her expression. "You don't know?"

"I guess not."

"Have you heard of the Front Patriotique?"

"France for the French, or something —?"

"Stéphane. Someone using a fake voice telephoned the Se-nior Terrorist Investigator's office this morning and stated, 'The Front Patriotique has executed Virgile Philadelphie, the mulatto mongrel of Martinique.' "

Stéphane stared. She put out her cigarette. "I didn't know that," she said softly. "That scares me. That practically puts it in the family."

"Exactly. Now, what I need to know . . . is this strictly a family story? Or is it common knowledge?"

"It's family."

"But Délice told you, and you're not family."

"Délice treats me like family."

"Didn't Virgile have other girlfriends?"

"Of course."

"If Délice told you after less than a year, couldn't she have told them?"

"I don't think so."

"What about Virgile's fiancée?"

"Angélique? I don't know. Délice and Honoré didn't much care for Angélique. They thought she was permanently out to lunch." She smiled. "But they adore me." She tossed some hair over her shoulder. "They wanted Stéphane and Virgile to make babies. Délice said, 'Honoré and me, we love diversity! You make them, we take them! We raise them on this radiant isle! And we don't let their heads be get wet!' "

"What's that mean?"

"It's voodoo-obeah belief that water, especially dew, is a powerful magnet and solvent for spirits, and that a man's spirit dwells either in his shadow or his head."

Alex wondered if this abrupt change of subject was deliberate or scattered. He decided to give Stéphane the benefit of the doubt. "Voodoo? Délice practices voodoo?"

"No. But she plays her cards. She acknowledges any religion that may be useful: her own, Catholicism; Honoré's, Judaism; her Pakistani art supplier's, Muslim; and voodoo, just in case." Stéphane clapped her hands once. "Yesss; I'm family. Délice not only told me the story, she gave me the book."

"The book?"

"The genealogy of the family; leather-bound, written and illustrated by her. It's gorgeous. It begins in 1761 with a miniature portrait of Joseph Tascher de la Pagerie in the female slave quarters of his plantation, his trousers around his ankles and his white bum in the air between a pair of pretty bronze thighs, recumbent on a straw pallet. The book ends, many pages and many black and white ancestors later, with Honoré adopting the six-year-old Virgile. There's even a sketch of the banana schooner leaving Fort-de-France for Philadelphia. Délice enclosed a note to me that said 'I just wanted you to know what you might be getting into.' "

"Where is this book?"

"In my room at the flat."

"Who's seen it?"

She shrugged. "Virgile."

"No one else? A guest? Cleaning man or woman? Corazón?"

"I'm sure not. Certainly not Corazón."

"And you've told the story to no one?"

She shook her head.

He turned to Philippa. "You said you'd heard most of this before."

"Not this part," Philippa replied.

Alex turned back to Stéphane. "Does Délice know that her son is dead?"

"Yes. But I don't think she knows he was murdered. When I called her late last night, I didn't know. And when I found out this morning, I didn't have the heart to call her back. Besides, she and Honoré are probably already on their way to Paris. They want to take Virgile back to Martinique."

The ship's clock suddenly struck five bells. It was 10:30. Philippa said, "Alex, Stéphane has a nine o'clock class."

Alex switched off the cassette and walked to the chart table. He opened a drawer and took out a stainless steel key attached to a plastic float shaped like a navigational buoy. He carried it to Stéphane. "This is the key to the companion hatch padlock." He placed it in her hand. "For the moment, you can consider yourself part of our family."

She looked at the key, raised her eyes to his for an instant, then quickly turned away and fanned her face with her hand.

Philippa missed it. She was collecting the snifters.

Just before 6 A.M. the next morning, Alex was awakened by a slight movement of *Le Yacht Club* alongside the quai, a movement imperceptible to anyone but a mariner intimately aware of his vessel's trim.

From across the forecabin corridor, he heard Philippa stir. After a moment, she murmured, "Alex?"

"Yes?"

"What was that?"

"Dunno. I'll see." He untucked his long frame from the

berth and, clad only in a T-shirt, took a step toward the corridor. At that moment, he remembered Stéphane, asleep in the saloon. He slipped into his jeans and padded into the corridor. Halfway to the companion ladder, he noticed that the settee had been made up and the bedclothes neatly folded on the table. There was a note on top of the blanket, together with the companion hatch key. The note, folded in half, was for Philippa. He delivered it to her stateroom.

As Philippa opened the note, Alex untangled her upper lashes from her lower, a persistent problem for Philippa in the morning. She read:

> *Chérie: Your boat is no place for these bones. I suddenly remembered Marcia has a spare room. Ten thousand for the hospitality, but I know it will be better for everyone if I bunk ashore.*
>
> > *Hugs,*
> >
> > *S —*

7

Varnas

HE HAD SLEPT POORLY. He awoke before daybreak with aching calf muscles and a stiff neck. "Not yet Nureyev," he muttered as he struggled out of bed and limped painfully to the bathroom for a long soak.

While he waited for the tiny claw-footed iron tub to fill — a long process on the fifth floor with an antique, curved copper spout of insignificant inside diameter as a faucet — he went to his closet kitchen and made a glass of strong tea, laced, Lithuanian-style, with strawberry jam and vodka.

Later, soaking and sipping, he examined the day ahead. The Commissaire's orientation meeting with Research was at 8. As Alex would be there, Varnas could miss it. It would undoubtedly consist of a recapitulation, one way or another, of Demonet's Dictum. In the absence of a suspect, the Commissaire's First Law was harmlessly appropriate:

> *Here is Demonet's Dictum:*
> *Learn all you can about the victim.*

At nine o'clock, Dactyloscopy and Photolab would descend on de la Pagerie's sealed flat in Rue de Tournon, for dusting and Polaroids. Forensics would arrive at 10 and, given the obsessively fussy Forensics Chef-Inspecteur Chartier, probably remain through the week. Chartier was a small, fastidious man whose giant condescension toward all but science lab police officers increased exponentially yearly. He was a man who would allow no speck of dust or chip of paint to escape analysis by "that brightest jewel in the Forensic crown, the gas chromatograph mass spectro-metre."

Those were Hippo's words, Varnas recalled. It occurred to him that Hippo (Hippolyte Maurice Ludovic du Temple, be-loved Chef of Ballistics) would not be on the case this time since no conventional weapon appeared to be involved. Moreover, Hippo was taking his habitual autumn holiday. A pity. Hippo was good company.

Much relieved after forty minutes in the tub, Varnas tow-eled and exited the bath. Since the drain was as obstinate as the faucet, he decided to postpone rinsing the tub until to-night.

He shaved and dressed. First, clean undergarments; then a fresh, Madame-Roget-laundered-and-starched white shirt, followed by Madame-Roget-pressed black trousers, vest, jacket, and polished shoes to match. He knotted his dark ma-roon tie, wound his pocket watch, and stretched the gold chain before placing watch and fob in opposite vest pockets. It was 7:15 A.M. He put on his hat. He would go now to Virgile de la Pagerie's flat in Rue de Tournon, arriving an hour early, to have a look round before the lab techniciens made a mess of the place.

Orly

Air Martinique's Flight 3041 landed thirty minutes ahead of schedule due to a powerful westerly eddy in the jet stream.

The flight had been undersold and, as most of the passengers were citizens of France, the Customs and Immigration process was accomplished without delay.

At 6:25, Délice Géronte strode out of the arrival building wearing a lavender head scarf, a knee-length sable coat over a gray running suit, and gray suede ankle boots. Heads turned as the slim but full-figured black woman passed. Her skin shone like polished ebony. But while her colour betokened darkest Africa, her facial features were conspicuously and perfectly European: the nose was small and Venus-straight, the mouth small but full. However, what amazed were the large, almond-shaped eyes of piercing, indigo blue. The effect was striking and profoundly aristocratic. No one would've believed she was forty-six.

Behind her, dragging a quantity of matching luggage, strapped to a two-wheeled baggage cart, came an older white man in a blue running suit and panama hat with a pale pink, paisley band. He had the aquiline nose and gently ascetic, but slightly yellowed, face of a saint in an unrestored Renaissance painting. This was Honoré Bloch. He was fifty-three and looked ten years older.

Outside, Délice hailed a cab, got in, and departed the airport for Paris. Next in line, Honoré hailed a cab, helped the driver place the luggage and cart in the cab's trunk, settled in the back seat, and departed.

At 7:05, Délice arrived at the Paris flower market and told the cab to wait while she embarked on her round of purchases. A few minutes later, Honoré arrived at the Hôtel Madison in Boulevard St-Germain, where he had booked a small suite for himself and Délice for the week. He left the luggage with the bell captain, and reentered the cab, which took him to the Rue de Tournon address of his stepson, arriving there at 7:20. Ten minutes later, Délice appeared, her taxi filled with fresh sunflowers, African and white daisies, chrysanthemums, asters, anemones, foxgloves, and four boxes of orchids.

They let themselves into the building and, carrying half the flowers, took the small lift to the private, fourth-floor landing opposite Virgile's flat. There they saw a red and white vinyl tape plastered across the front door, bearing the legend "Entry Forbidden, SN."

"Forbidden!" Honoré exclaimed.

"Shh," Délice whispered, "you'll wake Stéphane." She studied the lettering on the tape perfunctorily. "This is not for us, amour," she said. "The 'SN' stands for Stéphane Nikolaides. Go down and get the rest of the flowers."

While Honoré reentered the lift, she inserted her key in the door, which opened in, and entered the flat, tearing the tape.

Délice tiptoed across the white marble floor of the sun-drenched, high-ceilinged grande salle, lined with white, silk-curtained dormer windows. She moved noiselessly up the corridor leading to the bedrooms. In spite of herself, she stopped where the corridor split. Here, a narrow passageway led to the roof garden. Next to the door opening on the roof garden was a small room which had once been used to store tools and potting soil but that, since her last visit to Paris, had been transformed. Now the tools were gone. The walls had been replastered and papered in a repeating pattern of soft, pink-and-white summer clouds that formed castles in the air. Beneath the clouds, boys and girls in nineteenth-century costume — the girls in pantaloons and bonnets, the boys in sailor suits and straw boaters — flew kites in the warm, summer air. The only furniture in the room was an antique bamboo-and-wicker crib.

Délice remained there for a moment, then moved to Stéphane's room, across the corridor from Virgile's study. "Study" was the word Délice used. Actually, Virgile's study was an elaborate bedroom-office-library, with a four-poster the size of the Luxembourg Gardens, and twin bathrooms.

She peered through the open door into Stéphane's room. Stéphane was not there. The bed was made. Odd. Well, there would be a rational explanation for all this soon enough. She went into Stéphane's bathroom, festooned with laundered tights and leotards, and filled the bidet with water. She did the same to the bidets in the twin bathrooms of Virgile's study, and in the guest bathroom off the grande salle.

Honoré had returned and was whispering. Délice said, "You don't have to whisper, amour. She's not here. You do the bidets. I'll do the rest."

Honoré gathered up the orchids and carefully made a tour of the flat's bathrooms, emptying a boxful into each of the four bidets.

On the white marble floor of the grande salle, orange, pink, and turquoise rugs formed islands of colour on which floated Empire chairs and sofas in textured fabrics. Adjacent to these pieces were a dozen low tables of teak, rattan, and glass, which Délice now covered with vases, bowls, and dishes, crammed with fresh-cut flowers.

When she had finished, the room, dazzling in the morning light, resembled a sun-struck ice palace in which an autumn garden grew.

They stood in the middle of the room. "It is entirely fitting," Honoré said gravely, and kissed his wife's hand.

She said, "I will rest now, amour, until the funeral director arrives." She went to Virgile's study and stretched out on the chaise longue under her sable.

Honoré, who did not feel tired, went to the kitchen to prepare a café filtre. Previously, he had used his stepson's old-fashioned *machinetta*, a sort of double drip pot, to make the coffee. But since the renovation, the kitchen had acquired a machine that made any kind of coffee you fancied, as in a restaurant. He read the instructions and manipulated the appropriate buttons and handles. While he was waiting for the steam, he heard a sound behind him, turned, and there in the kitchen doorway beheld a very small man wearing a black suit and homburg.

Honoré said, "Good morning."

"Good morning," Varnas replied.

"You will be the funeral director."

"Pardon?"

"You are very early for your appointment, monsieur. We were not to meet until ten. But come in, come in. I am Honoré Bloch. My wife is resting. Do you wish coffee?"

Varnas learned that Délice and Honoré, upon learning of their son's death, had made plans for a private funeral in Paris at the Église St-Sulpice in two days' time. They had arranged with Air Martinique to fly the casket home the day after, with burial planned for Saturday in Trois Îlets.

It was plain that neither of them had seen a telecast or newspaper since they'd left Fort-de-France. Sitting across from Honoré at the kitchen breakfast bar, Varnas silently thanked Philippa for his sore legs, without which he would not have awakened early, would not have come to Virgile de la Pagerie's flat early, and would not have been the one selected, instead of some barbarian lab flic, to tell them their son had been murdered.

Honoré examined Varnas's ID. He read every word, including the validation dates, the Interior Ministry stamp, and the government form number. "So," he whispered, "in the present circumstances, 'SN' means Sûreté Nationale, not Stéphane Nikolaides." He paused and gazed at Varnas. "Well, inspecteur, you are investigating something in my son's home. Are you investigating something he did to someone, or something someone did to him?"

Varnas told him. Honoré Bloch's light brown eyes darkened. After a long silence, during which the only sound came from the refrigerator ice-maker, he rose and said, "I must inform my wife. Please excuse me."

Fifteen, then twenty, minutes passed. Varnas inspected the gas range with its two electric ovens, the microwave, the pantry, freezer, and laundry room. Finally, at 8:30, he left the kitchen and took the direction Bloch had taken. Reaching a corridor hung with blazing watercolours of tropical vegetation and long-tailed birds, he moved noiselessly to his left. After a few paces, he came to the open door of a large bedroom with bookshelves. There, in the centre of the room, stood Honoré and Délice, clinging to each other. They had stood like that, without moving, pressed together, wordless and inconsolable, for nearly half an hour.

Varnas called a cab, removed the police tape from the doorway, and escorted the Blochs back to their hotel. Not a word was spoken until they entered the hotel lift. There, Délice exclaimed, "We will require police protection!"

Honoré emphatically demurred. "Amour, we will not require police protection!"

"We will!" she cried. "The bastards are everywhere!" With that she punched a button and the elevator doors hissed shut.

The Maison

Sûreté Commissaire Henri Demonet had a small vein in his right temple that pulsed when he was impatient. It was pulsing this morning, Alex noted, somewhat mitigating the Commissaire's habitual poise and immaculate exterior: the well-shaped head, the glossy, slightly Brilliantined black hair, combed straight back from the distinguished, if somewhat receding, hairline, the dignified traces of gray in the sideburns. Alex looked again. The dignified traces of gray in the sideburns were not there this morning. Nor was the Commissaire, presiding as usual at his massive cherrywood desk, wrapped in his official blue pinstripe, but in white flannel trousers, blue blazer with brass buttons, and a white shirt, open at the neck, that partially obscured an untied Hermès foulard.

Alex wondered if there was any truth to the rumor that this immensely civilized and respected man, who could easily become Directeur of all Sûreté operations in France someday, a man married to the same woman for thirty-two years, might be dyeing his hair and adjusting to a more youthful lifestyle for some clandestine purpose not associated with the federal police.

The Commissaire glanced at his watch as the Sûreté's grizzled Research specialist, Chef-Inspecteur Isabelle Fauré, entered and took the seat next to Alex.

The meeting began. Alex switched on the office tape deck and played back the message phoned to the Senior Terrorist Investigator's office yesterday.

The robotic, artificial voice intoned: "The Front Patriotique has executed Virgile Philadelphie, the mulatto mongrel of Martinique, for blasphemy and crimes against the République. Long live —" Alex switched off the machine.

"Before we proceed," he said, "let me explain the genesis of the name Virgile Philadelphie." He briefly reviewed Stéphane's testimony, including Delap's alleged blood tie to the Empress Joséphine.

The Commissaire appeared sceptical. "These legends from the sugar and spice islands of the Lesser Antilles do not travel well, Alex. Be selective. Be careful. The judge expects facts, not folktales." He drummed momentarily on the desk top. "What about the zombie voice on the tape?"

"A variation of the 'Lectro Larynx, I expect. The sound box removes all speech characteristics: pitch, emphasis, even accent. Man, woman, child, robot, all sound the same. Nevertheless, we'll run the tape by the sound lab."

The Commissaire nodded absently and turned to his Research specialist. "You have something, Isabelle?"

Chef-Inspecteur Fauré was a tough Interior Ministry snoop, somewhere in her fifties, who regularly played the horses and had successfully predicted the winner of the Euro football finals for the past five years. She held up a newspaper.

"It will come as no surprise," she said, "that the Front Patriotique has officially denied any involvement in de la Pagerie's death. It's in all the morning papers. They say, more or less, that they will not achieve their ends by violence or intimidation, but by parliamentary means, et cetera; their victory will take place at the ballot box, long live France, and so forth." She dropped the paper on Demonet's desk. "Naturally, I've been looking for some connection between the Front Patriotique and de la Pagerie. I found this. It was published three weeks ago." She handed around two pages of photocopy. The first was a news article from *Le Figaro*. Alex read,

FRENCH RIGHT DENIES EXISTENCE OF HOLOCAUST AND
VICHY COLLABORATION

Marseille, 15 August. Rallying his supporters to the cry of "Long Live France for the French," leader of the Front Patriotique, Jean-François LeSaut, affirmed his group's denial of the Holocaust. "We have the right to set the record straight," he said. "The so-called Holocaust was, and is, a public relations strategy fabricated by Zionists to extort money from banks, government, and industry. The few hundred thousand Jews — not six million — who perished during World War Two did so in their own filth from typhus and other diseases. There was no Holocaust. The Holocaust is a myth, just as Jewish allegations that Vichy France collaborated with the Nazis is a myth."

Monsieur LeSaut, who seeks the invalidation of all naturalization of Arabs and Jews since 1974 and is pressing for job priority for white French citizens, accused the Socialists of trying to declare his party illegal. He threatened to sue the Anti-Defamation League of B'nai B'rith and France's Masonic Lodge if they persist in their attacks against him.

The second photocopy was of an editorial page reply to the Front Patriotique's declaration, by Virgile de la Pagerie, published two days later in *La Revue Endimanchée*.

"It was his last article," Isabelle said.

CRITIC-AT-LARGE

Well, dear friends, the ruffians of the hard right have declared themselves the fascist party of France. At least we know where they stand. That's more than we can say for the government.

Irony Number One

Is it not mystifying that the Socialists routinely attack the Front Patriotique, that anti-Semitic, xenophobic band of tiny-minded hoodlums, who maintain the Holocaust and Vichy collaboration with the Nazis never existed, when the government itself behaves as if the Holocaust and Vichy collaboration never existed?

Where will the Élysée Palace find the mettle to bring to justice the ex-Vichy politicians and police officials who survive among us today; those still-free collaborationists who, from 1941 to 1945, participated in the deportation of 76,000 Jews from unoccupied France to German death camps?

Irony Number Two

Where does the Front Patriotique get its money? From candy sales and lotto? No, Bernice. The Front Patriotique earns 5% of its income from extortion. It receives its other 95% from the same wealthy, isolationist, nativist band of old conservatives in the south who supported the anti-Semitic views of the Vichy government in the '40s, who funded the legal defense of the surviving collaborationists in the '70s, enabling them to escape trial for their part in the deportation of Jews from unoccupied France that the F.P. insists never took place. Indeed, the F.P. is inexorably linked to the very process they say never took place. Thus does the tail wag the dog.

QED

Unless we terminate this circle of cowardice and complicity, we will all be wearing badges again: stars for Jews, crescents for Arabs, pansies for homosexuals, and little watermelons for blacks.

Commissaire Demonet put down the article and peered at Alex. "When did the theatre critic become a political animal?"

"I don't know."

"Find out."

"I will."

"And what is the interest of this native of Martinique, born ten years after the war, in the fate of the Jewish diaspora?"

"I don't know. His stepfather is Jewish."

The Commissaire got up and began his promenade. This short tour around his desk was vintage Demonet, designed to clear his mind and command attention from his subalterns.

"We have a universally disliked theatre critic whose death, at the hands of a vengeful thespian or theatre manager, would seem logical and clearly motivated. Even the producer-directeur, Auguste Pezon-Schwartz, has testified that only cowardice prevented him from performing the deed himself. Yet no member of the theatrical profession has emerged as a suspect."

The Commissaire stopped his stroll and began to tie his foulard. "Now, fade out the unpopular theatre critic, and fade in a fearless, heretofore unknown political muckraker who attacks the hard right and the racist legacy of Vichy on which the government has been dragging its feet for forty years.

"First. Why has the critic assumed this new role? Second. Has his attack stung someone, or something, sufficiently to invite retaliation? And third. Why did the killer use the code words Virgile Philadelphie, which narrow the field and spotlight him?

"Arrogance. Why did he phone the Senior Terrorist Investigator's office, which everyone knows is bugged?"

Isabelle interrupted. "Excuse me. If the Front Patriotique is really out of this, as they claim, why did the killer choose to blame them? Why not the musicians' union or the phone company? What's so special about the Front Patriotique?"

"I don't know that either," Alex said softly. "But if there's a reason, we'll find it. My strong sense, though, is that the Front Patriotique had nothing to do with this. Much as I disapprove of them, this crime is not their style. These are punks and bullies who intimidate and knock heads out of frustration, ignorance, and anger. They target minorities they imagine threaten their jobs, their women, and their Frenchness. It's an old story. When times are bad, the hard right depends on the biases of the out-of-work white lower class to deliver its message.

"Furthermore, I can't reconcile the sophisticated method used to murder Delap with a hate group whose weapons are sharpened coins and brickbats. And the choice of locale. A theatre in Paris, on the first opening night of the season. Whoever did it could have killed him anywhere else with a tenth of the risk and a tenth of the preparation. They could've killed him on the beach at Marbella with a rock."

The Commissaire finished his foulard, buttoned his blazer, and smiled mischievously. "But that would not have had the same resonance, would it, Alex? I mean, if you murder the Archbishop, you murder him in his cathedral, don't you?" He glanced at his watch. "I'm late. Check with Forensics when you have a moment. Keep me apprised." He nodded pleasantly and, with a wave of the hand, was gone.

Alex stared at Isabelle. "I was just getting started. Where's he going at eight-thirty on a Friday morning, dressed for croquet?"

Isabelle got up. "I'm giving two to one he has a trick, seven to two she's under thirty-five, and eight to five he'll never shag her."

8

Hippo

PARIS BALLISTICS Chef-Inspecteur Hippolyte Maurice Ludovic du Temple lowered his copy of *La Dépêche du Midi,* glanced out the window, then across the front seat at his companion driving the rental Renault.

"Slow down, Marcel," he said. "We are at the village of Pexiora. You are going ninety in a fifty-kilometre zone."

His friend grunted and decelerated. Hippo resumed his perusal of the newspaper. To a man with a lifelong addiction to the Paris dailies, *La Dépêche du Midi,* the voice of Toulouse and the south, seemed to lack seasoning. Still, it was something to read, something that, when held in front of one, hid the road ahead and helped one deal with the trauma of driving with Marcel at the wheel.

Hippo read the Narbonne news. Five new houses going up in Narbonne . . . a viola concert tonight . . .

Marcel slowed to a virtual crawl. Hippo lowered the paper again and gazed through the windscreen. The reason for the snail's pace became apparent. A tractor with flashing lights bounced along ahead of them, hauling a trailer-load of grapes.

The village of Pexiora, indistinguishable from the other white stucco and orange tile–roofed villages on the fluvial plain that stretches from the Garonne to the Med, was, like its sister hamlets, devoted to the cultivation of grapevines for the region's winemaking industry. September was the beginning of the harvest, one of the reasons Hippo and Marcel decided to take their holiday together.

But while the vaguely Spanish-sounding Pexiora was indistinguishable from Villeneuve-la-Comptal or Lasbordes, Hippo and Marcel, though roughly the same age of sixty-something, were as different in appearance and temperament as oil and water.

Hippo, the widely respected Senior Ballistics Chef, who possessed an encyclopedic knowledge of weaponry, from the Trébuchet — a mediaeval siege weapon that hurled rocks at the enemy — to the automatic Uzi, was a small, pink-faced man whose ascetic mien was closer to a cloistered friar than to a professional flic. His lifestyle matched his countenance. Hippo would not fly in an aéroplane. He chose to leave Paris two days ahead of Marcel, so that he could take the train to Toulouse. Hippo did not drive an auto, or a bicycle either. He was allergic to exercise. He wore indifferently tailored suits of gray or brown, cardigan sweaters, bow ties, and always a fedora or beret, like his late father; and he peered out at the world through flat, round, black-rimmed bifocals. His passions were, first, his Ballistics work in Paris, second, the European Society of Antique Weaponry (E.S.A.W.), which took him throughout the continent and over which he presided with monastic zeal, and, third, every aspect of viniculture, from the selection of the grape to the tasting.

But if Hippo, the flic, resembled a monk, his friend, Marcel Rivette, an ordained Jesuit priest, resembled a retired

boxer. He was about the size of Gérard Dépardieu. His rug-
gedly sculpted face, beneath shaggy brows and a full head of
iron-gray hair cut in the latest style, was bronzed the year
round from skiing or windsurfing. He never wore a hat or a
suit, except at meetings of the Society of Jesus or when summoned by his bishop. In addition to his appreciation of fine
wine, which he shared with Hippo, he had a fondness for
Scotch whiskey and Armagnac. He enjoyed American cigarettes, Cuban cigars, YSL sunglasses, and he wore a gold
chain around his neck to which a tiny Saint Christopher
medal was attached, in violation of recent church canon.

Marcel had joined Hippo's arms society, not out of any
passion for weaponry, but because of his fascination with
early Christian history, much of which seemed to have been
shaped by force. Marcel's great enthusiasm, however, was the
history of religious miracles, serial and public; shrine-
establishing apparitions, miraculous Virginal interventions,
signs, cures, weeping icons, and paranormal events. Hippo
did not approve of this avocation for a man of the cloth. He
believed, with the church, that paranormal events, featuring a
celestial cast of characters, verged on the pagan, and were a
distraction from, and a poor substitute for, the daily sacra-
ments. But out of devotion to his friend, he endeavored to
keep quiet about it.

Hippo, then, had come to the south of France to catalogue
a few antique weapons for the E.S.A.W., and for the wine
harvest. Marcel had come to investigate the appearance of
the Blessed Virgin to ten-year-old Marie-Rose Fournier in the
Haut Languedoc, and, of course, for the wine harvest.

Pexiora behind them, Marcel resumed his normal
secondary-road velocity of between 90 and 100 kph. Hippo,
weary of his newspaper, leaned back and closed his eyes.

Hippo had looked forward to this holiday for some time; looked forward to it, that is, until this morning, when, while watching the TV at breakfast, he learned of the theatre critic's murder in the Théâtre Bakoledis. The thought that an investigation was going forward in Paris while he buzzed through the vineyards of the Languedoc was nettlesome. His anxiety was only slightly soothed by the knowledge that Alex Grismolet, putt-putting at a sedate pace along the Canal du Midi with Philippa, probably shared the same misgivings.

A critic poisoned in his seat, Hippo mused. How? He reached back in his memory ten or more years to a weapon used by the KGB, or was it the Stassi? — a spring-loaded umbrella gun that fired a tiny needle into the soft tissue behind the victim's knee. All it took was the slightest contact in a crowded environment. The killer walked, or perhaps sat, behind the victim and "accidentally" touched the back of his knee with the umbrella. A few hours later, the victim felt some slight soreness, nothing more. Meanwhile, the killer was in Canada or Ulan Bator. The poison was deliberately slow-working. Death usually occurred after forty-eight hours. Cyanide could probably be used, though at some risk to the umbrella man.

Marcel was slowing down again. "We're coming to Bram," he said. "Isn't that where we turn?"

Hippo picked up the Édition Poncet route map. He located Bram. "Yes. We turn left on D4. From there it is only a matter of a kilometre to the canal, where Alex and Philippa will be waiting."

They entered Bram, a replica of Pexiora except for a diminutive railroad yard piled high with aluminum wine casks. It was lunchtime. A few tractors were on their last morning haul. Shops were being shuttered. It occurred to Hippo that they should bring a bottle of something to Alex and Philippa to drink with lunch. Marcel stopped the Renault on the sidewalk in front of an épicerie-boulangerie that had wine bottles in the window. The female propriétaire of the store was winding down her shutter.

Hippo lowered his window. "Closed until four," she said in reply to his inquiry.

Marcel had a piece of equipment on hand for dealing with just such emergencies. It was a black cloth dickey, velcroed to a split clerical collar. He reached into the backseat, slipped it inside his Val d'Isère ski sweater, and got out of the car.

The wine was a 1982 Château Villars, Côte du Cabardés red, bottled under the signed logograph *Frère Christophe*. Marcel had never heard of the label, but the alternative was a nonvintage rosé. The red would do for lunch.

They crept through the rest of the village and turned north on D4. Leaving Bram, the ubiquitous rolling vineyard closed in on all sides again except directly ahead, where, at a distance of less than a kilometre, a double procession of immense sycamore trees cast a cool green shade across their path from horizon to horizon. The Canal du Midi.

The hire-cruiser *Sirocco* would be docked at the quai below the bridge that carried D4 across the canal. Hippo felt a pleasant tingle of anticipation. It would be good to see Philippa again, and he was anxious to discuss his umbrella gun theory with Alex.

They approached the bridge. Marcel parked the Renault on the grass under a tree. A footpath led down to the canal.

Hippo climbed out of the car and followed his friend down the path to a stone quai where a small canal barge, moored to iron rings, was filling its water tank. There was no sign of *Sirocco*.

The young couple on the barge were Dutch and did not speak French. Hippo peered up the canal in the direction from which he expected Alex to come. Nothing could be seen there except the glass-smooth surface of the water reflecting sycamores, and the dark, leaky, lower gates of the lock.

They nodded to the barge couple, walked across the bridge to a towpath on the far side and, hoping the lockmaster had a telephone, strolled the one hundred metres to the stone steps that led to the lockmaster's house.

A small black-and-white dog, standing by the bassin, barked once and trotted into the house. A young woman, wearing blue jeans and a brown pullover, ventured out of the doorway. She sized up Hippo and Marcel immediately. She was desolate, she said, to report that the captain and crew of *Sirocco* had been recalled to Paris. But if messieurs were hungry, she would be glad to sell them a baguette and small saucisson for their lunch.

Alex recalled to Paris. Hippo not recalled to Paris. Most vexing.

They dined al fresco back at the quai below the bridge. The Dutch couple had left.

The saucisson and baguette were excellent, but, to their surprise, the wine was extraordinary, with all the nuance and echo of a far more sophisticated label. Indeed, it was so good that Hippo, momentarily distracted from events in Paris, decided to obtain a case to take home. Since Château Villars was on their route to Le Pré, site of the Virgin's appearance, Marcel had no objection.

They left the canal behind them and, within moments, were speeding west through the vineyard of the lower Cabardés. At Carcassone, with the thirteenth-century fortified cité floating in a mythic splendour above the Aude River bridges, they turned north and, in a short time, came to Villars.

The village, in the fertile foothills of the Montagne Noir, is slightly off the main road, surrounded by vineyard, and completely unremarkable, except for the sprawling stone château. This is a working monastery, with a moat, a walled keep, and four spectacular, witch-hatted storage towers that completely dominate the landscape.

Marcel decelerated appropriately through the village and climbed the tree-lined, gravel drive to the château entrance. At a checkpoint in the arched tunnel entrance, a young monk took their order and directed them to a cobblestone parking spot next to the ivy-covered monastery chapel, from which issued the mournful, hollow choral cadences of plainsong. This pious sound contrasted oddly with the air they breathed, air that was saturated, intoxicated, with the odour of fermenting grapes.

A tractor, driven by a rough-looking young worker in a cap, muddy overalls, and rubber boots, bounced over the cobblestones, towing a trailer. In the trailer was their single case of 1982 Côte du Cabardés. The young man vaulted from the tractor seat, slung the case onto his shoulders, and slipped it under the hatchback into the Renault. He handed Hippo a slip for 310 francs. Hippo gave him 320 francs and told him to keep the change. The young man produced a crooked smile of appallingly bad teeth and raised his cap, showing a shaved head.

Marcel followed signs to the exit at the opposite end of the compound, and turned out the narrow road leading back to the village. The road ran parallel to the outside of the sandstone wall surrounding the keep. Marcel began to accelerate as they approached the end of this structure, when Hippo shouted, "Halt!"

Marcel braked. The Renault skidded to a stop.

"Dear God!" said Hippo, and pointed.

The graffiti on the wall was crudely done in black spray

paint, so that some of the letters had drizzled and run. An attempt had been made to remove it, but the message was still legible and unambiguous.

OUT! OUT! NIGGERS AND KIKES!
OUT WOGS! FAGGOTS AND DYKES!

9

Rue de Tournon, Paris

FORENSICS had finished their work at Virgile de la Pagerie's residence earlier than expected. This occurred for several reasons: The dwelling was forensically monotonous. Everything was new, identifiable, and spotless, except for a quantity of fresh-cut flowers, two coffee cups in the kitchen, and the mildly stimulating presence of a female dancer's wardrobe in the spare bedroom. The principal cause of the squad's early departure, however, was that Chef-Inspecteur Chartier was absent. He'd sent an assistant to the flat while he remained at the lab on other business. This "other business" would later be referred to as "Shit's Revenge."

Consequently, the apartment was turned over to Alex and the Operations Section in the late afternoon. Alex immediately assigned a laundry list squad of File inspecteurs to inspect and inventory Delap's books, papers, correspondence, and software.

Varnas was not present. He had earlier reported his surprise encounter with Monsieur and Madame Bloch, including her mysterious, exclamatory remark. "The bastards are everywhere!" He had not learned the significance of the phrase, nor was he likely to in the immediate future, as the Blochs were still in their suite at the Hôtel Madison, while he remained downstairs in the lobby, providing what he characterized as police protection. He was, as usual, unarmed.

The de la Pagerie flat, an entire floor under the mansard roof of the building, had eight dormer windows and two fireplaces. Alex started his tour at the rose moiré-covered entrance foyer with its gilt reception table, mirror, and empty coat closet. He passed from there into the vast, white-curtained grande salle, where furnishings, layered in matching patterned fabrics and pillows, were awash in a flood of bright, local, fall blossoms. The flowers helped disrupt the designer's too static arrangement, Alex thought. Without their spontaneity, the room could have been a page out of *Architecture Today*. Still, it had style.

He picked his way round the flowers and moved through a portal of faux marble pillars into the dining room. This was no less grand. Under an antique brass chandelier, a stainless steel and beveled glass dinner table waited to seat twelve on identical maplewood, ladderback country chairs. Along one wall stretched a mahogany sideboard with a porcelain tea service. Along the opposite wall, a glass cabinet displayed enough Limoges china and crystal to serve the entire arrondissement.

Alex inspected the hotel-size, state-of-the-art kitchen and pantry. He then walked slowly up the corridor leading to the roof garden and encountered the first paintings: extravagant renderings of iridescent hibiscus, of variegated macaws and boobies, of cobalt and coral seascapes, all signed by DGB. He came to a small, unfinished room that contained a child's crib. Stéphane had not mentioned a nursery.

Stéphane's own room was not as he had imagined. That is,

it was not a mess. In fact, it was immaculate. What few clothes she had were neatly arranged in the closet. Tights hung in the bathroom. On a table next to her bed was a framed photograph of Virgile on the beach, smiling and making a sandcastle. Next to the photo was a leather-bound volume entitled "Lineage of Euphémie de la Pagerie." Alex leafed through the minutely illustrated genealogy. It was as Stéphane had described, down to the banana schooner departing Fort-de-France for Philadelphia.

He'd deliberately saved Delap's room until last, not only to give the File squad a chance to get started, but because a pattern was emerging that he sensed would be confirmed in the master bedroom.

The library, with its theatre collection, was no surprise, although there were a few eclectic pairings. Floor-to-ceiling bookshelves lined two of the four walls. The complete works of Racine, Corneille, and Molière appeared next to Kant's *Critique of Judgement*. The plays of Genêt, Giraudoux, Beckett, Ionesco, Sartre, and Camus shared a shelf with Babeuf's *Manifesto of Equals* and the *History of Bebop*. Elsewhere were the works of Wilde, Shaw, Ibsen, Strindberg, Lorca, Brecht, Düranmatt, Pinter, Williams, and others. There were play scripts as well, histories of literary and theatrical criticism, histories of art, of fabric, of printing.

Against the third wall was a working model of the stage machinery of the Théâtre Odéon, an Antoni Tàpies print, an abstract watercolour by M. Kanemitsu, and a very large framed cartoon, done in the style of Daumier, in which de la Pagerie, armed with a smoking quill pen, stood astride a battlefield littered with the corpses of recognizable actors and directors.

In a corner of the room stood a personal computer and printer, a desk with a phone, fax, and a small safe. There was a Rolodex next to the phone, and, next to it, somewhat anachronistically, a child's antique school slate held upright by a brass pivot. Painted across the top of the slate, in delicate cursive, were the words, "Emergency and Frequently Called Numbers." Alex guessed it must have been a gift. Nevertheless, the slate bore the numbers, in pink chalk, for Police, Fire, Joyce, Carlo, LFD, Madame Inge, and CRD. Out of habit, Alex jotted the names and numbers in his notebook.

Opposite the computer centre, he saw the turntable, tape decks, and CD player of a complete sound system. There was no TV here or elsewhere in the flat.

Finally, perpendicular to the fourth wall, was The Bed, the enormous, canopied four-poster; the temple, tabernacle, and indoor stadium, designed, constructed, and installed for no other purpose than to provide the perfect landscape for the consummation of conjugal love.

Stéphane had mentioned neither the nursery, the bed, nor the twin bathrooms. Yet it was plain that the physical transformation of the flat from bachelor pad to formal residence had been carried out by a man who intended to marry, to entertain, and to raise a family. Stéphane had mentioned his fiancée's name only in passing, but forgot, or deliberately neglected, to acknowledge the feelings he must have had for her to create such an optimistic monument to their future.

Stéphane's characterization of de la Pagerie as remote, and her perfunctory dismissal of Angélique as unloved by the Blochs (and "permanently out-to-lunch"), did not square with the physical evidence in this house on Rue de Tournon.

Alex's pager beeped. He switched it off and moved to de la Pagerie's desk, where a File Inspecteur was checking software. He called the Maison. The assignment desk immediately transferred him to the recently returned Commissaire.

Demonet was waspish. "Where the hell are you?"

"At de la Pagerie's flat."

"Simply magnificent! You're at an unlisted number! I've been trying to find you for half an hour! Come home immediately! I've already summoned Varnas!"

"We're not finished here, Commissaire."

The Commissaire chuckled. "Finish later! Your favorite colleague, the learned Forensics Chef-Inspecteur Chartier, says he's found the murder weapon!"

The Maison

Alex speculated that if ever he suffered a recurring nightmare, it would have as its centrepiece Chartier's smooth, smug face. His complacent, supremely self-assured countenance never varied, because Chartier had found the only truth, the scientific truth, discernible only in the Forensic Lab. Alex favoured the other truth: the fact that, at age forty-two, Chartier still lived with his mother and wore rubber overshoes to work every day, summer and winter. No one disputed Chartier's ability as a Forensics Investigator. It was the cloying indulgence he casually demonstrated toward the less exact police disciplines that annoyed his brethren.

"Can I get you aspirin?" Varnas whispered to Alex as they took their seats in the Commissaire's office, along with Isabelle from Research, and some people from Data Processing.

"Get me a sharp knife. Who's protecting the Blochs?"

"House detective."

Chartier, wearing a white surgical smock, cleared his throat. He had set up a drafting table opposite the Commissaire's desk on which to make his demonstration. He stood with his arms at his sides and his pale, schoolboy's face raised, as if he were about to sing.

"We ask for your close attention," he piped in his precise, treble voice, using what Alex had decided was the royal we, not the editorial, "so that we will not be required to repeat. And please, no smoking." Alex looked over at the Commissaire, who was just then loading pipe tobacco into Joan of Arc's meerschaum helmet.

The room settled down. "It seems," Chartier began, "that the victim, Virgile de la Pagerie, was asthmatic." Varnas glanced at Alex. Chartier held up a piece of black plastic. "This is the plastic cap that was recovered in the auditorium of the Théâtre Bakoledis yesterday. It was found to contain traces of the same compound of sodium cyanide and trichloromonofluoromethane that was discerned on the theatre carpet and, later, on the victim's clothing and in his shoulder bag."

Alex noticed the shoulder bag on the floor, next to the drafting table.

Chartier now held up a small, L-shaped, red plastic container. The tip of a metal cartridge protruded from the top of the L. "This," he said, "is a Ventil asthma inhaler similar to the one used by the victim, in the theatre, the night he died. It is manufactured by Société Pharmaceutique d'Oise, a subsidiary of the German pharmaceutical company Scheel A.G. in Pointoise.

"The inhaler contains the compound Albuterol in an aerosol cartridge." He pointed to the tip of the cartridge, visible at the top of the L. "When depressed, the cartridge conveys medication, via the inhaler tube and mouthpiece, to the patient's bronchia." He pointed to the bottom of the L and depressed the cartridge. A fine spray emerged from the inhaler tube. "When it is not in use," he continued, "a cap is placed over the mouthpiece to provide sanitary protection and to prevent accidental loss of medication." He snapped the black cap onto the end of the inhaler tube. "We found the cap in the theatre and identified it, the poison, and the propellant."

The Commissaire interrupted. "Then this is not the murder weapon?"

"The cap is from what you refer to as the murder weapon, Commissaire. The victim's dispenser and cartridge were not recovered. These are exact copies that we acquired for demo purposes."

The Commissaire turned to Alex. "Did you know de la Pagerie was asthmatic?"

"No, Commissaire."

"Didn't his girlfriend mention it?"

"No, Commissaire."

Demonet raised his eyebrows. "I suggest you have another talk with her. Perhaps there are other things she hasn't mentioned. I can't imagine how a woman could live with a man for a year and not know that he regularly took medication for asthma."

"They had separate rooms," Alex responded lamely.

"Really?" He nodded to Chartier. "Continue."

Chartier made a little shit-eating grin at Alex. "To continue," he said. "Obviously the medication in the victim's inhaler was compromised at some point. We contacted the manufacturer and posited to him a hypothetical tampering case. He insisted that tampering at the source could not have occurred. And he voiced grave doubts that a foreign substance might be introduced into a Ventil inhaler from the exterior, given that the interior pressure is 17G, without losing the propellant which is metered to produce two hundred inhalations or enough for about twenty-five days, depending on dosage. Notwithstanding the manufacturer's claim, the device is clearly not tamperproof."

Chartier now removed the black cap from the inhaler and placed it on the drafting table. He then extracted the metal cartridge from the red plastic dispenser, placed the dispenser on the table, and, holding the cartridge at arm's length, said, "Operations may wish to note that the device is manufactured in three pieces: cap, dispenser, and cartridge. Of these, the cartridge is the most critical, not only because it contains the medication into which the cyanide was introduced, but because each cartridge bears a lot number, which might facilitate tracing, in the event the victim's actual cartridge is recovered." He held the cartridge aloft, like a torch, for emphasis, finally placing it on the table next to the other components. "This concludes our demonstration. We have examined the victim's clothing and the contents of his shoulder bag. There is nothing of forensic interest to report from either source, apart from the chemical traces already mentioned. Questions?"

Alex asked. "You say the device is good for two hundred inhalations, depending on dosage. What is the dosage?"

"Dosage, Chef-Inspecteur, is a prescribed number of inhalations at prescribed times of day. For that information, you may wish to contact the victim's personal physician."

To enable him to deliver this condescending piece of advice with the proper emphasis, Chartier had half-turned toward Alex. He now turned back and, in doing so, slightly nudged the drafting table. The pivoting table was not exactly level, and consequently, the nudge was just enough to start the metal cartridge rolling. Chartier, scanning the room for further questions, did not notice as the cartridge rolled down and off the table into Varnas's hand. There were a few more questions. During the exchange, Varnas closely inspected the cartridge, finally returning it to the puzzled Chartier, who had not missed it.

"Sleight of hand," Varnas said happily, placing his forefinger alongside his nose and winking like Saint Nick about to go up the chimney.

After the meeting, Alex and Varnas climbed the stairs to their shared office on the first floor. This windowless, airless, box stall, no larger than one of Delap's bathrooms, and reeking of a brand of disinfectant known only to God and the miserly maintenance section of the Interior Ministry, had not seen improvement, apart from the addition of a small computer and fax, since the days of the Third République. There were two back-to-back wooden desks, two desk lamps, two phones, the fax, a shared wastebasket, the computer on a separate stand, a few cardboard files lining the institutional green walls, and a safe, where Varnas kept his 25-calibre Baretta.

Alex placed Delap's shoulder bag on his desk and sat down. Varnas remained standing and studied his friend's somewhat dispirited expression.

"Alex, if French diplomat can make love to Chinese woman for eighteen years and not know she is man, it is possible Mademoiselle Stéphane can live with critic for one year and not know he has respiratory affliction."

Alex had overturned the shoulder bag and was emptying the contents on his desk. "I can't speak for the diplomat, but given Stéphane's breezy, big blonde affability and flirty curiosity, it seems unlikely."

"Why, if Delap doesn't want her to know?"

Alex was examining a small address book. "Why wouldn't he want her to know? Asthma isn't contagious or life-threatening."

"For men like Delap, is maybe image-threatening."

"Maybe."

"But, more important, now that we have inhaler information, we have new reason for Gus to run down aisle so quickly opening night."

"What reason is that?"

"To recover inhaler dropped by Delap in those few moments of confusion before house lights come on and doctor arrives."

"You think Gus has the inhaler?"

"Maybe. Except for black cap. By the way, does Isabelle finish dossier on Gus?"

"Not yet." Alex continued examining the address book. "Varnas. If Gus planned the murder, and, for his own reasons, planned to have it take place in a theatre before an audience, he could not have planned it better. Now, having accomplished this great success, both on a practical and dramatic level, why would he care about anything so pedestrian as the inhaler, much less grope around in the dark for it on his hands and knees? Let the inhaler be found! Let it be poisoned! So much better for the mystery, and the hype, and the box office!" Alex glanced up at his partner. "You seem poised for flight. Am I keeping you from something?"

Varnas smiled. "It is Friday, and dinnertime. Specialité de la maison at Chez Suzanne on Fridays is Chou Farci. I can think of nothing else."

Chez Suzanne was a diminutive café near the bottom of the funiculaire to Sacré Coeur. Run by an ex-madame from Limousin whom Varnas once liberated from the vice squad, it was his club, his social and gastronomique centre (Suzanne produced authentic provincial cooking, a different dish every day except Monday). It was, as well, a meeting place for the demi-monde and petty crooks who made up the nucleus of Varnas's list of useful police informants, the most exclusive list ever assembled by a Paris flic. Whenever Varnas made off to Chez Suzanne, it was seldom for the food alone.

"Bon appétit," Alex said, "stuffed cabbage notwithstanding."

Varnas left.

Alex put the address book aside and turned his attention to the critic's small tape recorder. He pushed "play." A markedly civilized male voice drawled, "As a young man, Jean Anouilh worked for an advertising agency in Paris. Unfortunately, advertising's loss was not the theatre's gain . . ."

The tape recorder clicked and was silent. Perhaps de la Pagerie had recorded his intended lead for his review of *Eurydice*.

Alex pushed "rewind." When the tape stopped, he pushed "play" again. The tape hissed for a moment, clicked, and a soft, clarinetlike female voice enunciated:

The man appears. The young girls watch him intently. He has found some tricks with which to enhance his worth in their eyes. He stands on his hind legs in order to shed the rain better and to hang medals on his chest. He swells his biceps. They quail before him with hypocritical admiration, trembling with such fear as not even a tiger inspires, not realizing that of all the carnivorous animals, this biped alone has ineffective teeth. And as they gaze at him, the windows of the soul, through which they once saw the myriad colours of the outer world, cloud over, grow opaque, and, in that moment, the story is over . . . and life begins. The pleasure of the bed begins. And the pleasure of the table. And the habit of pleasure. And the pleasure of jealousy . . . and the pleasure of cruelty . . . and the pleasure of suffering. And, last of all, the pleasure of indifference. So, little by little, the pearl loses its lustre, and long before it dies, it is dead.

The tape clicked and was silent, until the male voice returned to repeat the bit about Jean Anouilh. Alex had no idea who the woman was or what the speech meant.

He placed the tape recorder in his desk drawer and returned to the address book.

He was trying to find a doctor listed, de la Pagerie's personal physician: the physician who failed to come forward when the Medical Examiner's first diagnosis was made public, and, especially, when the toxicology report was released; more important, the physician who prescribed the asthma medication and could specify the dosage.

Alex went through the address book twice. There was no doctor listed. He took out his notebook in which he had scribbled the most frequently called numbers from the slate on Delap's desk.

He skipped Police and Fire and called the number listed for Joyce. A machine answered. Joyce was his hairdresser, and she was closed. Carlo, also closed, was a custom tailor. LFD was a catering service. Madame Inge was a masseuse. She had a client and was impatient to get off the phone until Alex identified himself. He asked if Monsieur de la Pagerie had any chronic disabilities or allergies that she was aware of. No, she said, apart from occasional lower back pain and muscle spasm. Alex rang off and called CRD. The telephone number was not a Paris number.

A female answered. "Centre for Respiratory Diseases."

Alex identified himself and asked to speak to the doctor who treated Virgile de la Pagerie.

"This is a clinique publique, monsieur, not a private practice. Patients are not assigned physicians. They are treated on a first-come-first-served basis."

"But you have records?"

"Of course."

"So you have a record that someone treated Virgile de la Pagerie. I wish to speak to that person."

She exhaled. "What is the patient's name again?"

Alex repeated it.

He heard some computer keys. In a moment she was back. "We have no patient by that name. Are you certain he was treated here?"

"Yes. Try Bloch. Or Géronte. Virgile Bloch or Géronte."

More computer keys. When she came back she said, "We have a Virgile Bloch, Bureau de Poste 473, Sixth Arrondissement, no phone. He was last treated by Doctor Louis Sélibaby."

"May I speak to him please?"

"Doctor Sélibaby is visiting his family in the Sénégal. What is it you wish to know?"

"The medication dosage prescribed by Doctor Sélibaby for Monsieur Bloch."

"I am not at liberty to divulge that information."

"Where are you located, mademoiselle?"

"Rue Émile Zola, Malakoff."

"You have a choice. I have told you who I am. You will either give me the information I've requested or the Senior Terrorist Investigator's office will cite you for contempt and close you down in the morning."

Alex was put on to the duty nurse. The dosage was simple enough: Ventil inhaler, two inhalations of Albuterol every four hours, at 8 A.M., 12 N, 4 P.M., and 8 P.M.

"Where was his prescription filled?"

"At our pharmacie downstairs."

Alex rang off. So. No personal physician. Sought help at a clinique in a rundown Paris suburb using a different name and address. Not even the doctor who treated him or the pharmacie that filled his prescription knew that a man named de la Pagerie was asthmatic.

He checked his watch. Still time to see Stéphane before half-hour. He took a cab to the Palais Garnier.

10

Philippa

THERE ARE ONLY twenty words in the French language that begin with the letter "W," and most of them are foreign-derived: wagon, walkrie, watt, weekend, whiskey, et cetera. And there are few, if any, French surnames that begin with W, apart from Watteau, which is Flemish.

Philippa, a French citizen, but of English and Irish parentage, inherited her mother's maiden name — Watten — when she was registered as Alex's ward.

The name had been nothing but trouble from the beginning. It was unpronounceable in French. It had to be spelled out when leaving phone messages, and it elicited curious glances from store clerks when charging things. "Mademoiselle Watt-ein?"

When she became a featured dancer, Philippa decided to change it.

"How about Watts?"

"There's Heather Watts in New York, chérie."

"What's wrong with Philippa Grismolet?"

"Too dark for ballet."

"Come on, Alex! How about Philippa Guerin? Or Guillem? Or Leclerc or Tcherkassky?"

"How about Philippa Watten?"

"Shit!"

It was the third day of her not-vacation. She had just finished giving herself class in the saloon of *Le Yacht Club* and was trying to decide whether to bathe first or call Alex at the Maison to plan dinner. She decided to call Alex. But when she reached for the phone, it suddenly rang, startling her.

She picked up and said, "I was in the act of calling you. My hand was actually on the receiver, when Brrrrring!"

Silence. Then a very English voice: "Miss Watten?"

"Oui? I mean, yes?"

"This is Nigel Philby at the Royal Ballet in London."

"Hi," she said rather clunkily, totally unprepared to speak English, a language in which she was no longer at ease.

"I tried to reach you at the Palais Garnier. They said you were on holiday and gave me this number."

"Oh. How do you do?"

"Very well, thank you. The reason for my call. We have Nicolaj Blixen, of the Royal Danish Ballet, with us for the fall season. I'm planning a production of Auguste Bournonville's *Napoli*. Nicky will dance Gennaro, and I'd like you to dance Teresina opposite him." Silence. "Hallo?"

"Please excuse me," Philippa said. "I'm trying to comprehend how to answer in English."

"Would you prefer to speak French?"

"Yes, please."

He spoke French quite correctly but with that flat, uncompromising British accent used by visiting prime ministers.

She was, of course, familiar with Bournonville, and knew Blixen by reputation (Stéphane said, "Young blond giant who jumps like a gazelle and screws anything that moves"), but she was not familiar with the ballet *Napoli*.

He briefly outlined the story of the young fisherman, Gennaro, whose only love, Teresina, is lost at sea and turns into a naiad.

"I'm deeply honoured by your offer," Philippa said, "but why me?"

"It was Nicky's idea, initially. He's seen your work and admires your clarity and energy, so essential to Bournonville. I saw your shades variation in *Bayadère,* last spring, and am very excited at the prospect of working with you." He paused. "Well. What do you say?"

"What do I say? I'm thrilled! I'd adore to do it! But, of course, it will be up to Rudy."

"Then I have your permission to speak to Rudy?"

"Of course!"

He paid her a few more compliments and rang off.

She hung up the receiver very slowly, took a deep breath, and uttered a shriek. She did a dozen fouettés and a cartwheel, and collapsed in giggles on the couch, kicking her feet. She then burst into tears. After a few good sobs, she felt a cool hand on her forehead. She grasped it with both of hers and covered it with kisses.

"What in the world?" Alex asked.

She whirled on the couch and threw her arms around his waist. "It's happened!"

They celebrated. While Philippa bathed, Alex went shopping. For dinner, he served her poached salmon with fresh dill mayonnaise, fresh asparagus with thyme butter, endive and watercress salade, a still-warm baguette from Pâtisserie Mariette, and a bottle of Sauvignon Blanc.

When it was all consumed, Philippa patted her tummy and

said, "My Last Supper. If Rudy says yes, it'll be tofu and gelatine from now until Christmas."

Alex replied, "If Rudy does not say yes, I will use my influence to persuade the government to make him a Chevalier of the Légion d'Honneur for his unselfish dance therapy work among the prisoners of French Guiana."

Philippa, who knew her man, sensed Alex was forcing the gaiety a bit with that last remark. She said, "So how is the murder in row E coming along?"

"Let's not spoil the celebration."

"Alex, this is Philippa calling."

He hesitated. "Recent developments make things look bad for your pal Stéphane. I went to the Palais to question her before the performance. The régisseur told me she was fired this morning. No one seems to know where she is."

Chez Suzanne

Suzanne waddled into the bar from her kitchen and gazed across the small, crowded room, at Varnas, who was just finishing his Chou Farci. Over the years, as they'd grown older (and she heavier), Suzanne had come to fancy Varnas. She'd invited him into her bed on several occasions, and when he invariably declined, she kept his attention by teasing, by inventing outrageous fictions: his uncontrollable virility, his talent as a telephone booth lover, what she'd heard from an unimpeachable source in the informant network about the impressive size of his member. These jokey vulgarities, heavily whispered into his ear while she sat next to him at his table by the café curtain, committed no one emotionally, and rendered her lubricity, while unambiguous, essentially harmless. However, when she heard he was living under the same roof with another woman (it didn't matter that they were four floors apart), she turned up the dial a notch.

From across the room, she yelled, "Chéri! Chéri! Do you like Italian food?" Heads turned. The buzz of male conversation and the slap of cards ceased momentarily.

Varnas, wiping his mouth, looked over at her and nodded in the affirmative.

"Good!" she cried. "Come in Tuesday. I make you Saltimbocca . . . unless you prefer a little Gnocchi!"

And so on.

That he was constantly the centre of her badinage actually enhanced his standing among the regulars.

He stopped at a few tables to kibitz the card games and exchange pleasantries with some low-level hoods who made a scant living fencing, among other things, Peruvian coca paste disguised as the American antacid Mylanta, and explicit mud-wrestling videos featuring young, naked women from the Philippines.

He left the café as Suzanne simultaneously smiled, blew him a kiss, and gave him the finger.

He walked to the Pigalle métro, took the No. 12 to the Madeleine and, from there, walked to Rue de Caumartin.

Théâtre Bakoledis

He arrived during the interval between acts two and three. Patrons were just leaving the sidewalk and lobby to reenter the auditorium. He went round to the side and entered the stage door.

An old man sat at a metal table inside. Behind him stretched an unpainted warren of message cubicles and hooks for dressing-room keys. "Nobody backstage during the performance," he mumbled, not looking up from his copy of *Paris Turf*.

Varnas slowly passed his ID under the man's nose.

"You were here before," he growled. "What's now?"

"I want to see downstairs."

"Downstairs is wardrobe."

"I want to see it."

The man sniffed. "Stairway to your right. And be quiet. The curtain's up."

The wardrobe room had been the orchestra room before the pit was covered and four rows of seats were added to the auditorium. It was a cheerless rectangular space under the stage, painted gray and illuminated by bare bulbs. It was now occupied by a number of pipe clothes racks on casters from which hung perhaps thirty costumes. To one side was a sewing machine and ironing board and a large steam iron. Opposite, in the middle of the downstage wall, was the old, sliding metal door that led to the former orchestra pit. The door, which opened to the left along an overhead track, had been immobilized by a wooden baulk wedged between it and a vertical beam.

Varnas listened. He could hear the squeak of the actors' footsteps overhead, but he heard their voices through the door to the pit. He inspected the overhead track. The door hung on rollers. He saw at once that, should he be able to remove the baulk, it was unlikely he could open the old door silently enough to avoid disturbing the performance. Then again, if he succeeded in opening it, he might yet be on a fool's errand because he was not certain whether that half of the orchestra pit under the stage had been isolated from the covered half in the auditorium.

He listened again. He could definitely hear the actors' voices through the door. A young woman spoke the line, "My darling, how long you've been!" This was followed by what sounded like rain falling, followed by a faint bump, followed by a storm of applause. The final curtain. He heard the curtain rise again and shouts of "Bravo!"

Without hesitation, he seized one end of the baulk and lifted with all his strength. It wouldn't budge. He looked around for a tool, spotted the large steam iron, unplugged it, and struck a blow with the flat of the iron to the end of the baulk. The baulk fell and the iron separated from its handle. He made an abortive attempt to rejoin the parts but realized the appliance was probably beyond repair. He placed the pieces on the ironing board and turned to the door. It slid open with surprising ease.

He switched on his pencil torch, entered what remained of the orchestra pit and, immediately, at eye level, beheld shoes, the shoes of patrons standing in the first row applauding; dozens of shoes seen beneath a short, red velvet curtain that hung on a brass railing from left to right. It was all that separated the auditorium from the vestigial space beneath the stage.

He swung the torch in the semidarkness. It faintly illuminated a single file of old wooden music stands lined up parallel to the ornamental curtain. He aimed the torch farther to the right and stopped at a music stand slightly higher than the others. There, the narrow beam of light found what he was looking for. The cartridge from Delap's inhaler had rolled down the centre aisle, rolled under the curtain, and come to rest on a music stand that bore the stencil "2nd Violin."

He pocketed the cartridge and torch and left the pit. He slid the door closed, replaced the baulk and was about to leave the wardrobe room when a silver-haired woman, wearing a brocade caftan and three pairs of spectacles that hung from her neck on fake gold chains, entered. She carried some costumes on hangers, and reeked of lavender toilet water.

She did not stop when she saw Varnas but moved briskly to a clothes rack to relieve herself of her burden. Without turning, she said, "The doorman told me you were down here." She spoke meticulously. "What could you possibly want with an old wardrobe mistress? Are you missing a button or do you want to hear the story of my life?"

Varnas said he wanted neither and confessed that, in the course of a routine inspection, he had destroyed her iron.

She finished hanging up the costumes and went to the ironing board. There, she picked up the handle, pressed a lever and effortlessly snapped the handle back onto the iron. She turned to him for the first time, spread her arms wide, and said, "Ta-dah."

She had a broad theatrical face, with prominent cheekbones and large, dark eyes. Varnas said, "You are once actress, madame?"

"Twice, actually," she replied. "Now, if you'll forgive me, I have to alter Julie's second act skirt. Gus says it hangs on her like a bag of shit." She took a costume from the rack and brushed past him to the sewing machine, leaving a trail of lavender fumes in her wake.

Varnas coughed slightly, thanked her, and turned to leave. "Oh, one more thing, madame."

"Mademoiselle." She sat at the sewing machine.

"Mademoiselle, how is it that you are not here yesterday when I question cast and crew?"

"I found voile on sale in the Marais for fifteen francs a square metre. The Palace Guard, mounted, would not have kept me away. However, had I been here, I would have told you that I thoroughly disliked Virgile de la Pagerie, and believe that whoever dispatched him deserves a medal!"

She placed a pair of pink, shell-rimmed spectacles on her nose and, with a sharp movement of her knees, set the sewing machine to chattering.

11

Palais Garnier

ALEX MANEUVERED THE BUG onto Rue La Fayette.

"Couldn't we have talked to Marcia by phone?"

"Are you mad?" Philippa said. "Trying to reach a dancer at the Palais by phone takes longer than the mail. Besides, I want to speak to Marcia without half the company hanging about in the hall."

They waited for the light at Rue de Chabrol. "I shouldn't be doing this," Alex said. "I should've put out an APB."

"An APB? Alex, you can't treat Stéphane as a common criminal."

"Why not? She disappeared. She's running."

"She's not running. She's hurting."

The light changed. "If she's not running, why did she jump ship this morning?"

Philippa sighed. "Dear Alex. Because she couldn't take her eyes off you. And because she cares for me."

"The Commissaire will cherish that explanation."

"Bugger the Commissaire! If Stéphane were running, she wouldn't have gone to class this morning. Park here."

He stopped the Bug on the sidewalk of Place Diaghilev and left the engine running. Philippa jumped out and raced to the Palais stage entrance.

He had not seen the gendarme. The white baton tapped on the windscreen. Alex lowered the window and showed his Sûreté ID. The gendarme regarded the scarred beige Bug with one purple fender.

"Sûreté cutting back?" he murmured, and returned Alex's ID. "Five minutes, chef, no more." The gendarme moved away as Alex's beeper went off.

Assuming the backstage phone at the Palais had a queue, he drove round the block and parked on the sidewalk next to the public phone at the Auber métro. He locked the car and dialed the Maison. His message was to call Chef-Inspecteur du Temple in the Haut Languedoc. "Hippo has something for you on the murder weapon," the Assignment Desk clerk said. The clerk gave him a phone number in Mazamet. Mazamet. The name of the town resonated slightly. He couldn't think why.

Alex carded the long distance number to the Maison and reached a Hôtel Jourdon. He was connected to room 204. Hippo answered. Despite his graduate degree in physics and keen awareness of modern advances in telecommunications technology, Hippo nevertheless clung to the notion that one had to yell to be heard on long distance. Alex held the receiver away from his ear as Hippo described his and Marcel's regret at having missed Alex and Philippa on the canal, a regret partially alleviated by their discovery of a marvelous local red wine. "I'll bring you a bottle," he said. He then launched into his umbrella gun theory.

Alex allowed him to finish. A description of any weapon by Hippo was a lesson in history, mechanics, and socio-economics.

"An asthma inhaler?" Hippo replied unenthusiastically. "That's a little out of my line. But, before I ring off, Alex, I must report that we have encountered the most appallingly xenophobic graffiti here." He described the explicit couplet on the wall at Château Villars. "The work is attributed to the local chapter of the Mountain Mafia, otherwise known as the Front Patriotique. They seem to be ubiquitous in the Haut Languedoc. We'll keep an eye on them." He lowered his voice. "I wish you needed me, Alex. I feel dysfunctional in the Midi. Tomorrow I accompany Marcel to the spot where the Blessed Virgin is said to have appeared to one of the local children. That's a bit out of my line, as well." He paused. "Well. Thanks for returning my call. Back in a few days. Love to Varnas and Philippa."

Alex walked back to the Bug. It refused to start. He took out the tire iron, raised the engine hatch, and delivered a blow to the carburetor that exactly coincided with the arrival of the gendarme, completing his patrol of the block. Alex fired up the Bug, waved to the white baton, and roared back to the rear of the Palais where Philippa was waiting.

Stéphane had not rented Marcia's spare room. She'd received two weeks' salary from the sous-régisseur, a wormlike syco-phant who did much of Rudy's dirty work. As Stéphane left in tears, Marcia said she heard him mention that the Folies were hiring.

"That little shit!" Philippa exclaimed. "Someday, *paf*, right in the dance belt!"

They drove back to *Le Yacht Club*. As Alex swung the Bug

onto Quai de la Charente, the headlights picked up the figure of a blonde, sitting on the midships bollard.

Stéphane

She was exhausted. Alex placed her in his captain's chair and offered Courvoisier. She declined. Actually, she was a little drunk. She'd found Délice and Honoré in mid-morning and spent the day with them in their suite at the Madison, drinking Calvados to ease the pain. "I've been fired," she said flatly.

Philippa embraced her. "We know, chérie. You can stay here forever."

Stéphane shook her head. "I've come to ask permission to leave Paris. I want to go to my parents in Antibes until I decide what to do next."

Philippa glanced at Alex.

"I'm afraid that's out of the question," he said. "At least for the time being."

"How long is for the time being?"

"That depends on you. We have new evidence that . . . uh . . . places the veracity of your testimony in doubt." Alex edited the unintentionally lofty syntax. "We think you're withholding information."

Stéphane frowned. "What information?"

Alex fetched his tape recorder, placed it on the floor in front of her, and knelt beside it. He switched it on. "Couple of questions for Stéphane Nikolaides. How long did you live with Virgile de la Pagerie?"

"From November of last year to September of this. Ten months."

"What prescription drugs, if any, did he take on a regular basis during that time?"

She frowned again. "Prescription drugs? He didn't take drugs of any kind, prescription or otherwise. He was a health freak. I never saw him take even an aspirin."

"You testified that you were never in his bathroom."

"That's true."

"So he could have taken something without your knowing about it."

"I suppose. But it would've been out of character. He was a fanatic about health. No pills, no cholesterol, no fat, no salt."

"Did he have any allergies?"

"No."

"Chronic disabilities?"

Stéphane was mystified. "I don't understand these questions. He never had a cold. He never had a hangnail. The only thing he protected himself against was the sun. It gave him freckles."

"Stéphane. Are you telling me you're unaware of the fact that Virgile de la Pagerie was a chronic asthmatic who took specific medication every four hours of every day of the months you knew him?"

Stéphane stared at Alex. "I don't believe you. This is some sort of cop trick. People with asthma don't run four or five kilometres a day on the beach or live with people who smoke."

"What time did your flight leave for Paris on Wednesday?"

She turned to Philippa with a look of helplessness.

Philippa said, "Answer him, chérie."

Stéphane reached into her dance bag. After removing half its contents, she produced an Iberia Airlines ticket folder. She opened it and read, "Iberia, Flight 1207, left Málaga at 11:50 A.M."

"Ten minutes before noon. In Málaga, did he leave you to go the men's room before the flight?"

"He went somewhere and got the Madrid and Barcelona papers."

"I see. Was your flight direct to Paris?"

"No. We flew to Barcelona." She checked the folder. "We arrived in Barcelona at 1:05 P.M."

"Isn't Barcelona out of the way?"

"Yes. The most direct flight to Paris is via Madrid. But he preferred Barcelona because of lunch at La Tortosa."

"A restaurant?"

"A Catalan restaurant in Mataro, about a half hour from the airport. Its specialties are sea turtle and octopus served in a green garlic sauce on a bed of eel grass and yellow rice. It was Angélique's favorite restaurant."

Alex was surprised to hear her mention Angélique in this context since she had scrupulously avoided mentioning her in connection with the renovated apartment. "And was it your favorite restaurant as well?"

"I don't eat lunch, Alex. And you can stop nibbling. I have no problem with the ghost of Angélique."

"Good. How long did this side trip to La Tortosa take?"

"Including the cab both ways, over two hours. We got back to the airport a little after three-thirty." She referred again to the flight folder. "Iberia Flight 4426 left Barcelona at four-fifteen, arriving Paris/Orly at five-thirty."

"What happened when you arrived back at the Barcelona airport?"

"I went to the ladies' and . . . ," she hesitated, ". . . he went to the men's."

"Yes. He went to the men's and took his last clean dose. What happened then?"

"We went to the departure gate, through that X ray thing where they make sure you don't have a bomb in your carry-on luggage."

"Did he surrender his shoulder bag to the attendant at the X ray counter?"

"Yes."

"Describe."

"Well, he gave it to a man who put it on the conveyor with my makeup case. Then we walked through. Something on Virgile rang the bell."

"Rang the bell? I thought his clothes were made without pockets."

"They were. The attendant said it was his belt buckle."

"Was it?"

"I suppose so. When Virgile removed the belt and walked through the second time the bell didn't ring."

"Describe the attendant."

"There were three. A short, polite, older man who placed our bags on the conveyor; a burly, bald type with a beard, guarding the walk through — it was he who took Virgile's belt — and a woman watching the X ray screen: typical airline chick, blonde, blue-eyed, have-a-nice-flight type."

"Were they Spanish?"

"They spoke Spanish."

"Was the X ray counter the only place his shoulder bag was not in his possession?"

"No. He put it under the seat ahead of him during the flight to Paris. And it was on the floor of the limo coming in from Orly."

"Did the chauffeur handle the bag?"

"Not while I was in the limo."

"Did you handle the bag?"

She met his gaze. "Never."

"I'm glad. Because sometime after he left the men's room in the Barcelona airport, and before he took his seat next to Philippa in the fifth row of the Théâtre Bakoledis in Paris, someone removed his regular inhaler from the shoulder bag and substituted one laced with sodium cyanide."

Stéphane gazed at Alex with shining eyes. She shook her head almost imperceptibly and whispered, "Poor Virgile. He had a flaw after all. Jesus. It's so fucking Greek. The sin of hubris. He didn't want anyone to know he wasn't perfect."

"Someone knew."

"Yes." She sighed and brushed her cheek. "Oh. I almost forgot. Délice and Honoré asked to see you."

12

The Maison

NEXT MORNING, Alex arranged for Stéphane to return to de la Pagerie's flat. She could stay there until the end of the month or until she was released to join her parents in Antibes, whichever came first. He called Isabelle, in Research, and asked her to contact Barcelona Airport to identify the attendants at the metal detector X ray facility servicing Iberia's Flight 4426 at 4 P.M. on Wednesday 4 September, and to acquire the passenger list and seating assignments from Iberia for the same flight on the same day. He then called Forensics and requested a metallic resonance test on Delap's belt buckle.

*

Varnas phoned the office to say he would be late. He was at the laverie, laundering a shirt.

"A shirt? I thought Madame Roget did your shirts."

"Madame Roget does not speak to me, Alex."

"Since when?"

"Since lavender toilet water."

"What?"

"Not to ask. I have something for you. Meet me Chez Suzanne at one o'clock."

"What's on the menu?"

"Boeuf en Daube Provençal."

*

The Directeur of the Paris Opéra Ballet summoned Philippa to the Palais Garnier.

*

A Sûreté vehicle, dispatched to bring Délice and Honoré to the Maison, had to wait an hour outside the Hôtel Madison, to allow Honoré time to finish arranging Délice's hair in cornrow dufils, each braided with gold and silver thread. The magnificent hairdo took five hours to complete.

Commissaire Demonet, pursuing his biweekly exercise regimen at the Croquet and Tennis Club in Neuilly, was not present at the meeting. Alex seated Délice in the Commissaire's swiveling, leather chair. She was dressed in a full, purple cotton skirt and fitted orange shirtwaist. She wore no jewelry or makeup and still managed to look like a Nubian queen ready to receive petitioners.

Honoré, in a white linen suit, preferred to stand. He stood, ministerially, next to his wife, his hands clasped behind his back.

With the Commissaire absent, it fell to Alex to convey condolences on behalf of the Sûreté and to express their gratitude for the Blochs' cooperation. That accomplished, he said, "You asked to see me. Do you wish to make a statement or would you prefer to respond to questions?"

"We wish to make a statement," Honoré said.

"Please proceed." The office recorder was rolling. Honoré cleared his throat.

"My name is Honoré Bloch," he began. "I was born in

Perpignan, in the south of France, in 1932. My father, Antoine Raoul Bloch, had twenty years at the time of my birth,
and my mother, Nicole Lazar, seventeen.

"My father went to war in 1939. He was wounded in the
Vosges and taken prisoner. When France fell in 1940, he was
repatriated and returned to Perpignan, where he and my
mother owned a small business that manufactured orthodon-
tic devices.

"During the winter of 1940–41, it became clear to my
father that the security of Jews in unoccupied France, under
the Vichy regime, was becoming increasingly at risk. Consequently, at the age of twenty-eight, he sold the business to a
consortium of non-Jewish dentists and, with the proceeds,
arranged passage for my mother and me, first to Dakar, then
to Martinique. He expected to join us at a later date.

"In the summer of 1941, while working as a fishmonger,
he was arrested by the Vichy police and imprisoned, without
trial, in the camp at Rivesaltes, outside Perpignan. During the
winter, he was deported to Germany. He perished in the con-
centration camp at Kleine Glatbach in the spring of 1942."

Honoré paused and glanced at Délice for just an instant.
He cleared his throat again and resumed.

"You will find documentation of my father's arrest and
imprisonment in the safe in our son's study. The documentation has been authenticated by the Fédération des Anciens
Combattants Français. In the safe, you will find also a copy of
the deportation order that sent my father to his death. It was
not signed by a German officer. It was signed by the député-
directeur of Vichy police for eastern Languedoc. His name is
Charles Fannois."

Honoré shifted his position slightly and now clasped his
hands in front of him. "Charles Fannois is one of four surviv-

ing police officials of the Vichy government who remains at liberty in France today."

Alex dimly recalled the name from the newspaper.

"In 1978," Honoré continued, "an attempt to bring these men to justice for crimes against humanity failed when an appeals court defined a crime against humanity as one carried out by a state 'practicing a policy of ideological hegemony,' not one that merely persecutes persons because of race or religion. The court held that since the Vichy government did not pursue a policy of 'ideological hegemony,' charges against former Vichy officials could not be sustained.

"The case was dismissed. Fannois was released and went into hiding, where he remains. For seven years, our son has sought to reverse the appeals court decision that freed this collaborationist-murderer.

"In the early 1980s, when, finally, the old men of the lower Vichy bureaucracy died off, many previously 'lost' or withheld files and transcripts surfaced in municipal warehouses in Vichy and Bordeaux. Our son uncovered evidence of fraud in the Fannois defense. He discovered that the magistrate who had brought the original indictment was mysteriously transferred out of his jurisdiction, to be replaced by the judge who found for the defense.

"With evidence of fraud, our son expected to persuade the government in Paris to reopen the case and, at last, to bring to justice the man who sent my father to his death.

"That our son was silenced before he could accomplish this task, we believe speaks for itself. We therefore name Charles Fannois an accomplice in the murder of Virgile de la Pagerie and demand his arrest."

Délice stood and embraced her husband. She remained standing, her arm about his waist.

Alex stood as well. Bloch's testimony was totally unexpected. But, while it was creditable, his assumption that the man who signed his father's deportation order in 1941 had a motive to murder his stepson in 1985 was long on circumstance and short on proof. Why would a seventysomething-year-old ex-Vichy official, safely in hiding for nearly a decade, suddenly risk detection and arrest by involving himself in the murder of a prominent theatre critic because the critic had reportedly assembled documentation alleging the Vichy official's complicity in the deportation of a French Jew to Nazi Germany forty-four years ago? In spite of the best efforts of Serge Klarsfeld and others, no Frenchman had yet been arrested for wartime crimes against Jews. An appeals court decision, tortuous to overturn, especially under French law, had dismissed the case against Fannois. Even if it were overturned, there was the spectre of double jeopardy. That could take another forty-four years. And what connection did any of this have to Delap's shoulder bag? Or Iberia's Flight 4426? None. Nothing connected.

Alex asked, "Monsieur Bloch, do you know anything about this man?"

"Yes. Before the war he taught art at the école normale in Perpignan."

"No, no. I mean do you know anything about him now? Where he might be in hiding?"

"No."

"Do you intend to bring charges?"

"Yes."

"Even though his whereabouts are unknown?"

"Yes."

Alex paused. "May I ask — do you think Fannois was familiar with the name Virgile Philadelphie?"

Délice interrupted. "Why not? The bastards can extract the juice from a mango without disturbing the skin!"

Alex wondered if Délice's tropical metaphors concealed more than they revealed. "What bastards are those, madame?"

"Vichy filth!"

He let it go and turned back to Honoré. "Very well, monsieur. If you intend to bring charges, you will have to remain in Paris indefinitely, and you will require an advocate. Sûreté specialists will examine the documents your son has assembled, and inform the Senior Terrorist Investigator of the evidence against the man you name as a suspect."

The meeting was over. They shook hands and walked into the hall. Still searching for a connection, Alex decided to pose one more question — to Délice. As she and Honoré were putting on their coats, Alex asked, "Madame Bloch, where did your son receive his education?"

She stood very straight, chin high. "Immatriculation, Institut Henri Vizioz, Fort-de-France, 1970, age sixteen. Baccalaureat, École Supérieur, Rouens, at eighteen. Sorbonne at twenty-one."

"And during that time, did he enjoy robust good health?"

She lowered her chin slightly. "Well, yes. Apart from an impacted wisdom tooth at fifteen."

"When did he develop asthma?"

Her eyes narrowed and she took a step forward. "When did he develop *what*?"

Alex immediately regretted the question. Too late, he remembered his own mother's reaction when a school district doctor, examining his skinny twelve-year-old chest, suggested that he might have had rickets as a baby. His usually mild-mannered mother went into orbit. She nearly destroyed the clinic.

Délice was outraged at the suggestion that her son was less than perfect. She shook off Honoré's attempt to restrain her. "He had the best of everything!" she cried. "He was a gros bon ange, with his soul manifested in his shadow! His eyes were clear as spring water, his breath sweet as mimosa!"

Alex did not pursue the question. Nor did he see any point in causing her further anguish by describing how her son had died.

After the Blochs departed, he fetched his anorak and left the Maison via Rue des Saussaies.

It was clear that both Honoré and Délice believed their son to be some sort of covert hero motivated by a sincere concern to correct an egregious political miscarriage of justice by a pigeon-hearted government. But, to Alex, this altruism seemed out of character with the acidulous, universally disliked critic whose demise had been so roundly celebrated in every greenroom from the Théâtre Antoine to the Variétés.

On his way to lunch with Varnas, therefore, he made a detour to the second-floor offices of de la Pagerie's former employer, *La Revue Endimanchée*.

A serious-faced young female receptionist in jeans, sweatshirt, and metal-rimmed bifocals sat behind what looked like a bullet-proof glass partition.

Alex showed his Sûreté ID. The receptionist was not impressed. He asked, "Has anyone replaced Virgile de la Pagerie as drama critic on the paper?"

She nodded. "Suzette Singer."

"Is she in?"

The receptionist punched some numbers on a phone. After a moment, she said, "Through that door, end of the hall, last cage on the left." She buzzed the door and Alex walked through.

Suzette Singer was about thirty, had blue eyes round as marbles, a thicket of bristly red hair, and freckles. She wore a black turtleneck, black mini, black hose, and high-topped black sneakers. She was lunching on a carton of vanilla yogurt.

After Alex's inquiry, she loudly replied, "I don't think he gave a shit about the Jews. I think he owed his stepfather."

"Owed him what?"

"Payback. Whatever. Virgile did not suffer indebtedness willingly." She slurped yogurt. "Before he came to work here, the old man supported him. So he owed. The diaspora bit was his cover to nail the Vichy cop and get his stepfather off his back guiltwise."

It seemed unimaginable to Alex that Honoré would be on anyone's back. He said, "You don't make Virgile sound like a nice guy."

She licked the last of the yogurt from the container. "Nice guy! 'Nice guy' is an inexact, punctilious expression used by bourgeois assholes concerned with appropriateness. Was Apollinaire a 'nice guy'? Was Céline?" She dropped the yogurt container in her wastebasket, already crowded with yogurt containers. "Actually, Virgile struck me as elitist and fundamentally anti-Semitic. At least, he never kissed me."

Chez Suzanne

Varnas was exuberant at lunch. He described to Alex the details of finding the Ventil cartridge in the Théâtre Bakoledis. However, with traces of lavender water still clinging to his lapels, he could not avoid reviewing his short scene with the wardrobe mistress last evening, or the longish scene this morning with Madame Roget, during which, shirt in hand, she accused him of betrayal and consorting with courtesans.

Somewhat in awe, Varnas exclaimed, "I think she really cares for me!"

After the laundry episode, he'd submitted the cartridge to Forensics, where the test was immediately positive. Forensics wrapped the still-lethal object in plasticene and consigned it to the deep freeze.

Varnas now produced a slip of paper that bore the notation *Z 31731, exp JUL 86.* "This is cartridge lot number, Alex. Sad to say, lot number does not trace inhaler to pharmacie counter where it is sold. Lot number is wholesaler number. I contact Société Pharmaceutique d'Oise, who put me onto wholesaler for entire Seine-Marne. In less than two minutes, wholesaler gives me printout of fifty-two pharmacies, all in Paris, that receive this lot number in July.

"Did any other pharmacies, not in Paris, receive it?"

"No."

"You still have a hell of a long laundry list. How do you expect to tell which pharmacie sold this inhaler instead of another one exactly like it?"

"This one is poisoned," Varnas said happily.

"Varnas! What if the inhaler was clean when it was purchased and the tampering occurred elsewhere?"

"My dear, we got to start someplace. Asthma inhaler does not sell like toothpaste or aspirin. Legitimate pharmacie sells it only with doctor's prescription. I look for illegitimate pharmacie." He tapped the table. "Listen, Alexei. If my sources can name twenty illegitimate pharmacies in Paris, eight of which are among the fifty-two that receive this lot number, then we already reduce laundry list to six. We are almost in the business." He smiled as the Boeuf en Daube arrived.

Suzanne served them. She loitered behind Varnas, sniffing.

After a moment she whispered, "What mountain lion pissed on you, chéri?"

Philippa

She sat in the directeur's empty office and listened to the ten o'clock company class in the big studio upstairs. The worm was in charge, his chalky voice shrieking, "Arabesque, plié, arabesque, tendu . . ."

Philippa marked the steps where she sat. At the same time, she ventured a very slow sum in her head. As math was not her strong suit, the sum was very slow in coming but eventually produced an astonishing figure. She realized she'd taken over eleven hundred classes since her first day at the Opéra Ballet School thirteen years ago.

She still believed the reason the school accepted her was because her ballet mother had been Alex. Alex, hugely splendid, hair and beard aflame in the bright, white studio, had dwarfed and rendered inconsequential the tricky, beribboned ballet mamas, all lined up against the wall, trying to look trim and turned out. Angela would never have taken Philippa to the ballet in the first place, much less listened to her child's wish to become a dancer.

Had it not been for Alex, Angela would have eventually returned Philippa to Wold Manor, the Methodist home for indigent children, on the barren plains of Lincolnshire, about as far from the ballet as one could get.

At Old Woldy, the secret of survival was to remain unremarkable. The great stupidity was to stand out. If one fell below the norm, punishment from the mother authority was inevitable. If one excelled, punishment from the peer authority was swift. Too tall, short, fat, thin; too dark, too light, too anything, punishment was waiting.

Philippa, the granddaughter of a Marchioness, viewed

childhood as a police state through which everyone was expected to pass; a dark forest of snares, entanglement, and
squalid odours, where one's constant companion was anxiety
and one's only weapon, vigilance; not exactly Angela's hal-
cyon playground of pony carts and morning glories.

Philippa had met her grandmother only once, during one
of Angela's doomed efforts at reinventing herself as the perfect mother. They met for lunch at an undistinguished restaurant in Lincoln, far from prying eyes and Watten House. Lord
Watten, who had already disinherited his daughter, would
not have dreamed of coming. Lady Watten, anxious to do the
right thing, drove herself to Lincoln in a Land Rover and dark
glasses.

Philippa remembered only that she had been allowed two
sweets, and that her mother and grandmother had argued in
harsh whispers the entire time.

Then it was back to Old Woldy. Always back to Old
Woldy, where Philippa honed her animal skills: learned protective colouration, learned to fade into the woodwork, to
diminish her presence, except when it became necessary to
defend herself, with fists and feet, against bully girls and
dirty-fingered boys.

She recalled her last fight, right here at the Palais Garnier
during her first year as a ballet student. She had learned that it
was now quite all right to excel. She was so exhilarated at the
prospect, and so famished for praise, that she outperformed
everyone in class every day. Finally, a boy behind her at the
barre, a tall, competitive redhead, had had enough. During
the *battements,* he delivered Philippa a hard kick in the backside. Without hesitation, she turned and decked him with a
single blow. There was no punishment. The boy later
dropped out and now teaches ballroom in Lille.

She glanced at the office clock. The directeur was already

half an hour late. She heard steps in the hall. Olivia, the ballet mistress, padded into the office and closed the door.

Olivia was a scrubbed, fresh-faced former soloist who looked fifteen but was probably thirty-seven. She knew every step of every ballet in the repertoire, and believed the sun rose and set in Rudy's crotch.

She leaned against the directeur's desk, crossed her feet and regarded Philippa with chaste, brown eyes.

"Philippa," she said and smiled serenely.

She's going to tell me how wonderful I am, Philippa guessed, as Olivia gazed at her with what appeared to be genuine admiration. That means I don't go to London.

"Philippa," Olivia said again. "You are a born dancer. You have it all: intensity, strength, beauty, line, technique, even incandescence. But Philippa, he wants you to progress naturally. He doesn't want to see you skip any of the stages of development essential to transforming a born dancer into a great dancer.

"You are not yet ready for Odette/Odile, chérie; or for Princess Aurora or Giselle. Nor does he think you are ready to dance Teresina in that piece of Bournonville crap at the Royal, especially opposite the likes of Nicolaj Blixen." She smiled.

Philippa shrugged. "Then the answer is no."

"No, no, no! The answer is not no! He's leaving it up to you! He has told Nigel Philby that if you insist on going, he will release you provided the Royal pays your Paris Opéra medical insurance, and that you are back in time to dance the Dewdrop in *Nutcracker*."

Part Two

FANNOIS

13

The Maison

BARELY VISIBLE through a haze of Balkan and Latakia leaf conflagrating in the meerschaum helmet of the Maid of Orléans, the Commissaire gazed at the 1941 studio portrait of young Charles Fannois in his custom-tailored Vichy police uniform. Waving away a lavaliere of smoke, he compared the portrait with the 1978 Agence France Presse wire photo of the aging former Vichy official, fatly waving from the municipal courthouse where charges against him had just been dropped.

"How do you know he's alive?" Demonet asked.

"I don't," Alex replied.

"If he's alive, how do you know he's in France?"

"I don't . . . until we find him. Monsieur and Madame Bloch understand that."

"Do they understand that the documents from Delap's safe that you sent to Comcentre contain absolutely no proof that he is an accessory?"

Alex hesitated. "Monsieur and Madame Bloch are confident that there is enough information to justify an investigation and that, with the computer's help, the investigation will produce the necessary proof."

"Mud pies. What else do you have?"

"I received a Science Lab report this morning that the artificial voice on the Senior Terrorist Investigator's tape was not produced by a sound box after all. The oscillogram showed sound wave amplitude variations inconsistent with sound box transmission."

The Commissaire vouchsafed Alex a tiny yawn. "Marvelous. Someone imitating a robot. My wife's great-nephew can imitate a robot. What else?"

"Iberia Airlines and the Supervisor of Passenger Service Personnel at Barcelona airport have acknowledged receipt of my inquiry concerning Flight 4426 on four September." He paused. "Varnas has a long shot pharmacist under surveillance. Isabelle is working on a dossier of Auguste Pezon-Schwartz. And Delap's belt buckle has enough carbon steel in it to build a small car. That's about all we have at the moment."

The Commissaire leaned back in his chair and studied his cuticles. "That noise I hear; is it a dynamo, or the sound of spinning wheels?"

Alex was not in the mood. He slowly got to his feet. "You seem out of sorts this morning, Commissaire. I hope your croquet game isn't off."

He returned to his office. The documents from Delap's safe were back on his desk. They'd been indexed by Comcentre after the information they contained was fed into Big Louie's newly programmed, amnesia-free random-access memory.

Big Louie had already swallowed the toxicology report from the Institut Médico-Légal, Gus's testimony, and that of his scene designer, Pierre-Yves Gastin, the testimony of the critic from *Le Télégraph,* of Stéphane Nikolaides, and of Honoré Bloch. So far, there were no signs of indigestion.

Alex sat at his desk and flipped open the top file. It contained Deportation Order No. 12073, dated 4 Nov. 1941 at Rivesaltes (Perpignan), consigning prisoners ABEL, I, BERKOW, W, BLOCH, A, FRANK, J, and ZWIN, L, to Transport Pool B, by order Directeur, under Criminal Code XIX, Section_____, subsection_____, paragraph_____f, as amended, Vichy, 1941. The document was signed by C. Fannois, Député-Directeur for eastern Languedoc.

Alex studied the distinctive signature. In France, a country where correspondence, even business correspondence, is often handwritten, much is made of calligraphy. A skilled handwriting analyst, or graphologist, can make a living in France. There is even a society of graphologists.

Alex studied the signature again. He opened his top desk drawer, selected a fine nib pen, and attempted to copy the signature's matching curlicues into his notebook.

Varnas

If his relationship with Madame Roget depended on nuance for its survival, Varnas's relationship with informants in the Paris underworld relied on delicacy.

Varnas used the informant network, which was invisible and unpredictable, much as a sailor uses the weather: If the wind is fair, he goes; if not, he stays. Actually, the analogy is not complete. While the weather can frequently seem malevolent, there is nothing personal about it, nor is there reciprocity.

Keenly aware that mishandled informant intelligence can lead to reprisal, humiliation, and the termination of a source, even the collapse of the network, Varnas pursued his search for an informant, in the matter of the illegal pharmacies, with extreme delicacy.

His rules of informant recruiting were simple enough. Rule One: To enroll an informant effectively, the candidate should be broke or need a favour. Under this rule, many qualified. Rule Two: The candidate should be personally motivated to provide data out of a manageable need for success or vengeance measured against reasonable risk. This rule reduced the field somewhat. Rule Three: The candidate must be discreet and understand the long-term consequences of his actions. This rule severely limited the field. Indeed, in this case Varnas found only one individual on his list who qualified.

He was a man of a certain age who made a comfortable living operating a clandestine fleet of motorcycle delivery vans that transported illegally imported goods, including some drugs, from airstrips, autoroute rest stops, and rail sidings to movable drops in the city.

His age and experience qualified him under Rule Three. He qualified under Rule Two when Varnas learned his fleet had suffered fuel contamination at the hands of certain illicit pharmacists. And he qualified under Rule One. While he was far from broke, he had a grandson who was a suspect in the robbery of a camera store. Varnas explained the circumstances to the juvenile court judge and got the boy released in the grandfather's custody upon payment of 1500 francs. Business could now go forward.

By cross-referencing the list of the fifty-two Paris pharmacies that received the Ventil inhaler lot number in July

against his informant's intelligence, Varnas was able to reduce the number of illegitimate enterprises that received the
inhaler to four.

There was one in the Eighth Arrondissement, another in
the Ninth, one in the Seventeenth, and one in the Eighteenth.

The investigation got off to a poor start. The pharmacist in
the Eighth had died of natural causes in July. His shop was
now a video rental store.

The propriétaire of the pharmacie in the Eighteenth, a female herbalist, had been sent to jail for dispensing the dried
leaves of *Narcissus jonquilla,* one of several poisonous herbs
of the amaryllis family, as medicine for the treatment of lower
bowel disorder. The police closed her store, and the one in
the Eighth, before the Ventil shipments arrived, a detail that
had not appeared on the wholesaler's printout.

There now remained two, one each in the Ninth and in the
Seventeenth. Varnas floated the rumor at Chez Suzanne and
elsewhere that the police were interested in questioning these
two in connection with a recent fatal poisoning. Both pharmacists were kept under surveillance to monitor their responses.

Next day, just after 9 A.M., the pharmacist in the Ninth
Arrondissement, a Corsican with connections to the Milieu,
left his store and, in the company of another man, drove directly to Sûreté headquarters in Rue des Saussaies. The man
who accompanied him, a well-known, low-level underworld
lawyer, threatened to sue the government if his client's name
was made public in connection with this affair. His client, he
said, was a responsible businessman who owned his own
store and the building in which it was situated. He would
never, could never, allow himself to be involved in any activity that would jeopardize his reputation, his livelihood, the
well-being of his family, et cetera.

Alex and Varnas knew that this man's pharmacie and the building it occupied were owned by a syndicate that controlled all trash removal in northwest Paris. As to the man's reputation, he had a record longer than his arm for selling prescription amphetamines without a doctor's blessing. Nevertheless, after twenty minutes, they sent him home with the stipulation that he report once a day to the local Commissariat of Police until further notice.

Nothing was heard from the pharmacist in the Seventeenth. He was an older Russian emigré named Boris Alexandrovich Popov, known by the soubriquet Doctor Zhivago ("Alex, when do you last see pince-nez with black ribbon attached?"). Doctor Zhivago, somewhere in his sixties, was a former physician, once celebrated for administering strength- and performance-enhancing injections of certain vitamins, steroids, hormones, and glycosides to athletes. Unfortunately, a sprinter succumbed to side effects directly attributable to the regime, and the doctor lost his license. He served one year of a five-year sentence. Subsequently, he became a probationary chemist and pharmacist. Probation was discontinued in 1980. His record since had been unremarkable.

His pharmacie, the small Pharmacie Berzélius, was located near the Avenue de Clichy factories. Home was a rented room he shared with a Russian woman in Rue de Vaugirard, a section of Paris in the Fifteenth Arrondissement that has been a centre for Russians in exile since the '20s.

The first evening, Varnas and an Inspecteur-trainee trailed Doctor Zhivago from his pharmacie to the nearby Brochant métro station. He took a No. 13 train to Montparnasse, a circuitous ten-stop ride. There he changed to the No. 12 and detrained at Convention, a block from his rooming house. He showed no apprehension. There were no uneasy glances. He sat quietly, reading a Russian-language edition of Nabokov's *Details of a Sunset.*

Next morning, he reversed the process, reaching the pharmacie at a few minutes before nine o'clock. He made no stops, side trips, or phone calls, or indicated in any way that he suspected he was under surveillance.

Varnas said, "Either he is smart or he is innocent. Both are bad. We wait. If he is smart, he does not alter daily pattern."

The decision was made to let him simmer. They parked an obvious, unmarked police car, with antennas, at the intersection of Rue Berzélius and Avenue de Clichy, forty metres from the pharmacie.

Le Yacht Club

After Nigel Philby's call, Philippa and Alex spoke only English at home. Alex could do a fairly fluent American English, learned as a teenager in the U.S. on a student-exchange program. Philippa, however, hadn't used English on a regular basis for thirteen years and was not remotely fluent. Worse, when she now made the attempt, the words dropped from her mouth like stones, and with the appalling gutter accent she'd acquired at Old Woldy.

She dropped her *h*'s; she said "toe-uhl" for "total," and "baw-uhl" for "bottle." Disaster loomed. About to be a guest star at the Royal, in a country where accent delineated class, she sounded like Eliza Doolittle before Rex Harrison.

There was no time for extensive speech therapy, but there were audiotapes: of Peggy Ashcroft, of Claire Bloom, Maggie Smith, John Gielgud, and Jeremy Irons. Unfortunately, Philippa got caught up in the narrative of each tape instead of paying attention to the accents. "Alex, I can hear the tune, but I can't sing it."

The night before she was to leave for London, her bags already packed and piled at the foot of the companion ladder, she and Alex tried to relax in front of the TV, with a bottle of champagne. They wandered through the channels several times, settling, finally, on an old musical film, produced before Philippa was born, that starred Bing Crosby, Donald O'Connor, Mitzi Gaynor, and the French dancer Zizi Jeanmaire. The plot of the film was utterly mindless, but Philippa had always admired O'Connor's dancing. At about the half-way point, however, she was taken with the way Jeanmaire dealt with English. Jeanmaire dropped all her *h*'s ("Eee's not 'ere at zuh moment"). She used the French, glottal *r*. She said "becohz" for "because," and "*beh*-gineeng" for "be*gin*ning." She demolished the language. But, with the accent, and occasionally substituting French words for those English words she couldn't pronounce, she managed nicely, without subtitles and with a certain charm. Philippa decided she could do that. If she avoided "ooh-la-la!" (which Jeanmaire didn't) and other saucy gallicisms that could give the game away, she thought she might be just convincing enough to persuade the English that she was not a person of poor quality.

Orly

Accustomed to leaving Philippa in Paris while he traveled on police business, Alex now found himself unprepared for this role reversal. He sought refuge in the papa-guardian figure.

He hovered. He made sure she had enough English pounds, shillings, and pence. He provided her with a letter of credit on Barclay's Bank. He armed her with emergency telephone numbers and the name and address of a colleague at Scotland Yard.

Stéphane, who accompanied them to the airport, watched

this performance with a mixture of amusement and envy. Alex checked Philippa's ticket and boarding pass for the third time. At the last minute, he bought her a copy of Chichester's *Guide to London* and made certain she understood how to get from her hotel — The Jane Austen, a security-conscious lodging place for young, professional women that placed a vigilant housekeeper in bombazine next to the lift on every floor — to Covent Garden.

Finally, when her flight was called, Philippa hugged Stéphane, turned to Alex with a tear on her cheek, and whispered, in her new French-accented English, "You are my favoreet pain in zuh ass!" With that she kissed him on the mouth and was gone.

Stéphane watched Alex watch the airbus take off, bank to the northwest, and disappear.

14

The Maison

EARLIER, with the acquiescence of the Commissaire and the Senior Terrorist Investigator, information and photographs of Charles Fannois, address unknown, had been dispatched to Sûreté directeurs in Bordeaux, Toulouse, and Marseille. The information was sent by air courier to ensure confidentiality. The suspect's postwar affiliation with Vichy interests and, possibly, the Front Patriotique, were noted. It was emphasized that any work undertaken was to be covert all the way.

Alex dropped Stéphane at de la Pagerie's flat in Rue de Tournon, and returned to the Maison. As he entered his first-floor office, a Research Inspecteur delivered Isabelle's long-awaited dossier on Auguste Pezon-Schwartz.

Alex placed the file on Varnas's desk. While he didn't share his partner's preoccupation with Gus, particularly now that the case against Fannois was under way, he was nevertheless mildly curious.

He went to the hall water cooler and glanced at his watch. Philippa had landed at Heathrow by now. She'd be checking into The Jane Austen within the hour. To fill in the time until he could call London, he returned to the office, sat at Varnas's desk, and opened Gus's file.

The first section dealt with the directeur's background and adolescent forays into the theatre. It confirmed what Alex already knew from Gus's testimony.

He skipped to the next section, in which Isabelle attempted to reveal a relationship between Gus and de la Pagerie, much as she had attempted to show the connection between Delap and the Front Patriotique. However, as Alex read on, it became clear that the link here was far more tangible.

Isabelle had discovered that, of the six plays Gus produced and directed between 1978 and 1984, four featured the critic's fiancée, Angélique Églantine.

Gus had never mentioned Angélique in his testimony. Alex wondered whether this omission could be considered significant. Especially as Isabelle now demonstrated that the actress was central to the feud that sprang up between the directeur and the critic.

The feud developed over who was responsible for her success. Gus credited himself for shaping her interpretations of the great playwrights and for developing her artistry. Delap ridiculed this presumption, insisting that her genius was spontaneous and directeur-proof, and that her success would eventually be attributable to audiences and the discerning eye of the critic.

Reviewing Gus's 1980 production of Anouilh's *Léocadia* in Dijon, Delap panned the production but praised Mademoiselle Églantine's mercurial presence in an otherwise "banal confection."

With the Paris revival of Giraudoux's *Intermezzo* two

years later, Gus had a hit that ran for three hundred performances. Delap carped over the mise en scène and the physical production but predicted great things for Angélique. Isabelle believed that the Svengali-Trilby relationship was already under way by this time. Angélique and de la Pagerie began living together during the run of *Intermezzo*.

In 1983, the critic accompanied his then fiancée to St-Jean-de-Luz to review the opening of Gus's revival of *The Visit*, by Dürrenmatt. The critic lavishly praised her performance as Claire Zachanassian, the richest, most powerful woman in Europe, bone ugly, hennaed, crippled, a malevolent character thirty years older than the actress herself. He said he was now certain that Mademoiselle Églantine could successfully play any part in any repertoire, in any style, classic or modern, comedy or drama, and would never need to succumb to the cheap lure of commercial stardom.

"In the tradition of the great European character actors of the 19th century," he wrote, "Angélique Églantine has the transcendent genius to be virtually unrecognizable from role to role."

At the same time, the critic continued his attack on the directeur. He called Gus a "revival queen, a fourth-rate traffic cop without a clue to the fundamentals of ensemble acting, a directeur of clanking predictability." To which he added, "Right now, Jean Genêt is a better directeur than Pezon-Schwartz, and Jean Genêt is dead."

Of the scenery, which had been praised by other critics, de la Pagerie wrote, "The scene designer, Pierre-Yves Gastin, has become the toilet bowl Chagall. However, his work in *The Visit* suggests that, at some time in his pampered past, he was traumatized by the engravings of Rockwell Kent or, possibly, by Soviet socialist realism. In any case, the coffin that accom-

panies Madame Zachanassian to the village of Guellen, in
this Pezon-Schwartz revival of the Dürrenmatt classic, looks
like the *Orient Express* with handles."

Isabelle had included a sidebar on Pierre-Yves Gastin.

"In addition to being Gus's scene designer, Pierre-Yves is
Gus's sweetheart as well as his main source of financing.
Pierre-Yves is rich. His grandfather, a Swiss banker, left a
substantial trust with Pierre-Yves' father as sole beneficiary
until his death in 1979. At that time the trust was dissolved
and the principal distributed among the grandchildren.
Pierre-Yves and his sister each inherited a half billion francs
after taxes.

"If you are wondering why this Swiss half-billionaire
needs to work as a scene designer in Paris, the answer is that
Gus 'discovered' him doing windows for Chanel for nothing,
and saved him from a life of aimless dilettantism. He is said to
be extremely talented but needs Gus to motivate him."

Alex skipped the list of Pierre-Yves' credits and concentrated on a piece of speculative evidence Isabelle had dug out
of the theatrical press that attributed the breakup of Delap's
and Angélique's engagement partly to unsubstantiated reports of physical abuse but principally to a decision she had
made, against his wishes, to play the title role in a biographi-
cal play based on the life of the great nineteenth-century
French actress Rachel. Delap had wanted her to do *Hedda
Gabler* in a new, colloquial translation by a young Czech
playwright he admired.

Gus produced *Rachel*. It was a disaster. It closed after five
performances. And, for the first time, de la Pagerie excoriated
Angélique.

He confessed to having been dazzled by her spontaneity
and diversity. But he now reluctantly concluded that it had

been all smoke and mirrors, that her talent was roughly equivalent to that of a saltimbanque, a juggler or acrobat. He wrote, "Alas, there is nothing there, after all. This writer watched in dismay as she recklessly attempted to recreate the vocal and physical intensity of that greatest of French classical actresses. By the second act, it became embarrassingly clear that no intellect, no theatrical heritage or consanguinity informed this superficial interpretation of a complex artist. Mademoiselle Églantine is a skilled mimic, an impersonator, a sleight of hand artist. But she is no actress. She does not belong in the theatre, but in a circus, saloon, or, perhaps, on TV."

Isabelle concluded. "Gus's response to this assault was to lament that the French system of justice provided no forum wherein an artist could redress personal injury at the hands of an unscrupulous critic. He regretted that dueling had been outlawed. De la Pagerie responded to this with a single line in the next week's *La Revue Endimanchée*: 'Puff pastry at five paces?'

"As for the theatre community, it perceived Delap's trashing of *Rachel* as the ugly personal attack of a failed Pygmalion.

"*Rachel* cost Gus, or rather Pierre-Yves, 3 million francs. Angélique, suffering from anorexia, withdrew to a cottage in the village of Seigneur-sous-Tarn, in the Aveyron. She died there six months later, reportedly of malnutrition and dehydration. In Paris, on Sunday 9 June, Gus and Pierre-Yves gave a reception in Angélique's memory at Pierre-Yves' home. Next day, they went into rehearsal for *Eurydice*.

"Apart from his professional association with Mlle Églantine and his financial dependence on Pierre-Yves Gastin, the information contained herein does not materially alter what we already know about Gus: that he hated de la Pagerie and would have gladly strangled him years ago if he'd had the balls.

"As to motive, I suppose it could be argued that they all had a motive. But Gus and his designer must surely know by now that destructive, even malicious, criticism is part of the game in art as well as in commerce; certainly in the theatre, which is a combination of both.

"Who do you like in the rugby semi-finals?"

Alex concluded that, given Gus's facade of jokey optimism and promiscuous badinage, his not having mentioned Angélique in his testimony was probably less a significant omission than a disinclination to acknowledge failure — or pain.

Alex closed the dossier, left it on Varnas's desk, and rang up The Jane Austen in London. Miss Watten had checked in but immediately departed for the theatre. Alex left a message for her to call him at either the Maison or *Le Yacht Club* when convenient.

15

Place Adolphe-Chérioux

At THE CLOSE of the workday on Friday, Varnas withdrew the unmarked police car from the vicinity of the Pharmacie Berzélius (which closed Saturdays), and placed a motor scooter (female) on Rue de Vaugirard opposite Doctor Zhivago's rooming house.

She phoned in three times during the night (Varnas would permit no communication by transceiver; the frequencies were too accessible). She had nothing to report. He replaced her at 8 A.M. The replacement, also a motor scooter (female), was disguised as a vendor of fruit ices.

Saturday was warm and windless. The subject, accompanied by a woman, was observed as he emerged from his logement at 0945 and walked the three blocks to Café Lambert. He and the woman had breakfast there of hard-boiled eggs and tea. They returned to the rooming house at 1030.

At 1120, having changed clothes, the subject and woman reappeared with folding chairs and a picnic basket. They carried these articles to the small parc at Place Adolphe-Chérioux, where they unfolded the chairs in sunshine and ate a lunch of sardines, black bread, and beer.

They spent the better part of the afternoon there, he reading and she sunning herself behind an aluminum foil reflector.

At 1402, the subject waved me over and bought two ices, one lemon and one raspberry.

At 1534, he walked back to the rooming house alone. A few minutes later, he returned with a blanket which he placed over the woman's legs.

At 1630, they folded their chairs and returned to the logement.

Nothing further to report.

Varnas asked the stake if the subject suspected he was under surveillance; if buying the ices from her was a statement. She seemed slightly offended at the suggestion.

"He never noticed me until I began selling to patrons in the parc. I kept the scooter moving, in and out of Place Adolphe-Chérioux, up and down the avenue, ringing my bell. I was never still. He had his nose in his book most of the time, and she had wet cotton over her eyes. It was a simple stake. He suspected nothing."

"Very good," Varnas said. "But do not be distracted by subject inactivity or by Russian civility and signs of devotion. Please report everything."

She had sold 350 francs' worth of ices. Varnas let her keep half the cash.

Théâtre Bakoledis

Earlier in the afternoon, Varnas made inquiries and learned that an understudy rehearsal of *Eurydice* would take place after the Saturday matinée. Believing that the rehearsal would be a good opportunity for him to become reacquainted with Gus, who was still on his mind, he decided to attend.

He was disappointed. As the last of the matinée patrons filed out of the lobby, he was informed that the stage manager, not Gus, would conduct the understudy rehearsal. The house manager then called Varnas into the box office.

"I got something for you," he said. He produced a small, crumpled paper bag held closed by a rubber band. Varnas took the bag, removed the rubber band, and peered inside. There he beheld the final missing piece of the inhaler: the red plastic dispenser.

"Where do you find this?"

"Lost and found."

"Where is lost and found?"

"In the lower lobby, between the maintenance room and the men's pissoire. Prob'ly been there since opening night."

"Really?"

"Prob'ly a patron turned it in."

Hippo

On this same warm September Saturday, Hippo returned to Paris from holiday; not to Paris, actually, but to the suburb of Aubervilliers, where he lived in a former discothèque.

Neither Alex nor Varnas had known the Chef of Ballistics to live in an ordinary flat. No ordinary Paris flat was large enough to accommodate the huge and sprawling storage requirements of the European Society of Antique Weaponry, nor was any floor in any Paris flat sufficiently robust to support a three-thousand-kilogram, cast-iron, Turkish siege cannon.

Hippo's past domiciles included a former barracks, a former firehouse, and a former gymnasium, each located a greater distance from the centre of Paris than its predecessor. He was now the happy, sole tenant of the former discothèque (capacity 750), with its faded glitz, its octophonic, multiple track stereo, its cerise walls and starry ceiling, and enough antique weaponry to equip the armed forces of Andorra and

Monaco; all this, a stone's throw from Fort d'Aubervilliers, only a few minutes from the Gare de l'Est by métro, but, to most Parisiens, as remote as Elba.

The Palais de Justice sent a small truck to meet Hippo at the railroad station. In addition to his luggage and the case of 1982 Côte du Carbadés wine, he'd brought home a sixteenth-century arquebus matchlock musket. This smoothbore brute, lovingly restored to original condition by a local machinist, was nearly two metres long and so heavy it could not be fired without a forked metal rod, inserted into the ground to support the muzzle.

Now, safely arrived, and with help from the truck driver and his assistant, Hippo cleared an area adjacent to the disco's former bar to display the musket along with a sixteenth-century pikeman's helmet, armour, and weapon. When everything was in place, he focused an overhead baby spot and produced a pool of hot, pink, nightclub light that anachronistically illuminated the ancient weaponry. The truckmen glanced at each other.

After they left, Hippo set the table for dinner. The table was a heavy, oak country piece that had belonged to his mother. It now rested on the raised former bandstand, under a series of haphazardly angled acoustic panels finished in pastel colours.

He had planned dinner for four, but, with Philippa gone, it would now just be he, Alex, and Varnas. The purpose of the occasion was to introduce his friends to the Côte du Cabardés, to catch up on the murder case, and to explain to Alex and Varnas the reason his traveling companion, Marcel, had elected to remain in the village of Le Pré.

A half hour before his guests arrived, Hippo poured two bottles of the Cabardés into crystal decanters, placed them on the table, and inserted Boccherini's string quintet into the stereo. He then went to the kitchen and began preparing the dinner of leek soup, linguini with meat sauce, a mixed green salade, and a pear tarte. This was not a daunting task. The soup, in a box, had come from the super-marché, the meat sauce in a bottle from the local pasta takeout, the salade and prepared dressing from the neighborhood épicerie, and the pear tarte from Mariette's, the pâtisserie in Alex's neighborhood, one métro stop away. Hippo had ordered the ingredients the day before, from the train, with a single phone call to his cleaning lady. This excellent woman of patience, who believed Hippo was Saint Peter, had assembled everything in less than an hour and placed it in his institutional fridge. His greatest exertion now was to grate the parmesan cheese and slice the bread.

"Opulent!" Alex said, as he tasted the wine.

"Very excellent!" Varnas said.

Hippo looked pleased.

During dinner, which, for low cuisine, was surprisingly good, Hippo quizzed Alex and Varnas on certain secondary details of the case. What were the credentials of the Sous-Medical Examiner who made the initial diagnosis of cardiac arrest? Why did Gus leave the opening night party early? Why did Delap terminate his engagement to Angélique Églantine, or did she break it off? Did Délice's phrase "The bastards are everywhere!" refer to Vichyists or the Front Patriotique? He then asked if the Senior Terrorist Investigator's office had lately been in touch with HCU (Hate Crimes Unit), Marseille, to learn of the lengths to which the Front would go to influence political opinion.

Which was the cue for the pear tarte, for coffee, Armagnac, and Marcel's reason for remaining in Le Pré.

After coffee, Hippo began. "Alex and Varnas, I have endured arms buffs, auto buffs, ships, aeroplane, food, wine and sports buffs, but never — until recently — the obsessions of a religious miracle buff.

"Marcel knows every detail and eye blink of every catalogued heavenly intervention in history; and he kept me up until 2 A.M. the other night, detailing his scholarly research into the appearance of the Blessed Virgin to young Marie-Rose Fournier at Le Pré in April of this year.

"He pointed out the similarities between Le Pré, in 1985, and the miracle of La Salette, in 1846. In both events, the children, Mélanie Calvat at La Salette, and Marie-Rose Fournier at Le Pré, were shepherdesses who knew their catechism at age seven, had difficulties with their stepmothers, and suffered emotional hardships that coincided with the appearance of the Virgin. Yet, the church accepted La Salette and has dismissed Le Pré. As you must know, paranormal events do not normally occupy my attention. But I feel obliged to tell you that, in this case, Marcel has convinced me. The reason the church does not recognize Le Pré is because it is bad for business.

"In preparation for our visit to the shrine, Marcel obtained a copy of the land engineering report, ordered by the local Catholic diocesan council to explain away the miraculous appearance of a mountain spring in the Fournier pasture. The report flatly states that the spring was a coincidental aquiferous event in an area of known seismic instability.

"As you can see, the church has abandoned Le Pré. Nevertheless, the pilgrims come. The pastures of the village have been turned into parking lots for the tour buses and caravans. Believers, wishing to undergo a direct spiritual experience, are turning up by the thousands. Ripe for an entrepreneur, the shrine has been taken over by the Front Patriotique and transformed into a fundamentalist theme park. Nothing is free. They charge for parking. They charge admission to the shrine itself, an ugly stone-and-log pergola shrouded in mist halfway up the mountain that contains the spring and a hideous, illuminated, glass-fibre statue of the Virgin. They sell T-shirts with photographs of Marie-Rose and her dog. They sell the water from the spring in one-litre bottles. They sell plasticene envelopes of dirt from the pasture. And they sell a xenophobic political message. They have taken the words the Virgin spoke to Marie-Rose and altered them. What was originally 'The people of Le Pré must do penance, say the rosary, and build a new stone church' has become 'The people of Le Pré must do penance and say the rosary, but first destroy the forces of Satan whose leaders are Zionists, Muslims, Pan-Africans, and pederasts.' No new church has been built. The chapel is padlocked, there have been no services, and the chaplain and girl seem to have disappeared. That is why Marcel has remained in Le Pré."

During this narrative, which did not directly concern them, Alex and Varnas sipped their Armagnac and nodded at appropriate intervals to acknowledge that they were listening, much as they would if a friend were describing his insurance policy or stamp collection.

Ever intuitive, Hippo asked, "Why am I telling you this? Because, for you, Alex, the story goes beyond mere anecdote.

"The day before Marcel drove me to Carcassonne to catch the train, we encountered a woman who had just arrived in Mazamet. Visitors to Le Pré must stay in Mazamet because there are no accommodations in the village. The woman is the girl's aunt." He glanced at Alex. "Her name is Thérèse Chalant. Does that name ring a bell?"

"No."

"She is the wife of a restaurateur whose establishment is on the Canal du Midi at Castelnaudary. She says she knows you."

Alex, temporarily dislocated, now recalled why the town of Mazamet had seemed familiar when he phoned Hippo. The restaurateur's wife had mentioned it as her place of origin.

"I remember her," he said. "She has my canned goods from *Sirocco*."

"You must have made quite an impression," Hippo added. "She is convinced Marie-Rose has been kidnapped, Alex. And she says you are the only policeman she knows."

Alex sighed. It had been a long day. Philippa was gone. He'd forgotten about the Front Patriotique. The possible kidnapping of a fanciful child who imagined she saw the Virgin Mary in the Haut Languedoc had little to do with his present agenda. Still, kidnapping was a federal crime. "Why didn't the locals investigate?"

"Marcel and I believe they were intimidated."

"When did Thérèse suspect her niece had been kidnapped?"

"When she received a letter from Marie-Rose's father in which he complained that the child had become uncontrollable. He appealed to Thérèse to come to Le Pré to persuade the girl to cooperate."

"Cooperate how?"

"By playing the role of divinely appointed intermediary. By appearing daily at the shrine. By receiving petitioners, healing the sick, and so on. Thérèse was alarmed by the letter because she knows Pierre Fournier can neither read nor write, and because Marie-Rose has never been uncontrollable."

Alex stood. "That's not evidence of kidnapping. Still . . .

maybe Delap was right. If we don't do something, we may all be wearing badges. Varnas."

"Alexei?"

"Alert the Senior T.I.'s office to the situation at Le Pré. Mention the possibility of an abduction."

"Yes, my dear."

He turned to Hippo. "Does Thérèse have an address in Mazamet?"

Hippo gave it to him on a slip of paper. Hippo also gave them each a bottle of Côte du Cabardés to take home.

Le Yacht Club

As Philippa had not called, Alex rang The Jane Austen again. Miss Watten had picked up her messages but was not presently in her room.

He rang off, walked into the galley, and removed the bottle of wine from its wrapping. Before placing it in the wine rack, he examined the label. It seemed conventional enough.

Château Villars

(A small watercolour of the château)

CÔTE DU CABARDÉS

Appellation Cabardés Contrôllée

Priory of the Holy Redeemer, Propriétaire

Mis en bouteille

au

Château

L. Hébert, 11411 Carcassonne, Négociant

He then glanced up at the small signatory label, just below the bottleneck. What he saw there made the hair on the back of his neck stir. He carefully placed the bottle on the counter, went to the saloon for his notebook, and returned to the gal-

ley. He switched on the light over the sink and compared the
signatures.

On the label,

Frère Christophe

1982

In his notebook,

C. Fannois

16

Marcel

THE DAY AFTER HE SAW HIPPO onto the train, Marcel was inspired to return to Carcassonne to seek an audience with the Bishop of Aude. He drove down from Mazamet and up to the Basilica of St-Nazaire in the ancient walled cité.

While he was unaware of the bishop's political views, he was certain that the spiritual leader of the diocese in which Le Pré was located would not condone events as they had transpired in that tiny, Catholic village, where no mass, confession, or communion had taken place in weeks.

Marcel wore his clerical collar and dickey under the only jacket he'd brought on holiday, a sort of blue-green, tweed sport coat shot through with orange dots. The elderly apostolic chamberlain who received him in the bishop's paneled antechambre held Marcel's Society of Jesus credentials a centimetre from his trifocals and slightly moved his lips as he read. When he became aware of who Marcel was, the foxy old monsignor endeavored to conceal his expression of alarm. In conservative clerical circles, the presence of a Jesuit is only slightly more acceptable than that of a Communist insurrectionist. The sport coat merely confirmed the chamberlain's worst fears.

He gingerly returned Marcel's papers and, in a low, adagio growl that resembled a leaky contra-bassoon, declared that, as the bishop was attending a diocesan retreat, an audience was out of the question. He added that the chaplain at Le Pré had been dismissed for deliberately disobeying His Grace's disavowal of the alleged Marian apparition as unworthy of the assent of human faith. He would be replaced in good time. As to the appropriation of the site by unscrupulous persons, it was, if true, beyond the purview and interest of the apostolic directorate.

Marcel, who could have demolished His Grace's peremptory dismissal of the miracle by reciting the *De servorum Dei beatificatione* of Pope Benedict XIV — in Latin — nevertheless refrained. He'd reluctantly decided Hippo was right. This was a matter for the police, not the clergy. In the meantime, however, he wanted satisfaction. Come what may, he would say mass at Le Pré.

He drove back to Mazamet. Arriving there in the late afternoon, he went directly to the rectory of the Église St-Sauveur, where Thérèse was staying. With the cooperation of the prelate, who was her cousin, he obtained a hundred communion wafers and purchased three litres of sacramental wine. He loaded these into the boot of the Renault. He then drove to the Hôtel Jourdon, where he and Hippo had stayed, ate a light supper in the hotel restaurant, and changed into wool slacks and pullover. He paid his bill and walked back to the Renault, which he had left locked in the hotel car parc. Thérèse was waiting there, perched on the bonnet of the vehicle. She wore a wool head scarf and hiking boots and carried a paper sack. It was just sundown. A pale gibbous moon hung low in the eastern sky.

She climbed down as he approached. "Good evening, Father," she said softly. "I have meat pies, a thermos of coffee, and cognac. We'll need them to keep us going through the night."

Marcel frowned. "We? Us? What are you talking about?"

Thérèse smiled shyly. "Father Marcel. The people of Le Pré don't know you. You will not persuade them to leave their houses and come to mass without me. You will not be able to get into the chapel without me, much less locate the candles, candlesticks, chalice, plate, crucifix, and vestments that are hidden all over the village. Moreover, the inside of the chapel lies under centimetres of dust. There are birds' nests and mice. There is a curfew and no electricité after eight P.M. Who do you imagine knows the chapel well enough to clean it by moonlight?"

"Saint Thérèse?"

She blushed. "No, Father. The ladies of the altar guild."

Le Pré

Some called it the Second Miracle.

That night, about 10 P.M., when the news of tomorrow morning's mass had spread selectively through the village, it began to snow. To the people's anxiety at the thought of openly defying the Mountain Mafia by celebrating mass was now added the risk of moonlit tracks in the snow, leading from a dozen doorways directly up the single village street to the chapel; the tracks of altar guild ladies and of those loyal parishioners who had concealed the chapel artifacts and were now returning them.

Someone said, "But there cannot be a moon and snow at the same time. Either the moon will disappear behind a cloud or the snow will stop. What to do in the meantime? In the meantime, hurry. Before the curfew jeep comes."

By midnight, with the ladies of the altar guild safely inside the chapel and the bearers of artifacts in their beds, it began to snow harder. By one o'clock, not a track could be seen. Yet the moon shone. And the rough mountain pastures surrounding the village turned pale blue, like dessert bowls into which fell a blizzard of bright Christmas blossoms. There had never been snow this early before. And the curfew jeep never came.

The sleeping young Député-Directeur of Shrine Sécurité (DDSS), deep in a recurring erotic dream in which the magnificently bosomed daughter of the postmistress was about to lower herself onto his pullulating phallus, sat up in bed with a terrible start. The phone was ringing.

Still half asleep, he grasped the instrument on which his mind was most wonderfully concentrated at that moment, and endeavored to bring it to his ear. "Allô!" he cried, then "Aiee!"

The phone continued to ring. Slowly, the iron bedstead, the quilt, the casement window filled with gray morning light, came into focus. He answered the phone. It was his boss.

"Allô-allô!" the DSS shouted. "There's twenty-three centimetres of duck shit on the ground! Grab your socks!"

The DDSS looked out the window. Snow. Jesus. Snow was an emergency for which the organization had not yet prepared itself, either in equipment, personnel, or planning. Snow on the busiest day of the week. The village thoroughfare, the access road to the administration building, the shrine promenades, and the four parking pastures had to be cleared of snow by nine o'clock.

The young DDSS climbed into long underwear, two pairs of socks, his brown uniform, Doc Martens, military belt with shoulder straps and holster, and his white beret with the French tricolour patch and initials of the FP. He brushed his teeth at the bathroom sink that he shared with the shrine electricien, and examined the peach fuzz on his cheeks in the mirror. He'd shave later.

His rank as Député entitled him to the use of a rebuilt World War Two jeep. He trotted down the stairs on the outside of the barracks building, shoveled the snow out of the front seat of the jeep, jumped in, pulled the choke, pumped the accelerator, and kicked the starter. The engine fired once and died. Minutes later he was chopping ice out of the fuel filter.

This scenario was repeated all over the village that morning, wherever an FP vehicle had been parked outside.

At 7:30, while his men prepared to pound on doorways to confiscate locally owned tractors and trucks capable of snow removal, the bell in the chapel began to toll. As rumors of sabotage and the sudden appearance in the village of a maverick priest had already begun to circulate, the tolling of the chapel bell had a profound effect on the young DDSS. He knew that the Front Patriotique would countenance no revanchist challenge to its politicization of the shrine and the miracle of Le Pré. Consequently, he now turned and faced his men, and with that swaggering bravado that the fear of combat compels, ordered them back to their headquarters in the municipal garage, on the double. They ran, in step, shouting and punching the air.

According to tax records, the permanent population of Le Pré hovered around eighty-four souls, up some years, down

others, but down lately as more and more young people left
for work in the cité.

The village chapel contained twelve pews, six to a side,
each capable of holding six persons for a capacity of seventy-
two. With this geometry in mind, the old chaplain, Père Labatt, had been able to tell at a glance how many parishioners
were present at any given time. The pews were not always
full, not even at Christmas or Easter; nor were the dozen or
so folding chairs, stacked along the wall in the back, ever
pressed into service. Until now.

Thérèse, who had delivered the two altar boys, in their red
cassocks and white cottas, to the chapel just in time for the
mass, estimated the congregation at the beginning of the service at ninety-one, ninety-four counting Father Marcel and
the altar boys. But at the end of communion, there was only
one wafer left, which meant ninety-six had actually attended
(ninety-nine counting Father Marcel and the boys). Thérèse
attributed these record numbers to devotees from neighbor-
ing villages, including three nuns who came by snowmobile.

Now, as the service was coming to an end and Father
Marcel turned to the congregation to deliver his Benediction,
the chapel doors burst open and a column of young paramili-
tary thugs in brown uniforms and white berets stormed in,
arms swinging in cadence and boots thundering on the hard-
wood floor. When they were halfway up the aisle, their leader
shouted "Halt!" They stamped to a stop and fell into an alert
parade rest, each man holding a weighted baton. There were
seven of them, including the leader. Thérèse, who now sat on
the aisle in the second pew, saw that none of them was from
the village, and that none could be over the age of eighteen.
Indeed, the young leader, a fair-complexioned, lumpish-
looking boy with a layer of feather-down on his cheeks, dis-

played a fresh crop of adolescent pimples that traveled across his forehead, roughly parallel to the leather band of his beret.

The leader moved several paces up the aisle toward Marcel, stopped, and shouted, "Everyone in this building is under arrest for unlawful religious assembly!"

Silence.

Marcel walked slowly to the edge of the chancel, descended the few steps to the floor of the nave, and came face-to-face with the young leader — face-to-face in a manner of speaking only, for Marcel towered over him, so that the boy's eyes came to Marcel's chest, presently draped in Père Labatt's old, embroidered chasuble, recently let out by the ladies of the altar guild for the occasion. Marcel gazed down at the boy. Very quietly, and evenly, he said, "Take . . . off . . . your . . . hat."

The boy's face flushed. He took a step back and tapped the tip of his baton in the open palm of his left hand. But, no sooner had he made this gesture than every head in the congregation turned slightly to the left. The reason for this was that they had all heard a sound, a sound from a long way off, a sound familiar to anyone who'd ever watched a dubbed-into-French rerun of *M*A*S*H*. The sound they heard was the *thup-thup-thup* of a helicopter's rotor blade, demolishing the distant air.

Marcel may have heard the sound first, for he smiled and opened his arms. "And there appeared a great wonder in heaven," he declared. "A woman clothed with the sun, and the moon under her feet, and upon her head a crown of twelve stars!"

The *thup-thupp*ing was now multiple and louder. There were two, perhaps three, machines coming.

The young leader, muddled by this unexplained heavenly

intervention, turned and fled from the chapel. His squad followed. Some in the congregation, anxious to satisfy their curiosity, started toward the doors. But Marcel's dignified presence before the chancel brought them back to their pews.

The *thupp*ing, now ubiquitous and deafening, filled the chapel.

Marcel raised his right hand. The congregation knelt.

"In nomine" ... THUP ... "patris" ... THUP ... "filii" ... THUP! Rrrrrrrr ... "et spiritus" ... ROARRR-RRRRRR ... "sancti. Amen."

Marseille

After a year's delay, the Police Air Wing of the Justice Ministry, Marseille, took delivery of three Aérospatiale *Alouette* single-turbine, seven-seat, high-performance helicopters, as well as a heavy-lifting Aérospatiale *Puma* sixteen-seater. The Police Air Wing was anxious to deploy this new equipment to monitor performance and fuel-burn versus the fifteen-year-old hardware just replaced. But, apart from a few traffic accident evacs and a single SAR operation on a Corsican trawler crew, August and September had been quiet.

Now, at 6 A.M. on this Sunday morning, came a yellow alert from Hate Crimes Unit No. 1. There had been yellows before. Nevertheless, fueling and preheating were ordered.

The late-night transmission of Varnas's message concerning the situation in Le Pré via the Senior Terrorist Investigator's office modem flickered indecisively on the computer screen at HCU No. 1; it flickered and trembled like a baby bird afraid to fly until it was joined, a few moments later, by a Sûreté directive naming what was believed to be the whereabouts of Charles Fannois, also known as "Frère Christophe," at the Priory of the Holy Redeemer, Château Villars.

Fannois was wanted for questioning in connection with a
Paris homicide. As Château Villars and Le Pré were only
twelve kilometres apart, according to the latitude-longitude
coordinates included in both alerts, and as the area around
the château had lately received some attention as the possible
site of an illegal, right-wing satellite television station calling
itself the Pays d'Oc Inspirational Network, the scramble flag
at Air Wing finally went up.

The three *Alouettes*, each with a strategic weapons and
tactical squad and a video cameraman aboard, took off for
Le Pré at 0715, ETA 0840.

The big *Puma*, carrying two squads, a camera crew, and
two pilots, took off for Château Villars at 0720, ETA 0850.

Château Villars

Satellite subscribers to the Pays d'Oc Inspirational Network
were taken by surprise when the organ music playing under
Brother Benedict's Sunday morning homily ("The Jewish ho-
mosexual as anti-Christ") suddenly stopped.

The camera was tight on Brother Benedict's ruddy face at
the time. He was seen to frown slightly and to shift his twin-
kling blue eyes slowly to camera right. He then said something that sounded like "Holy shit!" and the screen went
dark.

A title — WE ARE EXPERIENCING TECHNICAL DIFFICULTIES,
PLEASE STAND BY — slid in, underscored by an audiotape of
Johnny Halliday singing the French lyric of Barry Manilow's
I Write the Songs (That Make the Whole World Sing). Then
the screen went dark again, and that was it for the Pays d'Oc
Inspirational Network.

The strategic weapons and tactical squads had hit the
ground running while the *Puma* still hovered a few centi-

metres above the abbey courtyard. The illegal TV station, situated in the old wine cooperative behind the priory chapel,
was secured within minutes. This episode, and the one at Le
Pré, twelve miles to the north, were videotaped in detail and
shown on every major network in France that evening.

Viewers saw the "Liberation of Le Pré." It was like the
liberation of Paris in '44, but shorter. Villagers cheered and
wept and waved little tricolour flags as the Front Patriotique
hoodlums were rounded up despite a rogue snowfall that had
made the streets nearly impassable.

The priest who conducted the forbidden morning mass for
the people of Le Pré was shown flanked by two young altar
boys. The camera came in on the smaller of the two boys, a
spiky-haired, rosy-cheeked child with a heart-shaped face,
and huge, percipient hazel eyes, who gazed solemnly at the
camera, ventured a smile, waved, then hugged a large sheepdog.

The footage shifted to the taking of Château Villars.
Viewers witnessed the surrender of vineyard and winery
workers, and the arrest of a score of monks and their abbot.

At the conclusion of the TF 1 telecast, the anchor announced a late bulletin from Marseille:

"Observers agree that the operation against the Front Patriotique at Le Pré was totally justified. However, sources
close to the government now suggest that both the Senior
Terrorist Investigator's office and the Sûreté Nationale in
Paris may have acted prematurely, even improperly, in ordering the action at Château Villars.

"While the so-called Inspirational Network and the Priory
of the Holy Redeemer are thought to be connected to the
white supremacist, radical, evangelical wing of the Front Patriotique, the primary objective of the raid on the château

was not to secure the satellite station or to detain priory personnel. It was to apprehend a man wanted for questioning in connection with the murder of Paris theatre critic Virgile de la Pagerie. The suspect, Charles Fannois, a.k.a. Frère Christophe, is an ex-Vichy official believed to have been in hiding at the priory since his acquittal of Nazi collaboration in 1978. It now appears that the Sûreté was either misinformed as to the suspect's whereabouts or that he was warned of the raid in time to evade capture.

"A spokesperson for the priory, a well-known local producer of Cabardés wines, disavowed any connection to either the Inspirational Network or the Front Patriotique, and denied that Charles Fannois had ever sought sanctuary in the abbey. He added that 'Frère Christophe' was not a person but simply the commercial logogram for their popular carignan-grenache red table wine.

"The Sûreté has confirmed that Charles Fannois was not among those apprehended today."

(*Full-screen: 1978 black-and-white still photo of Charles Fannois*)

(*Voice-over*)
"Viewers with information regarding the whereabouts of this man are urged to call the following number . . ."

17

Judge Jean-Paul Ariel Céstac

THE JUDGE finished his perusal of the micrographologist's report asserting that the signatures *C. Fannois* and *Frère Christophe* were unquestionably written by the same hand. He then dropped the report on his desk, and, to Commissaire Demonet's considerable annoyance, began to extemporize.

"On the one hand," he said airily, "we could take the position that Marseille simply overreacted. They were impatient to test new equipment. They were in their commando mode. They sent five SWAT units and four aircraft when a pair of resolute HCU Inspecteurs would probably have sufficed. On the other hand, the results were unambiguous, and we know that, in future, the *Alouette*s and *Puma*s can be relied upon to perform flawlessly."

During these improvisational remarks, the judge had presented his profile to the Commissaire and Alex. The hairless cranium, the distinguished brow, the Bourbon nose, and cleft chin only wanted a crown of vine leaves to qualify the Senior Terrorist Investigator for that pantheon of celebrated profiles immortalized on Paris balustrade and pediment, in bronze or marble.

He now swiveled his chair behind the desk and faced them, wearing an enigmatic expression.

"On the one hand," he said again, "we received a very poor press. On the other, and here is the key, they chose to use the phrase, 'sources close to the government,' which, in my experience, is mediaspeak for the Élysée Palace." He hesitated. "Has anyone called you?"

The Commissaire shook his head and glanced at Alex.

"No, monsieur," Alex replied.

The judge tapped his desktop. "In my opinion, it is probable the government was not prepared for our unannounced move against Fannois. It is also probable there was a leak somewhere down the line."

The Maison

Alex and the Commissaire returned to Rue des Saussaies. The Duty Officer handed the Commissaire a memo requesting that he contact the office of the Minister of the Interior at his earliest. The Commissaire settled into his office chair and studied the memo.

Alex remained standing. "Do you think there's a chance the government's shielding Fannois?"

"No. But you have to remember the government's position on Vichy. The government's position on Vichy is that, please God, Vichy should go away. The raid on Château Villars was a violation of that position. The government believes that neither the république nor the people of France should be held responsible for acts committed by an illegitimate state half a century ago, and it is at pains to discourage anything that revives the memory of that moment in our history. Not only that; there are still a few éminences-grises around the Palais-Bourbon and the Palais-Luxembourg who believe that, if

Général de Gaulle was the sword, Maréchal Pétain was the shield."

Alex waited. But the Commissaire appeared to have finished. "So, what are my orders, Commissaire?"

"To leave the government to me. And to get back to work." He turned his back then and picked up the phone.

Alex left. From the hallway, he could hear the Commissaire's affable voice buffing up the Minister for a round of golf the following weekend.

The political ramifications of the raid on Château Villars were of no importance to Alex. What troubled him deeply, however, was that the fundamental precondition for the apprehension of his suspect was gone. Forever. When that priceless ingredient of the hunt, the element of surprise, is lost, the quarry gains the advantage and you cut to the chase. Hounds and hares. Cops and robbers. There is no more humiliating sign of an investigation in chaos than "Viewers with information regarding the whereabouts of this man are urged to call . . ."

He climbed the stairs to his office. There were two messages on his desk.

One, from Varnas, was written in longhand on his "While-You-Were-Out" memo pad, a gift from Madame Roget when they were still speaking. It said, "Fingerprints on inhaler dispenser from theatre lost and found all Delap's except single thumb and forefinger, not on file. Dactylo enters unidentified print in AFIS database. I am home (4 P.M.)."

The other message, neatly word processed, was from Isabelle in Research.

"Alex: It appears the Priory of the Holy Redeemer is blameless. The family Villars, who owns the priory land, has leased it to the monastery over the years for a symbolic tithe of 5 hectolitres of wine annually. In principle, therefore, the abbey and winery have operated rent-free, and tax-free, for over a century.

"The local regional council, mostly landowners sympathetic to the far right, threatened to remove the monastery's tax-free status unless they allowed the Front Patriotique certain priorities (hiring vineyard workers, setting up the inspirational network, etc.). The person at Château Villars with whom I spoke said the FP has been bullying them for a year. But more to the point of your inquiry, the 'Frère Christophe' logo, which appears on the label of their Cabardés red, was created by the art department of an advertising firm called Binoche, Boulmerka, Delage, et Olivier, located at 3, Boulevard des Minimes, 31000 Toulouse."

Varnas

Madame Roget collected her tenants' refuse at 8, Rue Georges-Berger every day at 5 P.M. The flats in the building were so arranged that each kitchen pantry was connected to the basement via the elevator shaft of a simple, rope-operated dumbwaiter. At 5 P.M., Madame Roget stationed herself next to an elaborate system of bell-pulls below and rang each flat when she was ready to receive. Only Varnas's fifth-floor residence was exempt from this network. Actually, since he did little cooking in his rooms, this was no great inconvenience. However, on Mondays, the one day of the week that Chez Suzanne was closed, he sometimes prepared his own meal and, consequently, had some small amount of trash to dispose of.

On this Monday, he assembled his few items in a plastic bag and, at 5:08 P.M., walked down the six flights to the basement, where he expected to find Madame Roget ringing bells and nimbly operating dumbwaiter ropes.

But when he reached the top of the basement stairs, he saw that the lights were out and Madame Roget was nowhere to be seen. This was most unusual. While it was true that he and she had been estranged for the better part of a week, he was certain that this slight emotional encumbrance would not interfere with her custodial responsibilities. From the top of the stairs, he called out, "Madame?" No answer. Perhaps a fuse or circuit breaker. He threw the light switch in the stairwell. The lights came on immediately.

He called once again. "Madame Roget!" Still no answer. Perhaps she was ill. But before he had a chance to act on this speculation, he heard distant women's voices coming from the direction of the elevator shaft below. It was well after 5. Four floors of tenants, accustomed to Madame Roget's punctuality, were discussing this unexplained divergence of schedule among themselves via the elevator shaft.

Varnas hurried down the basement steps, deposited his small parcel in one of the large dustbins, and, before tenant curiosity turned to tenant hostility, assumed command of the dumbwaiter on behalf of his friend.

The task took nearly forty minutes because he had to repeat, to each floor, his story that Madame Roget had been delayed in her return from a funeral of a friend at the Église de Notre Dame du Bon-Conseil, a church Varnas dimly remembered from the days when he lived in the Eighteenth Arrondissement.

In the end, he transferred twelve refuse bags to two large dustbins. These he wheeled outside to the allée for early-morning collection. He reentered the basement, bolted the outside door, secured the elevator shaft, and examined his hands. The old manila ropes of the dumbwaiter had left both hands punctured by tiny rope splinters, microscopic slivers of hemp that he could not remove with his fingernails. Too late, he noticed rubber gloves hanging nearby.

Holding his palms open, he climbed the basement steps, extinguished the lights, and started across the marble-floored foyer. Halfway to the curving staircase, it occurred to him that, in spite of their present misalliance, he should see for himself if Madame Roget were indisposed. He turned and walked toward the propriétaire's loge. As he arrived there and reached for the bell-pull, her door silently swung open. He stared at the empty door frame.

"Madame?"

A small voice behind the open door: "Please come in."

He entered. She closed the door and stood before him in a floral-print, quilted dressing gown worn over a long, white, cotton nightgown. Her feet were bare and her thick, black hair, which she normally wore brushed back in a chignon, was down. It came nearly to her waist and shone in the dim light of the hallway. Her eyes were swollen.

She looked small and vulnerable, and pretty. Varnas had an immediate and, for him, utterly alien reaction. He longed to hold her; to put his one hand in the arch of her back, and the other on the glistening hair at the curve of her neck. Instead, he said, "Are you ill, madame?"

"No," she replied. Then, "Maybe. I don't know." She gazed at him and suddenly reached for his hand. Varnas flinched.

"What is it?"

"Sorry. Splinters. From rope on dumbwaiter."

She examined his hand. "Dear God!" She seized his wrist and let him into her sewing room where she placed him in a chair on one side of the sewing table, and took the seat opposite. She reached into her sewing basket, extracted a small pair of tweezers, took his hand in hers, then abruptly closed her eyes and gasped. She dropped his hand and averted her face. She seemed to have trouble breathing.

"Madame?"

"I need my glasses," she said and left the room.

She was back in a moment, carrying a small, oval pair of wire-rimmed reading glasses. As she settled into her chair, she made a brief, distracted smile, and placed the glasses on the end of her nose. "I need them for close work," she said.

This was news to Varnas. He'd known Madame Roget for three years, stood next to her in church where small print prayer books and hymnals were de rigueur, and watched her knit and make floral arrangements, all without glasses. He wondered now if it was some small vanity that had kept the glasses out of sight in the past. Or was it that she knew all the prayer-book responses and hymns by heart? Or was it possible she wished to look her unencumbered best in front of him? Until now?

But, as she took his hand again, and peered with solemn gray eyes through the tiny lenses on the tip of her nose, and as her heavy hair brushed the table, Varnas thought he'd never seen her so lovely.

She carefully removed the splinters, one by one, first the right hand, then the left, dropping each splinter methodically into a wastebasket. When she finished, and there was nothing more to do, no further service to perform, she removed her glasses, turned her hands palms down on the table, and lowered her head.

Softly she said, "I want to do things for you; to care for you. And I want you to care for me." Relieved of the weight of that confession, she began to weep.

Varnas gently placed his hands on top of hers. Her response was electric. She seized his hands and covered them with kisses. She wept unashamedly. She reached across the table and held his face; she grabbed his ears. Varnas got to his feet, circled round the table and lifted her. She seemed weightless. She came up and pressed against him, stood back trembling, and pressed against him again, her arms tight about his neck. As they stood in this miraculous first embrace, the phone rang.

They froze. She lowered her forehead to his chest, grasped his shoulders and shook him. She rubbed her eyes and cheeks on his shirt, kissed him on the chin, and went into the hall where the phone continued to ring.

"Allô?" she said shakily. "Yes. One moment." She held out the phone.

He took it from her. "Allô? Yes, Alex. Toulouse? When? Tonight?" As he spoke, she gazed at him with a look so beseeching, so tender and unguarded, that he could scarcely concentrate on what Alex was saying. Something about a graphic artist in Toulouse who might be Fannois.

"I can't go tonight, Alex," Varnas heard himself say. "Madame Roget is ill."

She took his free hand, brushed it with her lips, and placed it under her heart.

"Tomorrow? Yes, tomorrow is fine. Tomorrow morning, eight-fifty, Orly West, Air Inter. I be there, Alex. Yes, I tell her. Good night." He hung up.

She came to him and placed her cheek next to his. He put one hand in the arch of her back, and the other on her glistening hair at the curve of her neck.

She whispered, "I love you, inspecteur."

"Oh, madame!" he said.

18

Toulouse

A TALKATIVE, MIDDLE-AGED SERGEANT from the local Sûreté, breathing garlic and Gauloises, met them at the airport. Driving down from Blagnac, he provided a sedate lecture-tour of Toulouse, the capital of the Département of the Haute-Garonne. This included the Sports Palace, the Université of Social Sciences, Le Capitole, the Cathédrale of Notre Dame des Graces, the railroad station, and, ultimately, the Canal du Midi, which, for its first western kilometres, ran parallel to the Boulevard des Minimes. No. 3 on the boulevard was a small, modern office building of white brick and glass, in a quiet block between two bridges over the canal.

They took the lift to the second floor and emerged into a reception area dominated by a spectacular bare wall, finished in black acrylic, on which appeared the lowercase stainless steel letters identifying binoche, boulmerka, délage, et olivier.

In front of this, in a cutout at the intersection of a paraboloid mahogany reception desk, sat an extremely pretty young African woman dressed in a robe of Kente cloth, painting her fingernails orange. She wore a tiny, curved microphone and earpiece that seemed colour-coordinated with the fabric. She did not look up until Alex identified himself and Varnas, and then only cursorily. She murmured something into the mike, finished a nail, and, in the honey-dipped accent of the Sénégal, said, "Monsieur Boulmerka will see you. Please be seat-ed."

In a moment, another pretty girl, this one blonde and mini-skirted, smiled them into the office of the art director, Habib Boulmerka.

Monsieur Boulmerka, linen-smocked, fortyish, Algerian, and unsmiling, looked up from a light box of colour transparencies. As the girl left, he came forward and silently shook their hands. He didn't ask them to be seated but gazed first at Alex, then at Varnas, then back at Alex. "May I see some identification?" he asked.

They produced their ID wallets. Boulmerka took them, inspected each carefully, and handed them back. He pointed to some contour chairs. "Please sit down, messieurs."

He leaned on the edge of his desk, frowning slightly. "As a result of the television coverage, we have received some attention here. I've spoken to several reporters. But a man who came in yesterday and asked about Charles Fannois said he was Inspecteur Garimet of the Sûreté." Alex and Varnas waited. "I had no reason to doubt him. He was well dressed, about your age, Chef-Inspecteur; well-spoken, professional. He looked like a detective. Perhaps foolishly, I didn't ask him for identification."

"What did you say his name was?" Alex asked.

"Garimet."

Alex asked to use the phone. He carded a call to Isabelle in Paris and had her check the national directory for the name. She came back in less than a minute. "No Garimet," she said.

"Actually, I don't think it's a name. Wait." He heard some clicking keys. "Alex?"

"I'm listening."

"Garimet is an anagram — for Maigret."

"Thanks." He rang off.

Alex guessed the man was a reporter with mischief on his mind. No one else would trouble to anagram the name of Georges Simenon's world-famous fictional detective for this purpose.

"What did you tell this Inspecteur Garimet?" he asked Boulmerka.

"Just what I will tell you, Chef-Inspecteur. That the man who did the Château Villars logo was named Christophe André. He came to us in 1979, unsolicited. I was reluctant to hire him at first because of his age. He was in his late sixties. But when I saw his portfolio I couldn't turn him down.

"He was an excellent graphic artist. He understood texture. He understood paper. He could even make paper — out of flax, or cotton. But, aside from his work, there was very little I could learn about him. Until later. He kept to himself. He had a small flat in Lalande. I don't know if he was married or had friends. Perhaps he didn't have friends. There was a haunted quality about him."

"Did you say 'haunted,' or 'hunted'?"

"Maybe I meant both. He was always very still, as if listening for something. Then, one day, quite out of the blue, he talked about the war. He told me he was a war veteran, entitled to veteran's medical benefits. Two months later, he checked himself into the Military Hospital in Pournonville."

"What for?"

"He said he was under surveillance by Mossad, the Israeli secret police. He thought he'd be safer in the hospital."

Alex glanced at Varnas, and felt the case against Fannois beginning to slip.

"Actually," Boulmerka continued, "he was found to be mildly diabetic. They treated him for that, then transferred him to the psychiatric section."

"Is he still there?"

"In the psychiatric section? Yes."

"And he's been there since 1983?"

"Yes. I went to see him for the last time about a year ago. He was inside the loading dock of one of the hospital warehouses, in a space where there were dustbins filled with soiled bandages and other items to be thrown out. He was busy painting faces on the screens of derelict television sets. He recognized me. He smiled and said he was getting ready for his first one-man show."

"Maybe he is faking," Varnas said, as they descended in the lift.

These were the first words Varnas had spoken since their arrival in Toulouse. Alex studied his friend's face.

"You look funny. Are you all right?"

"I'm fine. Time to go home."

"After one more stop."

The Sergeant drove them to the Military Hospital. While Alex entered the huge pile of asylum-gray stucco, the Sergeant directed Varnas to a nearby super-marché. In the regional produce and delicacies section, he purchased a confit of duck, a frozen Cassoulet, and a bottle of Château Villars Cabardés red to share with madame this evening in Paris, on the occasion of the successful completion of their first day together. Deeply aware of madame's sensibilities, and feeling fragile himself, Varnas had said nothing to Alex.

*   *   *

Alex checked the visitors' roster and satisfied himself that the pseudonymous Inspecteur Garimet had not followed up his inquiry at Binoche, Boulmerka by visiting the hospital. At least he hadn't signed in.

After a short interval in a cheerless hallway inexplicably decorated with the flags of the United Nations, Alex was directed to the office of the Chief Psychiatrist.

The Chief Psychiatrist, a naval commander, confirmed what Alex already suspected: that the pursuit of Charles Fannois had been a fool's tour of compound errors and assumptions. What he heard from the doctor also explained why de la Pagerie's investigative work, while accurate as far as it went, failed to bring Fannois to earth.

During his therapy, Fannois had revealed that, subsequent to his acquittal in 1978, the government had placed him in a witness protection program (thus the alias) in exchange for testimony leading to the conviction of certain employees of the national railroad for their part in a World War Two profiteering scheme. It seems that, in addition to Jews, the railroad had transported items of real value, such as black-market flour, cognac, cigarettes, coffee, and sugar into Germany. Alex expected he would eventually hear this tale told again, possibly after the Commissaire's golf game with the Interior Minister.

While Délice and Honoré Bloch would find nothing remotely amusing about this turn of events, Alex, perhaps because he was beginning to feel slightly giddy, now saw that he and Varnas had missed a moment of high hilarity by only a whisker. The spectacle of the Sûreté, the government police force, pursuing a government-protected felon for his testimony against the government's railroad seemed more the stuff of Feydeau or Offenbach than the *Police Manual of Strategy and Tactics*. The libretto was avoided only when the

government learned late that Fannois had been institu-
tionalized, and dropped him from the protection program.

Notwithstanding its demise, the Fannois episode had accomplished something. It placed Marie-Rose Fournier and
Vercingétorix in Castelnaudary with Marie-Rose's aunt
Thérèse. What else it accomplished would become evident
sooner rather than later.

19

Gare de Lyon

THE AIR INTER FLIGHT from Toulouse to Orly landed at 4:50 P.M. A Maison driver was waiting in one of the new Citroëns. In spite of the heavy traffic on the A6, he got Alex and Varnas to Gentilly in a little over twelve minutes. As they passed under the Boulevard Périphérique and entered the Fourteenth Arrondissement, the mobile phone in the front seat jangled. The driver answered and immediately handed the instrument back to Varnas.

The call was from Motor Scooter (female) No. 2. She was the stakeout at Doctor Zhivago's residence. She reported that the pharmacist had closed his shop at lunchtime and returned to Rue de Vaugirard.

"Is he ill?"

"No, inspecteur. Subject reached his home at two P.M. There was no activity until four forty-five, when he and his companion left their residence on foot. Apart from her purse, they have no luggage but appear to be wearing several layers of clothing. It's not cold today, but he was covered himself in a heavy wool overcoat. She's wearing a squirrel jacket over a long dress of some metallic material, and very high heels. I chained the scooter at the Convention métro and followed them to Austerlitz via Montparnasse and the Odéon. It took almost a half hour. They have just crossed the boulevard and are entering the Jardins des Plantes in the Fifth Arrondissement."

"Are you alone, mademoiselle?"

"Affirmative."

"Very well. Keep phone line open, keep talking, and don't let them out of your sight. I am there in ten minutes."

Varnas gave the driver instructions. To Alex he said, "Doctor Zhivago has made his move."

"Which is?"

"He goes to Jardin des Plantes with lady friend. Jardins des Plantes, on left bank, is perhaps six hundred metres from Gare de Lyon, on right bank, via Austerlitz Bridge. Gare de Lyon is Paris terminal for southeast rail network and TGV, Train of Great Velocity. Doctor Z. and woman both wear everything they own. My guess is that they plan extended holiday."

As the Citroën altered course across the Fourteenth and entered the Fifth Arrondissement, the stake kept up a running commentary on the subject's movements: "They have stopped in front of a large tree specimen and are reading its brass plaque."

"Where are you?" Varnas asked.

"Behind a statue of Baron Cuvier. They are about thirty metres from me. Ah, they are just moving on." This description was followed by a short interval of silence.

"Mademoiselle?"

"I'm here. They've stopped by the entrance to the Botanique Exhibit building. They are in conversation. I am pretending to be absorbed with the tree plaque they formerly studied."

A moment later, the Citroën skidded to a stop at the entrance to the Jardins des Plantes. It was 5:28 and beginning to get dark. Varnas handed Alex the plastic bag containing his purchases from the super-marché in Toulouse.

"Doctor Zhivago is mine, Alex. I take care of him." Alex did not comment. Jurisdictional independence was basic to their relationship. "But, before you return to Maison, please deliver groceries to Madame Roget, with my compliments, and tell her I am home soon."

"Then she's over her illness?"

Varnas nodded and, gathering up the cellular phone, stepped into the street.

The stake reported, "Subject has just kissed his companion good-bye. They appear to be separating. She is walking toward the Botanique Exhibit, and limping. The high heels hurt her feet. He has taken the opposite direction, across one of the promenades leading to the north end. Whom shall I follow?"

"Follow her. No. On second thought, follow no one. I am at Jardins entrance, mademoiselle, across from Austerlitz métro. Join me here."

"Inspecteur, we could lose them!"

"We don't lose them, mademoiselle. They have no interest in Jardins des Plantes. They have train to catch."

"Excuse me?"

"Never mind. They split up as diversionary tactic in case they are under surveillance. He probably goes to corner of Jardins where there is section of planting called labyrinth. If he can lure unsuspecting tail into labyrinth, he has chance to break away. His lady friend goes to Botanique Exhibit probably to sit down or to make pee-pee. Eventually, she will take Rue Buffon exit from Botanique and head for Austerlitz Bridge, Gare de Lyon, and golden years of retirement. You meet me here, mademoiselle. On second thought, it is not necessary for you to meet me. You are excused for today."

"Excused!"

"Yes. You have done excellent work, which I do not fail to mention in my report."

"Inspecteur! I've been on this case since the beginning. I want to assist in the arrest!"

"There is no arrest here, mademoiselle."

"No arrest?"

"No. Do as I tell you, please. I don't need you now. Go home."

"Inspecteur!"

"Varnas clear."

"Inspec —"

He shut down his phone and secured it in its case. She'd get over her disappointment. He'd already made up his mind to sponsor her for the Inspecteur-trainee program.

For the next half hour, Varnas shuttled between the garden entrance, where he had an unimpeded view of the Austerlitz Bridge, over which the pharmacist would have to pass, and the intersection of the boulevard and Rue Buffon, where he could keep an eye on the Botanique and the pharmacist's lady friend.

It was already dark when a taxi moved up Rue Buffon toward the bridge, its left directional signal flashing bright orange. It performed a U-turn and stopped at the curb opposite the Botanique. Almost on cue, the woman, in her fur jacket, limped from the building to the vehicle. When she was inside, the taxi immediately drove off in a direction away from the bridge and the Gare de Lyon.

Varnas experienced a moment of disquiet. He had not counted on darkness falling so rapidly. Nor had he considered the possibility that the pharmacist and his companion may have visited the Jardins des Plantes deliberately to mislead anyone shadowing them into believing their destination was the Gare de Lyon, when, in fact, it might be any one of several other railroad stations in Paris, or one of the airports. It was at this moment of unwanted clarity that Varnas heard running steps behind him.

"Inspecteur!" The girl, slightly out-of-breath, had not gone home as ordered. She said, "The woman has commandeered a taxi!" Varnas sighed. "She has just picked up the subject on Rue Geoffroy-St-Hilaire!"

"Ah. Well, maybe that is good," he said wishfully. "With luck, they circle round Jardins des Plantes and double back to Gare de Lyon. Mademoiselle, I am pleased to see you have sufficient character to disobey orders when appropriate. What is your name?"

"Joëlle."

"How do you do. I want you to run across Austerlitz Bridge as fast as you can. When you reach Gare de Lyon, attempt to locate subject who probably reaches station before you. If you cannot locate them, try to absorb track information from departure board for trains leaving Paris at approximately seven P.M. Reactivate cellular phone when you have information."

"Where will you be?"

"Behind you, running as fast as I can. Now go!"

She took off. She was small and light and ran like the wind. The time was 6:29.

In the darkness, individual automobiles were now nothing more than ambiguous shapes floating behind multiple, antennalike beams of light. Varnas could not tell if the taxi he had noted previously had crossed the Austerlitz Bridge or not. As he gracelessly jogged across the bridge himself, trying to activate his phone without dropping it, he could only hope.

At 6:35 he puffed into Rue de Bercy. His phone jangled.

"I don't see them," she said. "The departure board shows many trains leaving between 6:30 and 7:15, mostly locals. The train to Troyes has just left. However, there is one to Dijon at 7:02, and, at 7:13, the TGV for Geneva."

"What is track number of Geneva train?"

"Track four, Level one."

"Joëlle, go immediately to Track four. Be discreet. If you see them, ascertain only if they go aboard train. Do nothing to attract attention. I am almost there."

Varnas reached the station from Rue de Bercy. As he staggered round the newspaper kiosk at the entrance to the main waiting room, he nearly collided with the pharmacist and his lady. Unaware of him, and now perspiring profusely, they both moved briskly across his path; briskly because she was now wearing a pair of fluffy new house slippers. She carried the stiletto heels that had caused her such pain in a shoe bag.

Varnas called Joëlle. "I encounter them in waiting room. They are delayed at shoe store but now hurry to departure gate. Acknowledge."

"Joëlle here."

"Stay on line but remain out of sight in case I need you. And thank you for your help. You make the good flic someday."

"Thanks, Inspecteur."

Varnas followed his quarry across the waiting room and down a ramp to Level 1, where the commercial sights and echoing sounds of the waiting room were now muted, darker, and confined to dry announcements of arrivals, departures, and track numbers, eventually blending with the exotic smell of warm lubricating oil, and the tantalizing odors of the café car.

He followed them to Gate 4. They stopped before a filigreed, cast-iron archway that bore the white-on-black placard: TGV. PARIS–GENEVA (VIA LYON). DÉP 1913. Joëlle was nowhere to be seen.

Varnas had earlier decided that he would not apprehend the pharmacist in Paris on the chance that he might later be joined by confederates. If his plan of escape included co-conspirators, this was an arrest opportunity that would not come again. And the itinerary matched perfectly. The train stopped in Lyon before proceeding across the frontier to Geneva. The arrest, or arrests, therefore, would take place in Lyon.

Varnas waited until reservations had been processed and passports verified. He watched the subject and his companion pass through Customs and Immigration and board the train in the last car but one. He then presented himself to the SNCF police. The railroad constabulary would be responsible for the two passengers until the Sûreté came aboard at Lyon. He obtained a passenger list of the all-reserved train, including those boarding at Lyon.

As the bullet train pulled out of the station exactly on time, Varnas phoned the Maison with instructions to be forwarded to the Sûreté, Lyon. He then faxed the passenger list to Research, which would check the list against names of known criminals, as well as against any names associated with the case to date. The TGV would be in Lyon at 10:30.

He called up Joëlle. Together they flagged a taxi on Blvd. Diderot. Twenty minutes later, he dropped her beside her scooter at the Convention métro, then continued on to Rue Georges-Berger for his celebratory meal with madame.

Alex

The Commissaire had left when he reached the office. He checked his phone messages.

1. Philippa Watten called. "No message," the assignment clerk wrote on the memo. She'd been gone four full days and no message. Not even a message to call back. Well, either rehearsals were going wonderfully, in which case no single message to the assignment desk would suffice, or rehearsals were going shittily, in which case don't ask. At least she called.

2. His dentist, reminding him that it had been six months.

3. A request from the Directrice of the Childrens' Little Theater of Douarnenez (his hometown in Brittany), asking him to play *Tubby the Tuba* at their annual fund-raiser in June.

He went upstairs to the cubicle. On his desk he found thick envelopes from the Supervisor of Passenger Service Personnel, Barcelona Airport, and from Iberia Airlines, Madrid.

The task of reviewing this material at this precise moment after a disastrous day seemed insurmountable. He had Philippa on his mind. There appeared to be no heat in the office. He was hungry. He left the Maison and caught the No. 7 at Opéra.

Once on board and seated, he considered confronting Philippa. Since her departure for London, he'd called The Jane Austen a dozen times and left enough messages to paper a small closet. Surely the time had come to insist that she explain her silence. But how? Indeed, as the train rolled out of the Stalingrad station, he began to see, despite his indignation, that he was locking himself in the unenviable role of the meddling parent who will not mix out of his child's first unsupervised foray abroad. Stupid of him not to have recognized the signs earlier.

He reminded himself of his mother, who'd called him daily when he was a preteen at summer camp in the Vosges, where he suffered the indignity of wearing a 100-franc note in his shoe, redeemable only in case of emergency.

But of course this wasn't like that at all. Philippa was not his child, or even his ward now. She was his . . . second nature. So, the dozen calls to The Jane Austen were more about reassuring himself than about whether she was eating properly or staying warm and dry. Time to back off.

He got off the train at Porte de la Villette and made his shopping rounds for supper. He bought a salmon fillet to poach with a lemon and dill butter sauce, new potatoes to steam, and endive and watercress for salade.

After a half hour, he reached *Le Yacht Club* and checked the varnished teakwood letterbox next to the boarding ladder. In it was an electric bill and six postcards from Philippa, all mailed simultaneously yesterday. They were numbered one through six. He placed his shopping bag on a cockpit locker. Sitting with his back against the cabin bulkhead, he put the cards in order and, with mixed feelings of anticipation and anxiety, began to read them in the dying light.

(1) Saturday

Chéri: But quelle crise! Publicity photos on arrival at Heathrow with Nigel Philby and Nicolaj Blixen. Rolls-Royced me to Miss Austen's (a nunnery with elevators), flash check-in then on to the Ivy (posh restaurant) where Nicky ate two complete tournedos, one for each thigh. He is a lion! Love you — P

(2) Sunday

Chéri: All my phone messages at Miss Austen's were put in the wrong box. The film star Jeanne Moreau was here briefly. I got all her messages. Maybe they had us confused because we're both French. I've made a friend in the company. Her name is Cressida Pullinger. She dances Juliet in MacMillan's

R & J. She has a flat in, I think, Chelsea. I may move in with her and save myself 300 quid a week. Love you — P

(3) Monday AM
Chéri: Writing this backstage while waiting for Vassili Orloff to stop bitching at Nigel for cutting his 900th air turn. Vassily (Russsky and temperamental) is a jumper-turner, not exactly ideal for Bournonville. He dances the sea king, Golfo, and is supposed to get it on with me after Gennaro (Nicky) loses me at sea and I turn into a horny naiad. Why Nigel hired him is a mystery unless it's his basket which is said to be impressive. Love — P

(4) Lunchtime
Chéri: Lunch is lukewarm Chinese takeout egg drop soup. I seem not to have mailed any of these cards. I have this brain-dead thing that if I've written them I don't have to mail them. Plus I'm muddled about the postage. And busy! Rehearse 10 to 1 and 2 to 5, then class. And publicity, including tele appearance with Nicky, and costume fittings. Vassily's fitting took 3 hours. He's all seaweed and barnacles. Mine took 15 seconds. Nigel originally wanted me to dance the naiad naked! Can you believe it? French dancer bares all at Covent Garden! Of course I refused. Now it's a green body stocking and net skirt. I expect to acquire pneumonia. Love — P

(5) Mon. afternoon
Alex . . . I almost threw away card number 2, but then thought, no, better come clean. I lied about getting Jeanne Moreau's messages. Actually, I lied about Jeanne Moreau being at Miss Austen's. Jeanne Moreau wouldn't be caught dead more than a block from Claridge's, if she was in London, which she wasn't. Sorry. I'm suddenly in a fit of giggles about everything that's happening here, and *lots* is happening! — P

(6) Mon. PM

Nearly forgot. We open in 5 days, on the 21st. I booked a twin for you and Nana at Brown's Hotel. There will be 2 tickets at the Royal Opera b.o., Covent Garden. You'll be sitting next to Angela and the Marchioness. They saw Nicky and me on the tube and are dying to meet him.

"Me, too," Alex thought grumpily as he dropped the cards into his shopping bag and went below.

He fired up the galley stove and started to prepare supper. He noticed he was slamming things. Apart from the fact that slamming salmon was counterproductive, it did not take a leap of intuition to recognize that the postcards had triggered an emotion that had not heretofore emerged. She was having a marvelous time without him. She was not waiting by the phone for him to call, which was just as it should be, and he would be the first to acknowledge it if asked. So much for the official truth. The unofficial truth was that he felt discarded. Sharing a twin at Brown's Hotel with his mother!

His mother! Alex wasn't sure anyone had told Nana that Philippa was in London with the Royal.

He put the salmon in the poacher, started the potatoes, and made a call to Douarnenez. The phone rang a dozen times. There was no answer. It dawned on him it was Tuesday and Nana's night out at ladies' boules.

Nana had never flown. Indeed, Nana had never been out of the country, much less to England. As to England, her mistrust of the English went back to the Battle of Trafalgar. Moreover, she was a Bretonne, a Celt, who had always disregarded Philippa's English half while embracing her Irish half. Nana at the Royal? Nana in London, sitting next to Lady Watten and the Marchioness of Hardcastle?

Alex phoned Nana's next-door neighbor, the inspecteur of fisheries, and left a message for her to call back.

Supper was a disappointment. He forgot to make the butter sauce and the watercress had gone limp. He filled up on potatoes and endives and a half-bottle of Corbières. As he was rinsing the dishes, Nana returned his call.

She listened to his explanation of the circumstances. When he had finished, she said, "I'm very happy for Philippa." Pause. "Aren't you, Alexandre?"

"Of course."

"You don't sound very enthusiastic. Is everything all right?"

Jesus! He was thirty-seven years old and still couldn't beguile his mother. "Everything is fine, maman. I just burned the biscuits."

"It is understandable that you miss her, Alexandre. After all these years, I still miss you."

Alex took a deep breath and asked, "Will you be going to London, then?"

"No, chéri. The twenty-first is the Equinox and the Farewell-to-the-Light service at Église St-Jude. I never miss it. Do you remember who St-Jude is, Alexandre?"

"No."

"He is the patron saint of impossible causes. I'm sure Varnas knows that."

"I'm sure."

"Give Philippa my love. I'll wire her. Good night, chéri."

He rang off and finished the dishes. He decided he'd ask Varnas to go with him to London.

Alex unpacked his horn and started to read through the bassoon part of an old Alex Wilder octet he'd borrowed. But either he didn't have the wind for it, or the fingers, or the spirit, because he quit after a few pages and put the horn away.

He undressed, hung his clothes in his locker, and padded to the head for a shower. As he passed the sink he caught sight of himself in the mirror. He studied his reflection for a moment and thought he might shave off his beard.

Very good, Alex. That would certainly confirm Nana's suspicions. When jilted, women frequently cut their hair; men grow beards or shave them off.

He moved to the shower and was just turning on the hot water when he heard the phone ring. Certain it was Philippa, he ran naked into the saloon, quickly purloined a beer from the galley fridge and settled by the phone, anticipating the sound of her warm, mocking voice.

It was not Philippa. It was Stéphane. She had just auditioned for the Folies-Bergère and was hired on the spot. "I start a week after Philippa's opening," she said. "Come over tomorrow evening and help me celebrate. I have lamb chops, fresh asparagus, and a bottle of Merlot."

A faint, not disagreeable alarm bell rang in the pit of his stomach. He visualized the unblinking green eyes and the rude lips. "I'd like that," he said. "But I may be a little late."

"How late is a little late?"

"Seven, eight o'clock."

"Seven or eight is lovely. But if unfed by nine, I turn to stone."

"What can I bring?"

"Your stunning self and another bottle of Merlot."

Later, lying in his bunk, Alex entertained the rogue notion of inviting Stéphane to London for Philippa's opening, and sharing a twin with her at Brown's Hotel.

20

The Maison

COMMISSAIRE DEMONET silently read the item on the front page of *Le Matin*.

According to the Sûreté, local pharmacist Boris Alexandrovich Popov, 62, a.k.a. Doctor Zhivago, was arrested last night in Lyon. The Soviet-born Popov is believed to be an accessory in the death of theatre critic Virgile de la Pagerie. Apprehended with him was his companion, Nina Leonidovna, 56, a former gymnast from Kiev. Both are being returned to Paris for questioning.

The Commissaire looked at Varnas. "Did he have any friends on the train?"

"Negatarian, Commissaire."

"And your assumption that he is guilty is based entirely on the fact that he believed he was under surveillance and made a run for it?"

"Trust me, Commissaire."

"I have no choice."

*　　　*　　　*

Nina Leonidovna, who had been in tears more or less continually since her arrest the night before, was mildly sedated and placed in the Maison infirmary in the care of a police matron. The pharmacist was taken to a holding room, where he was given bread and a bowl of excellent fish soup from À La Cart, the awninged, fast-food franchise-on-wheels parked outside the Maison. He was then interrogated by Varnas in Russian.

They sat on opposite sides of a scarred wooden table, free of objects, except for Varnas's tape recorder and notebook. The pharmacist was stoic about his situation, possibly even relieved. However, his blink rate was somewhat high, and if he made eye contact, it was accidental.

"I received a letter at the pharmacie on Tuesday, twenty August," he began. "It arrived in a UNESCO envelope, postmarked the day before in Paris, Seventh Arrondissement. It offered thirty thousand francs for 'sensitive work with a pharmacological toxicant.'

"If interested, I was to go to the street-level public phone at the Brochant métro, two squares from my store, on Thursday, the twenty-second, at 0850. They said they would have me under constant surveillance. They would call between 0850 and 0855 and ask for Sampson. If I did not respond by 0855 the deal was off. The letter was not signed but bore the stamp of the Front Patriotique.

"I arrived at the Brochant métro at 0830 on the twenty-second and got into the queue for the phone. Three persons used it for the next eighteen minutes. At 0848 my turn came. I dialed the taped weather forecast and pretended to speak with my accountant. At 0850, a furious woman waiting behind me finally gave up and stomped away. I was then able to hang up the instrument. It rang barely ten seconds later.

"I picked up and said, 'Sampson here.' I spoke to a male voice with the unmistakable accent of the Midi."

Varnas interrupted. "A resonant voice, like an actor?"

"No. Quite light, actually. Perhaps an older man."

Not Gus, Varnas decided. Perhaps someone trying to sound like Fannois. "Proceed."

"He went right to the point. He asked if I was familiar with the Ventil asthma inhaler. I was. Did I have the item in stock? I did. He then declared that the dispenser must be cerise.

"I begged his pardon.

" 'The outer container, the plastic part with the mouth tube, must be cerise in colour, a sort of red.'

"I told him that, as far as I knew, all Ventil inhalers were cerise. Other brands were identifiable by other colours.

"He seemed satisfied. Then the music changed. He wanted to know if the Ventil aerosol cartridge could be broached; if a foreign substance could be introduced into the medication without compromising the effectiveness of the device.

"I played dumb. I told him that I didn't know. The medication in the cartridge was under pressure. Any rupture of the container could release the propellant and, with it, the medication. During this exchange, I was inspired to imagine a procedure wherein a liquid might be passed through the aerosol valve of the cartridge and into the medication by means of a very fine gauge hypodermic needle; the finest, probably a number thirty. But I said nothing.

"He remained silent for an interval. Finally, he said, 'We are looking for a person who understands the engineering of the Ventil inhaler, a person who will overcome the difficulties you describe, and successfully augment the prescribed medication with an appropriate measure of cyanide. Are you that person?'

"For some time I had longed for the opportunity to provide

an annuity for my Nina. This seemed like such an opportunity. Still, I was surprised at my response, particularly when I realized I'd already made up my mind to commit a crime when I accepted the phone call. I was surprised again when I calmly said, 'Thirty thousand is not enough for what you ask, monsieur.'

"He replied, 'We will see about that after we are satisfied you can do it. Can you do it?'

" 'I can try.'

" 'Not good enough. We must *know* you can do it. How will we know?'

"I'd already thought of that. It was now Thursday. I said, 'Give me the weekend. I will attempt to introduce a small quantity of purple dye into a Ventil cartridge. If I am successful, you will be able to test it yourself. When you receive the inhaler, you will simply depress the dosage button and direct the spray against a square of gauze, which I will enclose. If you are satisfied, we can proceed.'

"He was agreeable and now outlined the details of where and when I was to deliver the device.

"Within walking distance of my pharmacie is the Cimitière des Batignolles. In the southwest corner of the cimitière, in the third row off Rue Saint-Just, is a brown marble tombstone marking the grave of one Carlo Lombardo (1882–1938). Above the name, set in a glass-enclosed iron frame, is a tin-type photo of the deceased. Behind the photo frame, which can be slid in and out on a track, is a space approximately six by twelve centimetres.

"I was to place the test inhaler in its original package and wrap it with waterproof plastic. I was then to walk alone to the cimitière, deposit the parcel behind Lombardo's photo between 0830 and 0900 on Monday twenty-six August, and return without delay to the Pharmacie Berzélius. He said I would be under surveillance by the organization at all times during the delivery, and that any deviation from these instructions would terminate the agreement.

"All this cimitière stuff seemed a bit dramatic and amateurish to me. There are thousands of baggage lockers in Paris where drops and pickups are made every day. However, I said I understood their apprehension and asked when I would know the results of the test. He said, next day, Tuesday. They would contact me again at 0850, this time at the pay phone inside the Porte de Clichy métro station.

"When I rang off, I glanced at my watch. I had been on the phone for seven minutes, seven minutes that I sensed would change my life. As I walked back to the pharmacie, I experienced a moment of melancholic wistfulness for the young internist Boris Alexandrovich, who had dedicated himself to palliating the pain of the deserving poor. This feeling manifested itself in a mild ache beneath the sternum. But I took a deep breath and it was gone. I thought of my Nina in a sun-drenched room, with an unobstructed view of the Jungfrau.

"Passing the dye into the cartridge against pressure was not a piece of cake. At first, much medication was lost and there was dye all over me. It became a question of timing: Briefly press the aerosol valve. This eliminates the medication to be replaced by the additive. Quickly insert the hypodermic which I have now fitted with a rubber collar cemented in place by instant adhesive. Withdrawing the needle must be done smartly. Surgical mask, gloves, smock, and goggles are essential.

"Monday morning I delivered the test inhaler as instructed. Next day at 0850, I learned I had passed the test with flying colours. I then demanded sixty thousand francs and an open railway compartement reservation for two on the TGV to Geneva.

"This demand was not met with enthusiasm. However, after some negotiation, we agreed on fifty thousand and an open reservation for two seats instead of a compartement.

"It was now Tuesday, twenty-seven August. I knew the cyanide would have to be in soluble form. I decided I could best achieve this by forming a solution of sodium cyanide in the amount of three millilitres. The inhaler, containing the additive, was to be dropped before 0900 on Monday, September second, chez Signor Lombardo. I insisted on payment in advance. This resulted in grave warnings of the severe consequences to me, to Nina, to my flat, my pharmacie, et cetera, if I attempted any monkey business ('The Front Patriotique has limitless resources for retribution'). In the end, they agreed. The money, in old bills, and the railway tickets would be in place — and here I named the drop — in an overnight bag at the baggage counter, lower level, of the Gare de l'Est, on Thursday the twenty-ninth. They would mail me the baggage check at the pharmacie in time for me to make the pickup on Saturday the thirty-first.

"All went according to plan. I delivered the altered inhaler to the cimitière the following Monday. Three days later I read of the critic's death in the morning paper.

"Unfortunately, a reservation for two on the TGV to Geneva was not immediately available. You know the rest."

Doctor Zhivago now peered at the room with shining eyes made slightly larger by the magnification of his pince-nez. "I have told you the truth," he said, "and now I will tell you the truth again. Nina Leonidovna played no part in this escapade. She knew nothing about it. I told her, some time ago, that I was the beneficiary of a modest inheritance from an uncle in America. I told her as well that certain unscrupulous elements within the consulate of the USSR had extortion on their minds and had placed us under surveillance. She is terrified of the Soviets and saw nothing unusual in our sudden departure for Geneva without luggage." The pharmacist's eyes fluttered to the table, making temporary contact with Varnas. "She is innocent, monsieur l'inspecteur. Please believe me."

"She gets ample opportunity to prove it, Boris Alexandrovich. Meanwhile, how is it that man with Midi accent who claims to represent Front Patriotique chooses you out of all pharmacists in Paris?"

He shrugged. "I am known. I have a reputation. I am a doctor, an herbal pharmacologist, an anodynist, and a thalassotherapist."

"Thalassotherapist?"

"Administrator of algae and warm salt-water therapy. Very beneficial."

"And anodynist?"

"Specialist in the relief of pain."

Varnas was reasonably certain that Doctor Zhivago dispensed his pain relievers for recreational as well as medical purposes. But that was another matter.

Varnas now assumed his tabula rasa face, a face devoid of expression, a face impossible to read but from which mask he could detect significance in his subject's most insignificant response. He said, "Now I ask you please, Boris Alexandrovich, to identify following names."

The pharmacist nodded importantly and, fixating on the tabletop, assumed a visage of great seriousness.

Varnas intoned, "Virgile de la Pagerie."

The pharmacist slightly cocked his head. "The critic, deceased."

"Charles Fannois."

A small moue followed by a shake of the head. "I have heard or read of him only."

"Pierre-Yves Gastin."

No response. Unblinking eyes on the table, mien impassive. "No. I am not familiar with the name."

"Auguste Pezon-Schwartz."

Slight frown, eyes to the ceiling. "Man of the theatre, I believe. Producer-directeur."

Varnas checked the tape. Interesting. The only name that had elicited a unique response — that is, no response — was the name of the scene designer Pierre-Yves Gastin. It wasn't much. Not something you could hang your hat on. But enough to request a printout from PTT for calls made to both public phones at the times specified. Enough to monitor cash withdrawals from Gastin's bank account(s) yet to be investigated by Isabelle. And enough to transfer Joëlle and Motor Scooter (female) No. 2 to Pierre-Yves' fancy residence in the Sixteenth Arrondissement. Given the neighborhood, she could dispense *gelati* this time or small, corked glass containers of Herbes de Provence. Varnas switched off the tape.

Upstairs, Alex finished examining the documents from the Barcelona Airport personnel supervisor and from Iberia Airlines. Maddeningly, neither document sustained his theory that the altered inhaler had been put in Delap's shoulder bag after 4 P.M. at either the airport X ray facility, or during the Barcelona–Paris leg of Flight 4426. Alex was beginning to doubt his powers of deduction and intuition. He nevertheless summoned Inspecteur-trainee Biramoule and directed him to deliver the documents to the Commissaire's office for his boss's perusal.

Varnas came in and placed the tape of Doctor Zhivago's testimony on his desk. "Very detailed description of difficulties encountered while introducing three millilitres sodium cyanide into Ventil inhaler, followed by baroque scenario of passing inhaler to contact via Cimitière des Batignolles. He does not identify contact, except to say he represents Front Patriotique." Varnas sat. "At least we have first arrest, Alex."

Varnas was about to describe Doctor Zhivago's nonreaction to the name Pierre-Yves Gastin, when Inspecteur-trainee Biramoule reappeared.

"Gentleman to see you."

"Who?"

"Auguste Pezon-Schwartz."

Alex said, "Send him in."

Biramoule stepped aside and Gus slowly appeared, supported by a short, muscular man with a shaved head, walrus moustache, a tight T-shirt, and pumped-up pectorals. Gus didn't look well. His complexion was sallow, his chromium hair spikey and haphazard. He was out of breath from the single flight of stairs.

Varnas offered him a chair.

He declined. "I'll only be a minute." He turned to his attendant. "Arnaud, you may wait outside." Arnaud nodded and stepped out of the office. Gus said, "Arnaud is my new nanny. He's a registered nurse and a graduate of the Institut Culinaire." Gus then heaved a great sigh, leaned against the wall, and passed a hand across his forehead. "I need your help," he said softly. "Pierre-Yves is missing." The weight of the remark was suddenly too much for him. His eyes filled with tears.

"I'm frantic," he said. "Pierre-Yves left for Lausanne on family business several days ago. I called his sister this morning. She hasn't seen him. I don't know what to do. Can you help me?"

Varnas said, "We can contact Lausanne police. Actually, since Pierre-Yves violates his restraining order to remain in Paris, we can issue all-points bulletin for his arrest."

"Can that be done . . . um . . . discreetly? I mean, without a lot of fuss?"

"Main thing is to find him, Monsieur Gus."

"Of course. They won't harm him, will they?"

"No."

Gus wiped his eyes and nodded. "Good. At least he'll be safe. I can't thank you enough." He called out the door, "Arnaud." The male nurse reappeared and took Gus's arm. Gus suddenly stiffened and, glaring at Alex and Varnas, cried, "It's that prick's fault!"

"Which prick is that?" Alex asked.

"Fucking Delap! And I don't trust Bobo Botswana either!"

"Who?"

"That bizarre mama of his, with the Sheba profile, the weird Zoroastrian blue eyes, and the ju-ju voodoo! I know that bitch had the pins in Angélique! If she has the pins in Pierre-Yves, I'll set fire to her fucking dreadlocks!"

"Why would she have the pins in Pierre-Yves?"

"For fun!" Gus cried, and began to sob. "I swear, if anything happens to him, I'll —" He interrupted himself. "I mean this is the sweetest man on earth! He's a natural resource! He helps people! He helps me! He helps young artists get started! He supports actors who are on their ass! My God, he even took in Angélique after Delap threw her out!"

"Threw her out?"

"Threw her things out. Her clothes, her scripts. He threw everything she owned out the window into the street. I thought everyone knew that. Her stuff hung in the trees and telephone wires along Rue de Tournon for days. Why? Because he was a prick! If you ask me, he killed her!"

"Did that make you want to kill him?" Alex asked.

"I already wanted to kill him from before! I told you that!"

Varnas stood. "That is true, Alexei." He turned to Gus. "Monsieur Gus, does Pierre-Yves ever speak to you of Doctor Zhivago?"

Gus blinked. "I don't think he saw it. He hates Omar Sharif."

"Doctor Zhivago is pseudonym for pharmacist in Seventeenth Arrondissement named Boris Alexandrovich Popov. He is under arrest for preparing poisoned inhaler that kills de la Pagerie."

Gus stared. His mouth was slightly ajar. After a few seconds he clicked it shut and turned to the male nurse. "Did you ever hear Evie mention anyone by that name?"

"No, Monsieur Auguste."

Varnas added, "We have some evidence that Boris Alexandrovich Popov may know Pierre-Yves."

Gus seemed suddenly to recover his accustomed irreverence. He said, "Well, lots of people know Pierre-Yves, dearie. His largesse is legend, he's cute, and he drives a Ferrari." He nudged the male nurse. "Let's go." They started out. But at the door he turned. His momentary recovery vanished and he again projected an expression of submission and entreaty. "Then I can count on you to find him?"

"We do our best, Monsieur Gus," Varnas replied.

Varnas had noted Gus's open-mouthed response to the name Popov. "Do you think something is there, Alex?"

Alex, still preoccupied with the failure of his Iberia and Barcelona inquiry, failed to answer. Varnas repeated the question. "Do you think Gus's response to name of Popov is anything?"

"Maybe," Alex grunted.

"Do we put Gus's flat under surveillance?"

"No."

"Or tap a phone?"

"Why? So we can learn the nightly grosses of *Eurydice?*"

Varnas glanced at his partner. He had actually come upstairs intending to tell Alex about his new relationship with Madame Roget. But he now saw that the time was not auspicious. "I go to Research," he said.

He walked downstairs and left a note for Isabelle requesting a trace of all cash withdrawals from any Paris bank account in Pierre-Yves' name, between 27 August and 1 September. It was a precautionary measure only. Varnas was virtually certain that Pierre-Yves' principal assets were in Swiss banks and beyond tracing.

Meanwhile, Alex issued a low-urgency APB on Pierre-Yves. He added the notation: "Subject not considered dangerous."

He closed the office and went to a wine shop in Avenue de Marigny. He bought two bottles of Merlot and took a taxi to Rue de Tournon, where he deliberately intended to violate the directive in the Operations Manual that specifically forbids Sûreté officers from socializing with persons alleged to be suspects.

Stéphane

He heard the strains of *La Bohème* as the lift passed the second floor. *Musetta's Waltz* filled the fourth floor as he pressed the doorbell.

Stéphane, in a green silk, spaghetti-strap mini-dress, bare legs, and open-toe sandals, greeted him with a summer smile. She took the Merlot, hung up his anorak, and towed him past the reception table into the salon, where she'd installed an ice bucket containing two splits of Moët-Chandon.

"Welcome," she said, and kissed him lightly on the shirt front. She smelt of lilac.

Alex's taxi had leaked exhaust fumes. He sniffed his wrist. "I've had a bad day," he said. "And next to you, I feel unclean and loutish. Let me wash my hands at least."

"You smell delicious to me," she said, "but hand-washing is directly behind you in the little room with the lemon yellow lampshade and fresh towels."

Alex went there. She opened the splits, poured the champagne into flute glasses, and put out wheat crackers, Camembert, and smoked oysters. When he returned, she had arranged herself in the corner of a sofa.

The female ballet dancer is a breed apart. Close to physical perfection to begin with, her muscles are trained to perform tasks from which civilian muscles, with rare exceptions, are either exempt or in default. Over the years, this regime, if applied correctly, greatly enhances her already striking beauty.

From the age of five or six, the comely aspiring dancer is taught placement, balance, position, support, flexibility, spatial awareness, and, above all, line. Eventually, after years of observing herself in studio mirrors, she becomes acutely aware of how she looks, whether she's in the Rose Adagio or standing in line at the checkout counter of the super-marché.

For most dancers, this muscle memory, this learned physical behavior (the arched foot, the bent ankle, the pointed toe) becomes second nature. There is rarely a seductive component in the way she chooses to stand or sit. She's been standing or sitting that way in class for years, waiting for her moment to dance. Her body is her instrument. Her body is about beauty, not about sex.

Stéphane was the exception. At least that was Alex's idée

fixe of the moment. Philippa had told him that Stéphane once caused a three-car accident while crossing the Boulevard des Capucines at 5 in the evening in a borrowed Karl Lagerfeld cocktail dress.

This was attributed, variously, to the sinuous walk, the D-cup, to the fact that she was blonde, radiant, and Greek. Alex, for whom centerfold voyeurism was a distant adolescent memory, nevertheless had found himself viewing this evening with a certain expectancy. But now that he was here and alone with her, he felt self-conscious and culpable.

He sat at the opposite end of the sofa and made a rather wooden toast to her new job.

She was sitting with one leg tucked under her, and the other curved extravagantly over the edge of the sofa. After the toast, she shifted this leg and nudged Alex with her foot. "Relax," she said. "This is not an audition. You've already got the job."

He said, "I think I'm here for the wrong, reason."

Stéphane gave him her best unblinking green gaze. "You're here because Philippa's getting it on with Nicky Blixen."

He put down his glass and turned to her. "I don't have proof of that."

"Alex. Nicky Blixen has screwed every girl he's ever partnered. He can't dance otherwise. It's history. Besides, he's irresistible. He looks like an angel, jumps like Baryshnikov, and is built like King Kong" — she fluttered her eyelids — "I hear."

Alex felt his face flush. "All right! That's why I'm here! I'm here because I'm pissed . . . and that's a bad reason!"

Stéphane half-smiled. "What right have you to be pissed? Have you ever made love to Philippa?"

"No."

"Why not?"

He didn't answer.

"Because she's your little girl?"

"That's part of it."

"What's the other part?"

Alex glanced across the couch. "You're being pretty tough on me."

"Yes. What's the other part?"

"I'm a lot older than Philippa. I can't imagine she wants —"

"She wants! Trust me. In the meantime, do you expect her to remain immaculate until her prince decides she's no longer his little girl?"

"Certainly not."

"Good. Because she doesn't expect it of you either." She paused. "This is weird. Nicky Blixen aside, you actually have another reason to thank Philippa for being here tonight."

"What's that?"

"She never seduced you. If I'd been Philippa and you adopted me, I'd have nailed you before I was fifteen. We'd have six adorable, towheaded cherubs by now, and you wouldn't be here with Stéphane." She smiled. "Have a smoked oyster."

They finished the champagne and moved to the kitchen, where Stéphane began rattling pots and pans. She'd left a cookbook on the counter open to "Steaks and Chops." Very quickly it became clear that Stéphane was not at home in the kitchen. She didn't know a slotted spoon from a colander.

Alex prepared the meal. He broiled the chops with olive oil, garlic, and rosemary. There was no lettuce, so he made crudités of cauliflower, julienned carrots, and scallions, and served them with an herb mayonnaise and mustard sauce. At the last minute he steamed the asparagus. While this was taking place, she perched on one of the stools at the breakfast bar, crossed her legs, and silently watched him. From time to time she picked up a paper napkin and fanned herself.

Alex served. After the first bite she made a humming sound. "This is unbelievable. Are you free for breakfast, lunch and dinner tomorrow?" She looked up and watched him smile for the first time. "I've been waiting for that."

They ate slowly and talked. She said she'd just rented a TV, a VCR, and some videotapes. "I am TV and video-starved. Virgile would not allow them in the flat."

They talked about films they liked, about music, theatre and dance, family and friends, and the difference between fidelity and loyalty. Alex wasn't sure there was a difference. Stéphane insisted there was. She said, "Fidelity requires a vow that bonds you to a promise. Loyalty doesn't. Husbands and wives swear to be faithful and, because of that, either aren't, or are frustrated. Friends and lovers can be loyal with no restrictions."

Alex was not convinced. But it didn't matter. At this point he could choose to be faithful or loyal or not with impunity.

They rinsed the dishes and silverware and stacked them in the dishwasher. Stéphane put the pans in the sink, dried her hands on a dish towel, and turned to Alex. "Now for dessert," she said.

Making love to someone new involves risks: the risk of offending, of failing to satisfy, or of just failing. Until this evening, Alex had scarcely known Stéphane. Physically, she was a dream. She was every garage mechanic's fantasy, the tool-and-die poster girl posed provocatively on the cinderblock wall next to the socket wrenches. He'd never made love to anyone who looked like that. He wasn't sure he was up to the task.

He was certain that, aesthetically, Stéphane was nothing like the poster girl stereotype. Yet, while he'd been distracted by her promiscuous attention to him earlier, he was suffering, at this moment, from a severe case of first-night jitters.

Alex showered quickly, wrapped a towel around himself, and, dropping it at the last moment, slipped into bed beside her. He switched off the table lamp. At once, he felt her bare breasts on his chest as she rolled over and switched the lamp back on. She lay next to him. "Alex, I want to see you. And I want you to see me. We need to learn each other, and we can't do that in the dark."

With her hair down, her face in repose, and her wide mouth free of makeup, she seemed more beautiful, softer, even vulnerable. The love goddess faded. Alex felt a pulse in his neck, and a warm stirring in his belly. The jitters went away to be replaced, at some point, by a pressure so sensual and pleasurable as to become barely endurable.

Miraculously, there was no awkwardness. Between kisses, they compared hands and feet, wrists, ankles, shoulders, knees. After an hour, maybe more, of gentle exploration and contact he kissed the marble smoothness of the inside of her upper thigh. She whispered, "Alex, listen . . . you do that and I'll be ahead of you."

"I want to make you wet."

She stroked his hair. "Chéri, I've been wet since you rang the doorbell."

After perhaps another hour of pliant dalliance, she raised a knee and slowly drew him inside. The barely endurable was now unendurable.

Later, when he was deep, she held his face with trembling hands. They gazed at each other, neither daring to move. Finally, no longer able to defer the pleasure, she closed her eyes, whispered "Alex," and thrust. He detonated. His body contracted. She cried out once, seized his hips, thrust, cried out again, then threw her arms around him and wept for joy.

They slept. At something like 4 A.M. they made love again. Afterward, Stéphane closely examined his beard, his nose, his lips, teeth, ears. She kissed him on each eyelid and murmured, "I promised myself I wouldn't say this. But if I don't say it, you'll never know."

Alex realized how seriously he'd misjudged her. But he ran his fingers along her lips. "Don't say it."

She regarded him with a gravity he hadn't seen before. "All right. Instead, I'll take a bath and brush my teeth, and try to put you into some sort of sensible perspective. Will you do me a favor?"

"If I can."

"Make breakfast for me before you go?"

He showered again, dressed, and made cheese omelettes and coffee. Under the circumstances he guessed it would be fatal if he invited Stéphane to Philippa's opening. He *guessed* it would be fatal. He wasn't certain — of anything. He was so conflicted he couldn't distinguish his emotions. It was a miracle he'd managed the omelettes.

When she emerged from her bath, shining, in rose-coloured tights and a long, purple sweater, she announced, unsolicited, that Philippa had reserved a seat for her at Covent Garden, and that she would be spending the night in Chelsea with Philippa and Cressida. She came to the stove and pressed her cheek against his chest. "And Alex, if I wear a red wig, a false nose, and dark glasses, Philippa will know, the minute she sees me, that I'm in love with you."

Alex felt a frisson; but whether it was one of joy or guilt, he couldn't say.

They sat next to each other at the breakfast bar, Stéphane resting her foot on his. Halfway through the omelettes, Alex's beeper went off. She jumped. "Dear God! I nearly forgot! You're a working flic! Could that've gone off last night?"

Alex grinned. "I took out the batteries." He dialed the Maison and was immediately connected with Varnas.

"Hope I don't wake you, Alex. I just receive call from Dactyloscopy. AFIS, Automated Fingerprint Identification System, turns up set of prints that match thumb and forefinger on inhaler dispenser found in Théâtre Bakoledis lost and found."

"Whose are they?"

"DWI, arrested last night going wrong way on one-way street near Swiss border. He carries ID of Jules Garimet, fake Sûreté Inspecteur we almost encounter in Toulouse, looking for Fannois."

"Who is he really?"

"Driver's license shows name and photograph of Pierre-Yves Gastin."

"Was he alone?"

"Yes."

"I'll be right there."

He rang off and turned to Stéphane. She kissed the back of his hand. "I have a confession to make," she said. "I don't really have a job with the Folies. But I needed an excuse to get you to come over and celebrate." She made her summer smile. "Good-bye. See you in London."

21

The Maison

ALEX MET ISABELLE at the entrance to Reception. She lowered her voice. "Is it true we have Pierre-Yves Gastin's prints on the inhaler?"

"How did you hear about that so fast?"

"It's my job. Could that explain why he and Gus left the opening-night party early?"

"Maybe."

"You do good work, Alex."

Varnas was on the phone when Alex reached the office. He waved to a carton of coffee he'd left on Alex's desk.

After a longish silence, Varnas said, "Very good, thanks," and rang off. He sipped his coffee. "They bring Pierre-Yves to police bureau in town of Lons le Saunier in Jura. They helicopter him to Lyon later this morning, and fly him to us after lunch. Meanwhile, ten minutes ago, Joëlle spots woman letting herself into Pierre-Yves' residence in Rue Marbeau."

"A woman?"

"Joëlle says it is cleaning woman."

"Let's see for ourselves."

As they trotted downstairs, Varnas eyed his partner. "Do you lose a little weight, Alexei?"

"Possibly."

Rue Marbeau

The cleaning woman was a Romanian national with a legal work permit. The key she used to enter the house was attached to an aluminum tag stamped with the logo of Ménage Hausmann-Auber, the name "Gastin" hand-written in indelible black ink, and the address. By the time Alex and Varnas arrived, Joëlle had confirmed her identity with her employer, the same firm that cleaned the theatre. She was now disdainfully preoccupied, with feather duster and vacuum cleaner, in the main salon.

The downstairs rooms of the villa were furnished in Louis XV antiques, or copies. The decor was elegant without being distinguished — more hotel than château. However, upstairs was another matter.

At the top of the staircase was Pierre-Yves' studio. It occupied the entire floor. Along the white walls of this enormous room were rows of three-dimensional models of scene designs for *Eurydice, Léocadia, Intermezzo, The Visit, The Maid of Orléans,* and several other plays and operas. When Alex flicked on the light switch at the doorway, these models, built of translucent material, were breathtakingly illuminated, as they would be in the theatre. The illusion was astonishing.

In the centre of the room, on a large, white drafting table, stood a work in progress: a towering gray ruin of a mediaeval church or château within which appeared a rough, boulder-strewn clearing, tilted slightly in perspective toward the audience. Downstage of the model, and suspended from horizontal wires at proscenium height, were narrow strips of gray, transparent scrim material that extended to the stage floor.

Open on the drafting table was a large black leather notebook that contained sketches of mediaeval costumes in shades of bright yellow, black, and crimson, as well as research material on the Hundred Years War, 1337–1453, a mediaeval town plan of Reims, a photograph of the ruin of the fourteenth-century Château de Saissac, and a modern map of the village of Saissac in the Aude.

While Varnas examined the models, Alex wandered to the far end of the room, where he'd noticed a curtain of pale yellow silk. He ventured behind the curtain and found an antique, baroque brass bed with a low Spanish chest of drawers at its foot. There was a mirror in the ceiling. To one side of the bed was a door that led to a bath. Alex investigated this large, tiled space filled with marble and gold fixtures and stained wooden cupboards with white china door pulls. He opened a tall maplewood cabinet. The top shelves held sheets, pillow slips, towels, and bath gloves; the lower, a variety of toiletries and medicines, including a plastic container labeled $C_{17} H_{21} NO_4$. He removed the snap top and sniffed a white, crystalline alkaloid prescribed here as "Topical Anaesthetic." No doctor's name appeared on the label, which was imprinted with the name, address, and phone number of the Pharmacie Berzélius. Alex knew without tasting it that the compound was cocaine.

He pocketed the container and rejoined Varnas. They left the studio and climbed the stairs to the top floor.

Here were two adjoining rooms, both white-walled. Together they covered the entire upper floor. The first was an ascetic, Oriental-looking affair with tatami matting, a low table with floor cushions, and a Japanese bed.

Next door, separated by a short passageway and bathroom, was a sort of gymnasium-library-dance studio-dressing room. There were weights and pulleys, a stationary bicycle, a ballet barre and mirror, a sewing machine, sound equipment, a theatrical makeup table with mirror and lights, language tapes, dialect tapes, a pair of well-thumbed play scripts (*La Pucelle,* by Hanataux, *The Maid of Orléans,* by Françoise Bauré), and shelves of books: the works of Racine, Molière, Corneille, Voltaire, Maupassant, and others. There were books on fabric and costume design, on magic, mime, makeup, stage illusion and swordplay, and a dozen volumes describing religious miracles, including *The Third Secret of Fatima, The History of La Salette, The Miracle at Rue du Bac,* and something called *Marieverschijnin gen in Medjugorge.*

This must have been where Angélique came to live after Delap threw her out. But Delap couldn't have thrown this vast accumulation of stuff out his windows into Rue Tournon. Perhaps Gus made up the story.

They went downstairs. Alex called Ménage Hausmann-Auber and had them recall the cleaning woman until further notice. They left Joëlle on station.

The Maison

A few minutes after 2 P.M., Pierre-Yves, shackled to a CRS officer, was delivered to Sûreté headquarters. Apart from the fact that he had a bandage over his left eyebrow and a strip of plaster on his chin, Pierre-Yves most resembled a young Bavarian nobleman. He wore a magnificently cut blue velvet blazer, an open-neck orange shirt, and white flannel trousers that provided an ambient opulence in contrast to his cool, blond good looks. According to the officer, he'd resisted arrest. It seemed unlikely. Pierre-Yves didn't have a thread out of place, and the arresting officer was twice his size.

Alex signed a receipt for him. While Varnas escorted him downstairs to a holding room, the CRS officer was given coffee and repatriated to Lyon.

In spite of the circumstances, Pierre-Yves sat quietly in the wooden chair provided for him, and projected an image of such patrician privilege and certitude, that Alex, instead of wanting to bash him, was mildly diverted.

Alex said, "You are charged with violating your restraining order, impersonating a police officer, driving while under the influence, resisting arrest, drug possession, and conspiracy to commit murder."

Pierre-Yves shrugged. "I deny all charges."

"Monsieur Gastin, we have your fingerprints on the murder weapon."

"That's ridiculous. I drove Gus home opening night after the party and returned to the theatre to change the light plot. Act Two was too amber. I walked to the back of the house to reset the board and tripped over this thing in the aisle. I had no idea what it was. I assumed it belonged to a patron, so I put it in the L and F. You can't arrest me for that."

Varnas said, "You are telling us this story while sitting in same chair as your friend Boris Alexandrovich Popov when we question him."

Pierre-Yves ignored the remark.

"Do you know Popov?" Alex asked.

"No."

"He owns the Pharmacie Berzélius, where you obtain your jelly beans."

Pierre-Yves lowered his lids. His lashes were so long they cast shadows on his cheekbones. "I do not intend to speak to you," he said. "My solicitor will do my talking."

"Your solicitor can advise you but he cannot do your talking. Have you contacted your solicitor?"

"Yes."

"When can we expect him?"

"Her. When she gets here."

"When might that be?"

"I don't know. She's driving my Ferrari from Lons le Saunier. She's never driven a stick shift. It's over four hundred kilometres. It may take her a day or two."

Pierre-Yves had retained his sister, a corporate and financial juriste from Lausanne, Switzerland. As she would be precluded from practicing law in France, she'd agreed to act on his behalf in an advisory capacity.

Meanwhile, Commissaire Demonet arranged for a court-appointed defense counsel to represent Pierre-Yves. This man, a middle-rank, conservative Paris solicitor noted for compromise, arrived at the Maison at 4. He took a seat next to Pierre-Yves and, without so much as a nod in his direction, stated, "My client has nothing to say at this time. I wish to examine the accommodations you have provided for him while he waits for justice to be served."

After a cursory glance at Pierre-Yves' spartan holding cell, the court-appointed jurist huddled amiably with Alex and requested the opportunity to acquaint himself with the charges against his client before commenting further. With that he bade them good afternoon and left.

Alex and Varnas retired to their office. Alex turned his desk chair around and straddled it.

"This may not be so easy," he said. "His DWI, violating

the restraining order, impersonating a flic, resisting arrest —
if true — and drug possession, are all certifiable. But the
murder charge, based solely on two latent prints, is a long
way from conclusive, and the solicitor knows it." Alex
glanced at Varnas sitting at his desk with his hat on. "What
do you think?"

Varnas hesitated for a moment, then said, "I got something to say, Alex."

Alex, remembering his abrupt bad humor from the day
before, prepared himself for a lecture.

Varnas adjusted his hat and said, "I want you to be first to
know. I plan to get married and wish you to be best man."

Alex's jaw dropped. "Married? You?"

"Yes."

Alex suddenly grinned. "You? Married? The grand pan-
jandrum of celibacy? The proselytizer of singlehood? The
champion of uncommittedness who hustles me home every
time I'm distracted by a pretty face?"

"I save you for Philippa," Varnas said. "And don't laugh."

Alex wiped off the grin. "You're serious."

"Yes."

"Then excuse me."

"It's okeh."

"And congratulations."

"Thanks."

"May I ask . . ."

"Certainly. Madame Roget."

"Madame Roget. Isn't this rather sudden?"

"Not really. We are the good friends now for some time.
We don't realize how good a friends until lavender water episode. For first time, madame shows her feelings. Recently, we
have rather remarkable reconciliation in which I show my

feelings also. It is first time for me, Alex. Better late than
never."

Alex got up and circled his desk. Varnas rose to meet him.

"You sweet old son of a bitch," Alex said softly, and
hugged his friend. "I'd be honoured to be your best man."
Varnas, a half-metre shorter than his colleague, held on to his
hat until released.

He nodded. "Good. That's settled then. Maybe Philippa
can be best woman."

"The term is 'maid of honour.' I'm sure she'd be delighted,
if she gets back in time. When is the wedding?"

"Tomorrow."

"Tomorrow?"

"Or the day after. As soon as possible."

"What's the rush?"

"The rush, Alex, is that remarkable reconciliation is not
yet consummated."

"Oh, no!"

"Oh, yes. And madame does not permit it until she receives God's okeh — in church. Actually, ceremony is scheduled for ten o'clock, Monday, twenty-three September." He
glanced at his pocket watch. "That is three days and seventeen hours from now."

"I'll be there. And I'll wire Philippa immediately." Alex
felt a warm wave of affection and a new virtuousness wash
over him. He said, "Would you like to go with me to Philippa's opening in London Saturday? She's booked a room
for us at Brown's Hotel."

"That is sweet of Philippa, Alex. But I promise madame I
help her find wedding dress Saturday. And I need to rent dinner jacket." He paused. "Also you can do me great favour,
Alex."

"Anything."

"Go to Chez Suzanne and tell her. After so many years, I don't have a heart."

Chez Suzanne

Alex had never been to the café-bar without Varnas. As most of the regular customers didn't know him, his entrance elicited some uneasy glances. However, he nodded pleasantly to them and was careful not to appropriate Varnas's special table by the café curtain.

Suzanne waddled over with her hands on her hips. "Dining alone, chef-inspecteur?"

"Good evening, Suzanne. Yes, I'm alone."

She looked him over. "Euh . . . to what do I attribute the occasion of this . . . um . . . solo presence?"

Alex decided Suzanne should have remained a madam. Absent her somewhat increased avoirdupois, and her effulgent silver and gold bridgework, she was the perfect French Mae West *doppelganger*: the walk, the hands on the swaying hips, the insinuating cadence. He smiled and said, "I'm here for your exquisite Thursday night special, the Noisettes d'Agneau."

"Really? I'm flattered to hear that from such a fine figure of a man." But her expression darkened. "So where is he?"

"Varnas?"

"Who else?"

"He's home, Suzanne."

She looked skeptical. "I haven't seen him in a week. Are you sure he hasn't had an accident?"

Alex looked her in the eye. "It's worse than that. He asked me to tell you."

She exhaled, "Jesus. He's marrying the landlady."

"Yes."

Her eyes glistened. But after a moment she recovered and returned to her Mae West mode. "Well," she said, "I'll have to find a replacement. Meanwhile, what are you drinking?"

Alex ordered the specialité, the Noisettes, which were excellent. He drank a half-carafe of vin ordinaire, enjoyed a crème brûlée for dessert, and a cognac afterward. She would not allow him to pay. And it was later alleged that, for the first time in anyone's memory, Suzanne bought a round of drinks for the entire house before closing.

Le Yacht Club

He reached the barge at 9:30, checked the dock lines, fenders, the shore power cable, and went below.

He dialed the PTT and sent a wire to Philippa, c/o Royal Ballet, Covent Garden: "Varnas to wed Clothilde Roget 10 A.M., Monday, Église St-Charles de Monceau. Wants you as maid of honour. R.S.V.P."

He had no more than hung up the phone when it jangled. He considered letting the machine answer so he could be selective about returning the call. However, assuming it was Varnas or the Maison calling, he picked up. It was Délice calling. And she was roaring.

"Chef-Inspecteur! You will come immediately! Stéphane has made a discovery!"

"Stéphane?" He hadn't expected to encounter Stéphane again so soon. "What sort of discovery?"

"An extraordinary discovery! Don't waste time! Come! We are in Suite Three-D, Hôtel Madison, Boulevard St-Germain!"

22

Hôtel Madison

ALEX CONSIDERED CALLING DÉLICE BACK
and telling her to stuff it. He was not accustomed to being
summoned so magisterially. However, there had been something beyond imperiousness in her voice. And, given the Fannois debacle, perhaps he owed her.

He took the lift to the third floor, found 3D and pressed
the doorbell. Unaccountably, it played the first four notes of
Autumn Leaves.

Délice, magnificent in a gold lamé jumpsuit, answered the
door. "Come in, dear," she said affably. She took his arm and
led him into the room. The television set was on, but the
sound was muted. Honoré sat on a couch with his arm
around Stéphane. This was not the seductive and compliant
Stéphane of last night. She looked as if she'd seen a ghost.
Pale and drawn, she was simply dressed in jeans and a white
blouse. She looked smaller than he remembered.

They were drinking rum punch. Alex declined the rum and
accepted a beer. Behind the couch he saw the domed dishes of
a substantial room service dinner recently consumed.

Honoré had gotten up to get Alex's beer, and now stood next to the TV. Stéphane, responding to Alex's presence, rearranged herself on the couch. She piled her hair on top of her head, pinned it with an amber comb, and attempted a smile.

"Have you heard from Philippa?"

"Yes. Have you?"

"Not a word."

"Well, she's probably busy."

She slightly raised her eyebrows. "I'll bet."

Alex cleared his throat. "So. What is this extraordinary discovery?"

Stéphane fished in her dance bag for her cigarettes, lit one, inhaled, and, peering directly at Alex, said, "There's no TV in Virgile's flat. Since I haven't had a whole lot to keep me busy these days, I rented a TV and VCR. I rented some film cassettes as well, including a couple of tapes of a TV variety show I used to watch called *Vaudevillesque*."

Alex remembered the show. It had been off the air for a few years.

"I spent this morning watching old films. Later I ran one of the *Vaudevillesque* tapes. It dates from the late seventies and features Jerry Lewis, Bernardo Bertolucci, Cantinflas, an American singer named Julia Migenes, and the late Angélique Églantine."

"De la Pagerie's fiancée?"

"The same."

"But on a comedy program? I thought she was a serious stage actress."

"This was before she was a serious stage actress."

Alex waited. "Is that the extraordinary discovery?"

Stéphane flashed him a look of impatience. "I'd never seen

her before. When I watched her at home this afternoon, I couldn't believe my eyes. So I called Délice and Honoré and brought the tape here so they could see it. Now I want you to see it."

Honoré started the VCR. Délice released the mute button and Alex watched Bernardo Bertolucci finishing an impression of Anna Magnani doing Tennessee Williams in English. There was applause at the end, music, a commercial edited out, more music, and an emcee introducing Angélique Églantine.

Angélique, blonde, blue-eyed, and doll-faced, did a standup comedy sketch in which she played a dumb, giddily distracted, hopelessly uncoordinated airline flight attendant who, catastrophically, attempts to demonstrate to her passengers the aircraft's safety equipment: the seat belt, oxygen mask, inflatable life vest, the emergency exits, and the vomit bag. The sketch, frequently interrupted by laughter, ran about four minutes and finished to enthusiastic applause. Honoré turned off the set.

Stéphane turned to Alex. "Well?"

"Well what? I think she was very funny."

"It's the same chick!"

Alex looked blank. "The same chick?"

"Alex! The chick Angélique plays in that airline sketch is the same chick that checked our bags through the X ray counter in Barcelona!"

23

The Maison

Early next morning, Alex and Varnas stood before the Commissaire. On his desk were the Iberia and Barcelona Airport documents Alex had sent down. The Commissaire wore his darkest expression.

"The seating assignments on Iberia's Flight 4426 on Wednesday four September indicate that the only passengers who might've had in-flight access to Delap's shoulder bag were the passengers seated directly in front of him and Mademoiselle Nikolaides. They were the Spanish Minister of Agriculture, his wife, and his press secretary, en route to Paris for a Sabena connection to Brussels and a meeting of the European Community Council of Ministers." He paused for emphasis. "Can we scratch Iberia?" Without waiting for a response, he pushed the document aside and turned to the other document on his desk. This was the report from the Supervisor of Passenger Service Personnel, Barcelona Airport.

"We have here the names, ages, length of employment, biographies and photographs of the personnel in place at the metal detector gate on four September. They are Luis Ximinez, fifty-nine, baggage handler, Jaime Gutierrez, thirty-nine, gate monitor, and the woman, Lupe Santiago, twenty-six, X ray monitor. Lupe Santiago has black hair and wears glasses."

The Commissaire gave Alex his undivided attention. "Now you tell me that, notwithstanding the supervisor's report, Lupe Santiago, twenty-six, with the black hair and glasses, did not monitor the screen that day. Now you say it was monitored by the French actress Angélique Églantine, a person my usually reliable sources tell me is still dead!" He threw the photos on the desk.

"Alex and Varnas! If a whiff of this surreal hypothesis gets out of this office, I will be looking for work before the end of the week! So will you! One more Fannois embuscade and the Interior Minister will transfer this case to the Cub Scouts!"

Alex replied simply, "Has the minister told you yet that Fannois was in a government protection program?"

The Commissaire stared. "What?"

"I'm sure the minister will tell you eventually. In the meantime, Commissaire, let's leave Fannois out of the present discussion." Alex supplied no further details. It was enough that he had temporarily blunted the Commissaire's attack.

"It is undeniably true that Angélique Églantine is assumed to be deceased," Alex said. "I believe there was even a memorial program for her in Paris last summer. But let's presume, for a moment, that she is somehow not dead and managed to impersonate an airport employee at Barcelona. If that occurred, wouldn't you expect that de la Pagerie would have recognized her?"

The Commissaire shrugged.

"I thought the question important enough to ask it of Délice and Honoré. They said that if Angélique's appearance in the TV sketch matched her appearance at the airport, Virgile would not have recognized her. They didn't recognize her in the sketch, and she was nearly their daughter-in-law. They said if the emcee hadn't introduced her by name, they wouldn't have known who she was."

"Alex, that proves nothing! Délice and Honoré's remarks prove something only if Angélique was at the airport, and only Stéphane says Angélique was at the airport!"

"I know that. So I asked Stéphane how she could be sure it was the same person, since her original description of the woman was so offhand. She called her a 'typical airline chick, blonde, blue-eyed, have-a-nice-flight type.' Stéphane said she has been known to forget a face, but after years onstage with the Opéra ballet, she claims total cosmetic recall. She insists Angélique wore the same Lionne lemon mousse in her hair, the same Sahara number three pancake with a light street blush, the same Nuage cerulean eye shadow, the same mascara charbonne, and the same Sauvage number two carmine lip gloss. She's positive!"

The Commissaire vigorously shook his head. "No! No! No! This wild abstraction is based on the allegation of a woman of questionable morals and strained credibility who, herself, had unimpeded access to the victim's shoulder bag all the way from Marbella to Paris, and has yet to convince me of her ingenuousness! You will not pursue this line of inquiry, Alex! It stops here! *This* morning! *In* this room! Trying to incriminate a loony was bad enough! A corpse would be worse!"

"How does Commissaire's tango lessons go?" Varnas asked, as they waited for coffee and pastry at À La Cart.

"Tango lessons? I thought it was croquet."

"Whatever. We ignore him for now, Alex. Do you trust Mademoiselle Stéphane?"

"Yes. Although I suppose it's possible she's mistaken about Angélique at the airport."

"How can she be mistaken? Either she sees blonde air chick at gate or not. That is what we got to find out!"

They took their cafés-complets up to the office and sat down again with the Personnel Supervisor's report. The report was very complete. Indeed, it told them more than they needed to know. In addition to the descriptions and photographs of the employees in question, the report included a forty-page booklet of regulations covering employee training, appearance, behavior, and performance. One section dealt with grounds for dismissal. Baggage tampering led the list. There was even a hand-written, marginal notation, stating that there had been no incident of baggage tampering at Barcelona in twenty years. In other words, the report was professional, thorough, and, Alex thought, entirely too custodial. Questions remained. What if Lupe Santiago had needed to go to the bathroom on 4 September at 3:59 P.M.? Could a total stranger replace the X ray monitor without comment from the gate crew or the knowledge of the supervisor?

They decided to try the supervisor again — by phone. As neither of them spoke Spanish, they enlisted the help of a serious young programmer from Comcentre named Nora de Jesus.

She declined the offer of secondhand coffee and pastry and put the call through to Barcelona. Alex went to his work station and began typing the questions he wanted Barcelona to answer.

The Supervisor of Passenger Service Personnel was out of the country. They switched Nora to the Deputy-Supervisor.

The Deputy said he was familiar with the Sûreté inquiry. Indeed, he'd prepared much of the reply himself. Nora thanked him and asked if he would supply some additional information.

"I'll try."

She asked, "What happens when one of your employees becomes ill on the job or needs a short break?"

"We have a temporary replacement procedure."

"Can an employee be temporarily replaced without the supervisor's knowledge?"

"No. Well . . . yes, if the employee is flagged by a TPI."

"TPI?" She glanced at Alex.

"Terminal Proficiency Inspector. They're a squad of quality control officers that can appear at any facility, unannounced, to rate employee performance and monitor equipment."

Nora briefly explained TPI to Alex. He typed in the next question.

"Does the supervisor receive reports of these unannounced visits?"

"Only if an employee is censured, or if there is an equipment failure."

"In other words, if a TPI visited the metal detector gate X ray screen servicing Iberia's Flight 4426, at four P.M. on Wednesday four September, and Lupe Santiago was doing her job properly, the supervisor would not have been notified?"

"That is correct."

Alex finished typing. Nora said, "Thank you, señor. One more item. We have evidence that an unauthorized person may have temporarily relieved Lupe Santiago on four September, prior to the departure of Flight 4426."

"That is not possible."

"Why?"

"Because all terminal employees wear laminated photo

ident with a work number. Because security is tight. Because the gate people know most of the TPIs."

"But not all?"

The deputy supervisor sighed. "Señorita. If I question Lupe Santiago when she comes on duty today, and she remembers after two weeks, will you be satisfied?"

"Yes." Nora gave him the Sûreté fax number and rang off.

Varnas put on his overcoat. "I don't know, Alex. French actress, supposed to be dead, no airlines experience, no technical knowledge, walks up to X ray and, with a fluent Spanish, convinces gate crew she is Special Inspecteur?"

"Why not? And what do you mean, no airline experience? She made this trip with Delap dozens of times. Why would she need technical knowledge? All she needed was the opportunity to observe and absorb. As for speaking Spanish, don't forget all those months in Marbella, and visits to La Tortosa restaurant. Varnas, listen. If she could play Claire Zachanassian in *The Visit*, she could play a TPI in Barcelona."

"Maybe." Varnas tipped his hat to Nora and withdrew.

Alex thanked Nora and emphasized the importance of keeping the Barcelona call confidential.

Nora, feeling ordained, nodded gravely and left.

Alex sat quietly for a moment to gather his thoughts. There was something in the back of his mind that was trying to get his attention. He waited. It came, finally. It was the village where Angélique died. He'd seen the name in Isabelle's dossier on Gus.

He rummaged through his desk drawers. Remembering he'd left the dossier on Varnas's desk, he rummaged through Varnas's desk drawers. No luck. He called Research. Isabelle said, "We put it on your computer. Tomorrow is here, Alex."

With Philippa on the verge of stardom in London and

Varnas getting married, Alex had the illusion the world was leaving him behind. He fired up his work station and punched in the entering code. Gus's dossier dribbled down the screen like a small cataract.

He found what he was looking for. The village was called Seigneur-sous-Tarn, département of the Aveyron. He turned off the computer and pulled down his old atlas. He was able to locate the river Tarn, but the village did not appear on the small-scale map of south-central France.

On his way to lunch, he stopped at the Transport Pool and picked up a copy of the Michelin, large-scale, Carte Routière of the Aveyron. Seigneur-sous-Tarn was a tiny dot on a numberless back road, about fifty kilometres northeast of Castres. He tucked the road map inside his anorak and went to a brasserie on St-Honoré, where he spent an hour toying with a bowl of sandy mussels and a white bean salade.

During the meal, he made some notes in the margin of the map.

Aveyron, Dépt. No. 12, préfecture, Rodez.

Dairy country. Cheese. Why Seigneur-sous-Tarn?

Inaccessible?

Can you die of anorexia in six months?

Death certificate?

Funeral? Burial?

Gus?

He consumed half the mussels and most of the beans, chewed on a mandarine for dessert, and walked slowly back to the Maison the long way, via the Madeleine and Rue de Surène.

The Duty Officer stopped him on his way in. "There's a fax for you in Data Processing, Chef."

Alex concealed the road map inside his anorak again,

pulled up the zipper, and trotted down the single flight to Data. He signed for the fax and went next door to Comcentre. There he located Nora's frosted glass cubicle, placed the fax before her, and handed her a pencil.

Wordlessly, she wrote out the translation.

Screen monitor Lupe Santiago
reports no TPI inspection
occurred 4 Sept. Gate crew
confirm. Sorry.

Alex whispered "Shit." He thanked Nora again and climbed back to his office.

Someone was lying. Either Stéphane, because she switched the inhaler herself, or Lupe Santiago and the gate crew because they were afraid of something, or the Deputy Supervisor who, with a simple faxed denial, managed to declare the matter closed and his airport personnel inviolate.

Alex could not believe that Stéphane was capable of joining a murder conspiracy, even if she had a motive. Nor did he think her capable of inventing Angélique-at-the-gate. However, these judgments meant nothing. The Commissaire would be unmerciful if any aspect of the inquiry were not supported by hard fact, particularly as he had forbidden the inquiry in the first place. Varnas had it right. "Either she sees air chick at gate or not."

Either Angélique was alive or not.

Alex unfolded the Michelin Carte Routière on his desk and reviewed his margin notes. He had an impulse to take a shortcut and phone Gus. No. No calls to Gus until Stéphane's allegation was either substantiated or invalidated.

He surveyed the road map and noted the proximity of Seigneur-sous-Tarn to other towns and villages in the region.

After a few minutes, he made a decision. He called Research again. Isabelle was at lunch. He spoke with her assistant.

"Find me the Medical Examiner for the département of the Aveyron," he said. "I want a copy of the death certificate of Angélique Églantine, deceased Seigneur-sous-Tarn, 6 April 1985. Note any unusual circumstances. Start with the town of Rodez. That's the préfecture. And tell Isabelle this is an unauthorized inquiry."

An hour later, Isabelle summoned Alex to her office.

"I'm giving even money that Stéphane Nikolaides is telling the truth about Angélique Églantine," she said.

Alex felt himself jump-started. "What about the death certificate?"

"The death certificate is authentic, but it was not signed by the Medical Examiner for Aveyron."

"Why not?"

"Angélique's death was characterized as an 'unattended death.' That's fairly common in rural areas where the Medical Examiner is remote. The local or family doctor reports the death to the M.E., who, if he is satisfied that everything is in order, can 'deny jurisdiction' that permits the attending physician to sign the death certificate and contact the undertaker. The M.E. cannot deny jurisdiction if the body is to be cremated. But as cremation was not called for in this case, the denial of jurisdiction was in order."

"So?"

"So the local doctor from the town of Réquista, eighteen kilometres to the north, signed the death certificate. He would normally have then contacted the undertaker for embalming and burial. However, Angélique left instructions that she wished to follow the Orthodox Jewish practice of burial without embalming by sundown of the same or the next day. Under the circumstances, the doctor simply turned the body over to the local undertaker, who is also the mayor of Seigneur-sous-Tarn, and went home.

"The woman I spoke with at the Medical Examiner's office in Rodez said there was nothing unusual about that. She said that these people are all farmers, mechanics, carpenters, and anything else they need to be, and that they've been burying their own dead for centuries. She said her information was that the mayor and his son buried Angélique in the village graveyard next morning."

"I didn't know Angélique was Jewish."

"She wasn't. We have a copy of her birth certificate from the Bureau of Passports. She was Catholic."

"And she chose the Orthodox Jewish burial to avoid the . . . uh . . . inconvenience of being cremated or embalmed."

"Right."

"Where did the body spend the next twenty-four hours?"

"I don't know."

"You said she left instructions. Left instructions with whom?"

Isabelle shrugged.

"Who attended the funeral?"

Isabelle shrugged again. "Why don't you ask the mayor of Seigneur-sous-Tarn? Or the doctor at Réquista? Or both? Their answers might give this unauthorized inquiry a little goddam legitimacy."

Seigneur-sous-Tarn

Alex packed an overnight bag and caught the early afternoon turboprop to Rodez-Marcillac. He rented a Peugeot 106 at the airport and drove forty kilometres south to the village of

Réquista, in the Tarn valley. The air smelled of clover and cow shit.

The doctor's name was André Pujol. His surgery was in his home, a perfectly square two-story house of gray stucco and red tile on the edge of the village, in a perfectly square, fenced garden plot of beans, lettuce, squash, tomatoes, grapevines, and geraniums. The doctor was a small man, probably in his late seventies. He wore rimless glasses, baggy homespun trousers, and a brown knitted vest over a brown wool shirt. He was weeding his lettuce when Alex drove up. He appeared to be very nearsighted, and Alex detected a slight tremor when they shook hands.

The man was clearly a doctor whose best years were behind him but who still fulfilled the need for a rural general practitioner at a time when most young medical school graduates tended toward the more lucrative, urban specialties.

Alex did not wish to discomfit the old man. Indeed, when he showed him the faxed copy of the death certificate with his signature on it, it was not to call into question the doctor's competence but to refresh his memory and, Alex hoped, stimulate a discussion. But the old man merely nodded and returned the document. To get him to talk, Alex was inspired to ask if, in the doctor's opinion, there was any possibility that the young woman might have met with foul play.

The old man's white eyebrows knitted slightly. "In Seigneur-sous-Tarn?" he replied in a rheumy falsetto. "My dear monsieur, there hasn't been a crime in Seigneur since 1815 — I think that's the date — when a royalist shot a Bonapartist for some indiscretion that I don't remember. Foul play. No, no. There was not a mark on her. She was simply emaciated. She died of malnutrition. Moreover, if there had been any question of foul play, the Medical Examiner would have presided himself."

"Was anyone with her when she died?"

"I recall a woman. I didn't get her name."

"Was this woman the person who expressed Mademoiselle Églantine's wish to be buried according to Orthodox Jewish practice?"

"Perhaps. There was some question about whether that would be possible. No one seemed to know if the graveyard at Seigneur was a sanctified Christian burial ground. Apparently it was not, for I was later told the burial fee was paid and a casket provided."

"Was the body prepared for burial?"

"It was not embalmed, if that is what you mean."

"I mean, was it clothed or wrapped in any way?"

The doctor seemed confused. "I'm sure I've no idea, monsieur. When I placed the deceased in the custody of the mayor, I fulfilled my responsibility." The doctor peered at his lettuce. He seemed to have lost interest in the subject, or perhaps mislaid his next thought. At any rate, he now reached into his trousers, produced a large pocket watch, and blinked at Alex. "Perhaps you will excuse me, then. I have to wash up before I reopen the surgery." Having said that, he remained rooted to the spot.

Alex thanked him. They shook hands. Alex felt the old man's pale eyes on him as he returned to the Peugeot. He briefly consulted the road map, and drove off.

A few kilos south of Réquista, immediately after he crossed the river Tarn, he came to a nameless country road that curved off to the left through farmland and foothills. About the time he was sure he'd taken the wrong road, he spotted an ancient stone marker. Hand-carved in the stone, and barely legible, was the legend, SEIGN-S-TARN, 14 KM.

He saw the village across a narrow valley long before the winding road reached it. If one squinted, depending upon one's interest and fancy, one could imagine a gray caterpillar crawling up a distant hill, or freight cars stalled on a mountain siding. The village started with a pair of crowded, gray, rectangular houses facing each other across a road just wide enough for one vehicle to pass and ended in less than a hundred metres, with a final pair, indistinguishable from the first, except that some had cattle barns built on at the back. Surrounding the village were fields under cultivation and pastures with grazing cows. This was a design from the Middle Ages, when the farming family worked in the fields during the day and returned to the village at night for protection from marauders and wolves. No picturesque farmhouses here. Even today it would be considered profligate to cover a tillable piece of land with a house. There was one exception. On the crest of a low hill and isolated from the village by half a kilometre or so, was a small sandstone villa with a mansard roof, a chimney, and three glass doors that opened onto a low-walled veranda. This was not the Hôtel de Ville or the mayor's residence. This was either the estate of a country mouse who had prospered or the visible consequence of a country mouse who had had enough of the country and sold his ancestral acreage to a city mouse.

Alex ventured into the village, driving at a snail's pace on the impossibly narrow single street, made narrower by several autos haphazardly parked on the weather-beaten sidewalk. Midway through, he came to a café-tabac-bar, beyond which was a sign P, for parking. He turned into a cobbled lane that led to a small, rectangular courtyard. He parked the Peugeot there, left his bag in the car, and walked back to the café-tabac.

A trio of old men, poised over pastis, argued milk prices. When Alex entered, the conversation expired. He nodded politely to the men as a young boy appeared behind the bar.

" 'Jour, 'sieur," the child said and waited. Alex ordered a beer and asked if messieurs would join him. The old men looked at each other. Finally, one, leather-skinned and purple-nosed, said, "I seldom say no."

The pastis were served. Alex toasted their health. After appropriate exhaling and a cough or two, the purple nose asked, "So what shall you be selling?"

"Nothing, monsieur. I'm looking for the mayor."

"Ah. And which mayor shall that be, then? The mayor of land grants and acquisition? The mayor of building codes and restrictions? The mayor of veterinarian medicine and milk prices? The mayor of farm management? Or the mayor of holy scripture, embalming, taxes, and assizes?"

"Taxes and assizes."

"Ah. Then you will be the government. Good! I knew you shall finally get onto him. Follow me."

Alex paid up. The purple nose chug-a-lugged his pastis and led Alex into the street. He moved with surprising agility, given his age, avoirdupois, probable blood-alcohol level, and heavy rubber boots. Alex followed him across the street and along a gravel path between two houses with cattle barns. They came to the foot of a grassy incline, fenced at the top, on which a handful of sheep grazed. Beyond the fence, cultivation began, and continued in a pattern of parallel furrows that rose and fell as far as the eye could see, a green-and-white seascape, ocean swells of turnip, potato, cabbage, and leeks, that converged at the horizon. The purple nose pointed to the near distance. There a figure sat slumped in the metal seat of a stationary tractor, silhouetted against the sky.

"That shall be your mayor of taxes and assizes, monsieur. You've only to follow the turnip line." He winked, raised a thumb, and retraced his steps to the café-tabac.

Alex climbed the fence, located the turnips, and followed

the furrow to the top of the hill. He approached the tractor. The mayor, in a rumpled corduroy suit and wool cap, was asleep. However, even here under the sky, in the open air, fulsome with the scent of manure, loam, vegetation, and purest oxygen, Alex nevertheless detected the unmistakable fragrance of Armagnac. The mayor was sleeping one off.

Alex said, "Monsieur le maire," several times. He shook him, to no avail. Finally, making sure the gearshift was in neutral, he turned the tractor ignition key and pressed the starter button. The diesel roared to life. The mayor, whose foot was on the accelerator, recoiled, lifted his foot and nearly lost his balance. Had it not been for Alex, he would have ended in the dirt.

After a chaotic moment, the mayor's eyes focused. He realized someone was standing nearby and struggled furiously to regain his lost dignity. He switched off the engine. "What the devil passes here?" he shouted. "Who the hell are you?"

Alex held up his ID. The mayor reached inside his jacket and produced a pair of dusty reading glasses with the left ear piece missing. He studied the ID. "Shit!" he said, and removed the glasses. "Couldn't you make an appointment, at least?"

"Sorry," Alex replied. "I have come from your colleague, André Pujol in Réquista. He said you were a most accessible man."

"Oh yeah? What does the Sûreté want with the mayor of this meadow muffin in the middle of nowhere?"

"You buried a Jewish woman here on April sixth of this year. Pujol signed the death certificate."

"So?"

"Did you bury the woman?"

"Of course."

"The Sûreté has evidence that you did not."

The mayor glared at Alex. "I am the undertaker here," he growled. "That burial is in my record book! I have a copy of the burial receipt! I can show you the grave!"

"All in good time. Meanwhile, a few questions. Where did Mademoiselle Églantine stay in Seigneur-sous-Tarn?"

"In the villa." He jerked his head in the direction of the house across the valley. It was plainly visible from where they stood.

"Who owns the villa?"

"My wife."

"Then mademoiselle rented the villa from your wife?"

"She rented, yes."

"Did mademoiselle pay the rent herself?"

"The rent was paid each month by certified check drawn on the Crédit Lyonnais in Toulouse."

"What branch?"

"Don't know. My wife keeps all that shit."

"Did anyone live in the villa with Mademoiselle Églantine?"

"A woman. Véronique."

"Local woman?"

"No. From somewhere up north. She was a companion. What's this got to do with me?"

"Plenty. Now try to remember carefully, monsieur le maire. Who was it had custody of the body between the time Doctor Pujol signed the death certificate and burial next day?"

"Me. Who else? I'm the undertaker."

"And where is your undertaking establishment?"

"In the mairie — my house."

"Then you transferred the body to the mairie after the doctor left for Réquista?"

"Why the devil would I do that? I ordered the body left at

the villa for the night. What would be the point in transferring it to the mairie when the villa is closer to the graveyard than the mairie by eight hundred metres?"

"Did you prepare the body for burial?"

"I saw to it. The woman, Véronique, clothed the deceased in a burial costume. Together we put her in the casket. I closed the casket myself and nailed it shut. What else do you want to know?"

"I assume that, as undertaker, you provided the casket?"

"No. The lady knew she was going to die. The casket was already there. It's just as well. Everything happened so fast, I wouldn't have had time to order one from Toulouse."

"When was the funeral?"

"There was no funeral. Just a burial. Next morning. There was only me, my son, a gravedigger, and some weird guy from Paris who took a cab all the way from Rodez. Over sixty kilometres by cab! And sixty kilometres back!"

"Did Véronique attend the burial?"

"She said she couldn't face it. She left the village as soon as we moved the casket out of the villa."

"What did the weird guy from Paris look like?"

"Big, overweight, sissy. Cried like a baby when we put her in the ground. Is there anything else?"

"I want the body exhumed."

The mayor chuckled. He gazed patronizingly at Alex. "My wife has a better chance of becoming a film star — and you haven't seen my wife — than you do of obtaining a permit to exhume a body in this département. In thirty years, I've never heard of an exhumation. Permits are required from the Minister of Justice, Guardian of the Seals, and the Medical Examiner for Aveyron, each preceded by a rigorous investigation."

"All of which would reflect badly on you, monsieur," Alex

replied. "I am prepared to provide the authorities all the facts they need to verify the authenticity of my request. The result will be an investigation — of you and Pujol. The Medical Examiner, who denied jurisdiction because he was assured that nothing was amiss, will rereview the case from his special point of view. The consequences for you could be extremely grave. Now. All I need to see can be accomplished in a half hour with two shovels, no questions asked, no reports filed, no permits needed, and no rigorous investigations."

The mayor gazed across the valley at the villa. His property taxes were in arrears. His veterinarian's license was under review. After a moment's reflection, he leaned forward and started the tractor.

The grave was in the farthest corner of the cimitière away from the village. It was distinguished by what must have been a temporary marker, for it was made of wood, elaborately carved, stained, and varnished. The marker, in the shape of a theatre proscenium arch, had a small Star of David at the top, flanked, lower down, by the masks of Tragedy and Comedy. Below this appeared,

Angélique Virginie Églantine

1957–1985

"Little by little, the pearl loses its lustre
and long before it dies,
it is dead."
— Giraudoux

With three of them shoveling — the mayor, his huge son, and Alex — they struck the top of the coffin in twenty minutes. The mayor's son had rigged a rudimentary chain haul to a trapezoidal A-frame at the top of the excavation. By means of straps passed under the casket and brought up to a ring shackled to the chain haul, they were able to lift the box to ground level and swing it onto the sod.

The casket was dark blue and had handles. On the wide end, near the base, Alex spotted a small white stencil: "The Visit, Act One, Sc 1."

The mayor's son inserted the flat blade of a nail-puller under the cover of the casket and pried along its length. It screeched open. He raised the cover.

The deceased, dressed in a rich black velvet gown with gold lace sleeves and collar, was a bald, faceless dress mannequin. Lining the casket on both sides of her were approximately thirty kilograms of kiln bricks, roughly the weight of an anorexic woman of medium height, recently dead of malnutrition.

Part Three

ANGÉLIQUE

24

The Maison

A FEW MINUTES before he flew back to Paris that same evening, Alex phoned Varnas from Rodez. He asked him to set up an emergency meeting with the Commissaire and to request Pierre-Yves' solicitor to stand by.

"There is good news while you are away," Varnas said. "Isabelle locates bank statements showing cash withdrawals of twenty thousand francs from Pierre-Yves' account at Banque de France, and ten thousand from Banque Populaire. Withdrawals are made two days before Doctor Zhivago delivers inhaler. Probably other twenty thousand comes from Crédit Suisse. I set up meeting, Alex, if I can locate Commissaire."

The Commissaire, in evening clothes, had been forced to leave a dinner party at the Jordanian Consulate in the middle of the appetizer. He was therefore not in a sanguine mood when Alex reached the Maison nearly an hour late. However, when Alex made his presentation, he fell silent and studied Doctor Pujol's medical report.

"No pulse, no blood pressure, breathing imperceptible, no vital signs, and the beginnings of rigor mortis." He gazed over his desk at Alex. "Can someone fake that?"

"Evidently. Her last role was as the nineteenth-century actress Rachel. Rachel is said to have been able to stop her heartbeat in death scenes. In any case, there are plenty of recorded cases of misdiagnosis of death, even by coroners. The probability that Angélique is now alive somewhere appears to exonerate Stéphane Nikolaides and, Barcelona notwithstanding, places Angélique at the metal detector facility on four September. We now have Pierre-Yves' prints on the inhaler, bank statements that connect him to the pharmacist, and evidence that Angélique attempted to place herself beyond complicity by faking her own death."

Demonet vouchsafed Alex and Varnas the ghost of a smile. "You both have my grudging admiration," he said. "Ask the solicitor to come in."

The Commissaire acquainted the court-appointed jurist with recent developments. "Perhaps, under the circumstances, you might wish to persuade your client to reexamine his plea of not guilty."

The solicitor, ever affable, replied that these allegations would have to be presented to him en dossier before he could properly evaluate them. That would take time. Meanwhile, he could not possibly predict what his recommendation to his client might be. He suggested they meet again tomorrow at 2 P.M.

The meeting was adjourned. Alex and Varnas met outside in the hall. Tomorrow was Saturday. Alex was scheduled to fly to London at midday. "Go," Varnas said. "I cover for you."

Alex demurred. "You have a wedding dress to buy, a suit to rent, and marriage to contemplate. I'll manage."

Alex returned to his office and tried to reschedule his flight. The six o'clock was the latest he could take and still make Philippa's opening. It was fully booked. He was placed on standby.

He rang off and, without hanging up, dialed Stéphane to give her the good news that she was a free woman. There was no answer. He was surprised at how much he'd looked forward to telling her.

He locked his desk, grabbed his still-unopened overnight bag, and left the office. In the hall he heard the phone ring and hurried back. It was Hippo calling.

Hippo announced that his disco had become infested with India meal moths. They'd hatched in the songbird seed he stored in the former ladies' room. Not only did he have to throw out twenty kilograms of sunflower seed, but he'd had to call the exterminator, who was coming to bomb the place tomorrow. Hippo would have to stay away for twelve hours. Since Alex would be in London, Hippo asked if he could bunk aboard *Le Yacht Club* tomorrow night.

"I may not be in London after all," Alex said, "but you're welcome to stay. I'll leave a key at Pâtisserie Mariette."

He retrieved the overnight bag and took a taxi home.

Le Yacht Club

There was no mail in the box by the boarding ladder. He did his usual docklines inspection and went below.

Unpacking the overnight bag, he discovered a copy of the newspaper *La Dépêche du Midi*, which he forgot he'd bought at the airport in Rodez-Marcillac. He tossed it in the waste-basket next to the chart table.

He put away his toilet kit, showered, climbed into his bunk and, without moving, slept for ten hours.

Pierre-Yves

The solicitor spent the entire morning seeking to secure his client's cooperation in a defense strategy in which Pierre-Yves refused to participate. Pierre-Yves persisted in proclaiming his innocence, even when confronted with the cash withdrawals linking him to Boris Popov. And when the solicitor informed him of Mademoiselle Églantine's miraculous reincarnation, and Stéphane's eyewitness testimony against her, Pierre-Yves withdrew into a contemptuous, aristocratic silence.

The solicitor patiently reviewed his strategy. "I want you to understand that the evidence against Mademoiselle Églantine is good for you. I can now show that you merely provided the weapon, while she actually committed the crime."

Pierre-Yves would not respond.

The solicitor played his final card. "Right now you are in an advantageous position. In a few days you might not be. Right now, I can get you a reduced sentence, possibly even immunity, if you agree to become a witness for the prosecution."

Pierre-Yves examined the cuffs of his prison uniform. "This is *very* boring," he murmured.

"Not so boring as life in prison."

Pierre-Yves sighed. "What does being a witness for the prosecution entail?"

"You tell them what Angélique did . . . and you tell them where she is."

That Saturday was as warm and windless as a day in early spring. Pierre-Yves' sister had not arrived by the time Alex reached the Maison.

The inquiry convened at 2 P.M. Alex wouldn't hear of immunity. He was confident he could apprehend the suspect without resorting to what he considered juridical chicanery to negotiate — not achieve — justice.

However, neither the Commissaire, the Senior Terrorist Investigator's office, nor the Ministry of the Interior were deaf to expediency if it meant saving time and therefore money. Consequently, a deal was struck. Pierre-Yves was not granted immunity, but, in return for his testimony on behalf of the government, his sentence would be reduced from life to fifteen years, with a chance for parole after eight. While this agreement was processed with the case judge, the inquiry was recessed.

This sudden emergence of Angélique Églantine as a prime suspect was not only dizzyingly unforeseen, it placed Alex at a disadvantage. He'd never seen her and knew nothing about her, except that she was an actress. What he would learn about her would be disclosed piecemeal in testimony by witnesses, all of whom would characterize her to suit themselves. Consequently, the portrait would be indistinct, like a composite photograph: eyes from person A, nose from person B, mouth from person C, and a clown's body with one leg shorter than the other. There was no Angélique model to which she could be compared. Even Isabelle and Research had come up short. Who was this person, and what was her motive?

The inquiry reconvened at 4 P.M. Present were Pierre-Yves, his solicitor, Alex, and Commissaire Demonet. In spite of the evidence against him, Pierre-Yves never abandoned his supercilious profile.

He defied his solicitor's counsel from the very beginning. "The decision to murder Virgile de la Pagerie was entirely mine," he stated. His solicitor stared at the ceiling.

"What about Mademoiselle Églantine?" Alex asked.

"No. The idea was all mine."

"And Gus?"

"Don't be dumb," Pierre-Yves responded. "Gus had nothing to do with this. Gus is a poor boy with a sweet streak. No. I made the decision, and Angèle simply went along with it for the fun. I decided that if we were going to do it at all, we were going to have fun.

"At first I toyed with the idea of putting Angélique to work at La Tortosa — that's a restaurant near Barcelona where Delap and she used to stop on the way back to Paris. Angèle has a Catalan waitress she does that can fool anyone."

The Commissaire glanced at Alex. "What does that mean?"

"Simple," Pierre-Yves replied. "The owner of La Tortosa is a bastard. Nobody wants to work for him, and he can't keep help. Angélique dies in April. Four months later, Jacinta Tarragon, who speaks fluent Catalan as well as Spanish, is hired as a waitress. Simple."

"But doesn't the owner of La Tortosa know Angélique?"

"Sure. But he doesn't know Jacinta. Listen. We're not talking about Catherine Deneuve here. We're not talking about a public face. We're talking about a great actress who can transform herself absolutely. You've heard of the play *Intermezzo*?"

Alex nodded.

"In *Intermezzo*, Angèle played Isabel, an ingenue character with a pure soul and the face of a saint. She was the star. After the opening performance, which received twelve curtain calls, Gus gave a party at Narcisse. Angélique wasn't there. Everyone wondered where she was. She was there. She'd got herself up as Jacinta and was waiting on tables, actually serving the cast. No one recognized her. No one. Not even Gus.

"Still, I decided against La Tortosa. I couldn't find the slow-working, odorless, tasteless poison I needed to lace the octopus in green sauce."

The solicitor interrupted. "Excuse me," he said. "I wish to confer with my client." He put his mouth next to Pierre-Yves' ear. "Don't be a fool. Our defense is that she committed the murder and you were merely an accomplice. If you persist in claiming responsibility for every decision leading to the crime, persist in using the pronoun 'I' instead of 'we' or 'she,' our defense will crumble. From now on I want you to emphasize that the murder would not have been possible without her."

Pierre-Yves peered at his solicitor, smiled slightly, and turned to Alex. "The murder would not have been possible without me," he said. "But Angélique came up with the idea of the asthma inhaler."

"Then she knew about his asthma?"

Pierre-Yves gave Alex a look of patient contempt. "No, she didn't know. She just guessed. He had hemorrhoids and asthma and she got lucky and picked asthma. *Of course she knew!* She nursed him for nearly two years!"

"Did she know about Virgile Philadelphie as well?"

"Certainly. Delap didn't keep anything from her."

"Not even Fannois?"

"Especially not Fannois. Fannois was our alibi."

"How?"

"Delap had seven years' worth of material on Fannois. When he fell in love with Angèle, he'd just uncovered his grandfather's deportation order, signed by Fannois, and was about to blow the whistle on the crooked appeals court judge

with the contacts to old Vichy and the Front Patriotique. Angèle said that Delap actually believed his life might be at risk
if he published his Fannois information and he wanted to
make sure the woman he expected to marry was familiar with
the evidence in case anything happened to him. So Fannois
was our alibi."

"What about Délice and Honoré?"

"What about them?"

"Did they know their son's life might be at risk?"

"Yes. In fact we counted on it. Angèle knew the police
would find the evidence against Fannois in the office safe. She
knew Délice and Honoré would confirm the evidence, and
probably bring charges. What she didn't know was whether
Délice and Honoré knew she knew. Consequently, to place
her above suspicion, I decided it would be prudent if she retired to the country, developed anorexia, and died."

"That was your idea?"

"Of course." The solicitor sighed. "And it would have
worked, too, if Fannois, in hiding for seven years, had remained in hiding forever. But the raid on the winery at Château Villars ruined that."

Alex glanced at the Commissaire.

"When I heard Fannois was a graphic artist working for
an ad agency in Toulouse, I was determined to get there
ahead of the police and, one way or another, remove him
from harm's way. But when I learned he'd been in a psycho
ward since 'eighty-three, I headed for Lausanne."

"Go back a bit," Alex said. "You said de la Pagerie and
Angélique were in love."

Pierre-Yves made a small, scowling smile. "I said de la
Pagerie was in love. It happened during *Intermezzo*. Delap
had reached the point where he decided *he* was the reason for

her success. Can you imagine the arrogance? But what, for him, was a transcendent celebration of love and narcissistic gratification was, for her, simply an acting exercise.

"Actually, I can't imagine being in love with Angélique. She couldn't deal with love. She could *act* love. Brilliantly. She could be whatever he wanted: confidante, nurse, mother, whore, muse, virgin. So, you might ask, who was he screwing? Was he screwing the steady nurse who massaged his back and shoulders and cared for him when he had an attack? Or was he screwing the happy hooker who fucked like a snake but never had an orgasm? Or was it the astonished ingenue who, shrieking with pleasure, had her first? Take your pick. Just give her a minute to change.

"She once said to me, 'I don't know which me he loves. And if I did, I wouldn't want to play her every day, much less every night.' "

Alex asked, "What broke off the engagement?"

"Irresistible force meeting immovable object. Method meeting spontaneity. He was a programmed intellectual, a planner, a strategist who was wildly attracted to her spontaneity. At first. But he couldn't measure her. She was a will-o'-the-wisp, as slippery as a pumpkin seed.

"They argued about acting. He believed acting came from within, from the actor's life experience, from reality. She hooted at that. She said acting was deception, nothing more. She had no interest in reality, only the heightened reality of the performance. That was Gus's mantra as well, and it infuriated Delap.

"He broke it off, finally, when she wouldn't listen to him about playing Hedda Gabler in a deconstructionist translation by some Jacques Derrida freak from Prague."

Alex said, "Just a minute. She can't have been all that slippery. They lived together for two years. They planned to marry. He completely remodeled the flat for her. There was even a nursery."

"Yeah."

"Yeah what?"

"During the first year, while *Intermezzo* was still on, Angèle played Isabel eight times a week at the theatre and the rest of the time at his place. She played bewitched and adorable. But after the play closed and she started preparing for Claire, in *The Visit*, things began to come unglued. Plus, she spent more time at my place than at his."

"What do you mean?"

"Her studio is in my house. That's where she prepares. She had to retrain her body to play Claire. She had to decide what voice to use, what walk, what posture, what nose and mouth, makeup, clothes, jewelry. She worked eight, ten hours a day. She couldn't do that at his place."

"I was under the impression she moved in with you after Delap threw her out."

"Who told you that?"

"Gus."

Pierre-Yves smiled. "Poor Gussie."

"When did she move in with you?"

"Five years ago."

Alex blinked. "You lived together for five years? Was . . . was there ever anything —"

"Anything between us? Are you joking? Certainly not. But I understood her. And I made no demands."

"So it didn't bother you when she went to live with de la Pagerie?"

"Why would it? I knew it would be temporary. Besides, she didn't really leave. His place was a pied-à-terre for her near the Luxembourg Gardens. She liked the gardens. Don't imagine that I wanted to kill him out of a jealous rage or something."

The solicitor recoiled. "Monsieur Gastin . . ."

Pierre-Yves ignored him. Alex asked, "Why did you want to kill him?"

"Monsieur Gastin, you do not have to answer that question!" the solicitor cried.

"Will you shut up!" Pierre-Yves turned to Alex. He placed his hand alongside his cheek, like a child trying to remember a sum. "Why did I want to kill him? Principally because of money. I was facing financial ruin backing plays that were routinely eviscerated by this man, and only this man. And because he called me the toilet bowl Chagall. And because I knew Gus would never get his theatre with Delap alive."

"What was Angélique's motive?"

"She didn't have a motive." The solicitor closed the dossier in front of him and shut his eyes. "She viewed her part in the plan as the acting challenge of a lifetime: to deceive the doctor at Seigneur-sous-Tarn, to give a performance in Barcelona less than a metre from the nose of France's most notorious critic, a man with whom she'd had an affair, and fool him completely. She was intuitive, daring, thrilled by the risk, and totally oblivious of the consequences."

"She should have remembered the airlines sketch."

"What?"

"Never mind. You say Gus was out of it?"

"Completely."

"But I still want to know about you and Gus leaving the cast party early."

"I told you I drove Gus home, then went back to the theatre."

"To find the inhaler, not to fix the light plot."

Pierre-Yves shrugged.

"Did you plan to have de la Pagerie die in the theatre?"

"Yes. Except when he was late and Gussie held the curtain, I thought he might have already taken his dose. Obviously he hadn't. Actually, everything went as planned, except I thought he'd have time to put the inhaler back in his shoulder bag. I didn't count on his dropping it."

"Where were the cleaning ladies when you returned to the theatre?"

"Backstage. They hadn't started yet."

"Too bad. If you'd left the inhaler for them to find, you might have made it to Lausanne."

Pierre-Yves shrugged again. "Next time."

Alex checked the tape. In spite of the solicitor's objections that Pierre-Yves was incriminating himself, Alex suspected he was not telling anything like the whole truth. His motive for murder seemed insubstantial, and Angélique's was nonexistent. Come to that, why did he repeatedly incriminate himself? Was he taking the blame? Or the credit?

Alex glanced at his watch. It was 6 P.M. He was going to miss Philippa's opening. But if the price he paid was that the case was concluding, it seemed fair exchange. He turned to the Commissaire. "Any questions?"

"Not at the moment."

Alex turned back to Pierre-Yves. "All right then, monsieur, where is she?"

"I have no idea."

The solicitor leaned over and whispered in his client's ear once more. Pierre-Yves turned to the jurist and said, "Don't be stupid! How can I tell him where she is if I don't know?"

Alex reminded Pierre-Yves that if he withheld this vital information, he would be held in contempt, and could forfeit his reduced sentence.

Pierre-Yves smiled faintly. "Sorry. Nice try. You'll never find her."

Le Yacht Club

As he walked up the Quai de la Charente slightly after 7 P.M. on this relatively balmy September evening, he noticed that *Le Yacht Club*'s masthead and spreader lights were on, and that two men were enjoying drinks on the barge's foredeck. One of the men was a black-suited priest. As Alex came closer, he saw that the other man was Hippo. He'd forgotten Hippo would be spending the night.

"Thought you went to London!" Hippo cried. "Took the liberty of inviting Marcel to supper! Alex, Marcel! Marcel, Alex! This is the man we missed on the canal! Marcel's been to see his Bishop! Have you eaten, Alex? We brought a ton of bifteck! Plenty for all!"

Hippo's jovial mood contrasted with Alex's. As he went below to fetch a drink, he glanced at the ship's clock. Half hour to curtain time at Covent Garden. He poured himself a neat whiskey, climbed back up the companion ladder, and fired up the charcoal grill installed inside the taffrail. As it was now dark and turning chilly, he invited his guests below and attempted to join in their animated conversation, at least until the fire was ready for the steaks.

Alex noticed that the copy of *La Dépêche du Midi* he'd thrown away earlier was open on the chart table. Marcel was talking about someone named Catherine Labouré.

Alex tried to appear interested, but his attention wandered and he found himself gazing at the ship's clock: 7:40, 7:45. Fifteen minutes to go. Then, as if by divination, at exactly ten minutes to eight, the phone rang. Alex nearly spilled his drink. He answered.

"Where are you?" Philippa asked.

He explained.

"I've never had a debut, not even when I was in the corps, without you in the audience. I'm terrified."

"You're supposed to be terrified. I'd be worried if you weren't."

"This is different. Terrified without you here isn't the same as terrified with you here."

"Have you seen Stéphane?"

"Yes."

"Is your mother there?"

"No. The Marchioness is here, but no Angela. Alex?"

"What?"

"Tell me you love me."

"I love you. And I have absolute confidence in you. You'll be fine."

"No, no. Say 'Philippa, I love you.' "

"Philippa, I love you."

She exhaled. "Okay." She paused. "Tell Varnas I'll be at his wedding on Monday. But I have to be back here Monday night. There are three more performances." She suddenly giggled. "Varnas and Madame Roget! It's bliss! I can't wait!"

Alex heard orchestral music through the phone. She said, "Got to go. Wish me luck."

"Good luck, chérie."

"Thanks. I'm better now." She kissed the phone. "See you Monday."

He rejoined Hippo and Marcel and made an effort at conviviality.

Marcel was referring to yesterday's *La Dépêche du Midi* and speculating on some sort of coincidence. Alex climbed the ladder to check the charcoal grill. From the cockpit he heard Marcel say "Rue du Bac."

He placed the grill on top of the nearly ready coals and tried to remember where he'd recently seen or heard those words. He went below to oil and pepper the steaks.

He asked, "What is Rue du Bac?"

Marcel replied, "The cloister of Rue du Bac, in Paris, was the site of the Virgin's appearance to a nun named Catherine Labouré, in 1830. It was the first such miracle to be acknowledged by church authorities, and led to the dogma of the Immaculate Conception by Pius XI in 1854."

"Oh," Alex said. And then he remembered where he'd seen "Rue du Bac." It had been in the title of one of Angélique's books on religious miracles — *The Third Secret of Fatima, The History of La Salette, The Miracle at Rue du Bac,* and some other volume in a foreign language.

Hippo said, "We were struck by the coincidence, that's all."

"What coincidence?"

"Well, I fished your copy of *La Dépêche du Midi* out of your wastebasket to read while I waited for Marcel. When he arrived, I left it open on the table while I prepared our drinks. He spotted this ad with the name of the nun Catherine Labouré in it. That's what stimulated the discussion."

Alex glanced at the page in the second section of the paper devoted to activities in the département of Aude. On it was a half-page advertisement describing a sound-and-light production of Arthur Honneger's oratorio *Joan of Arc at the Stake,* produced by Windows-on-the-Theatre at the ruin of Le Château de Saissac in the Aude village of Saissac; two performances only, 8 P.M. Saturday 21 September (tonight) and Sunday 22 September (tomorrow night), starring Mademoiselle Catherine Labouré as Joan.

In the background of the ad was a shadowy silhouette of the ruined mediaeval château, the model of which Alex and

Varnas had examined a few days ago on the drafting table at Pierre-Yves' studio.

Acting instantaneously on the assumption that Catherine Labouré was Angélique Églantine, Alex made the decision to go to Saissac immediately. However, it was too late to obtain a police or charter-aircraft to fly him down tonight. He'd have to make the arrangements tomorrow.

He remarked on the relative commonness of the name Labouré and casually changed the subject so as not to alert Hippo's finely tuned attennae. He subsequently climbed into the cockpit and grilled the steaks.

During dinner, Hippo delivered a lecture on his sixteenth-century arquebus matchlock smoothbore musket that was both informative and amusing. After Courvoisier and conversation, Marcel departed on his BMW motorcycle. It was ten o'clock. A few minutes later, Hippo retired for the night to Philippa's stateroom.

Alex stood in the middle of the saloon and rehearsed the argument he would need to persuade the Commissaire to give him an aéroplane tomorrow. After several run-throughs, he called the Commissaire at home. There was no answer. He didn't bother trying the Maison. It was Saturday night. The Commissaire was out for the evening, possibly for the weekend.

He lay in his bunk in the dark and listened to the No. 7 métro rumble under the canal. His last thought before sleep was that it might be impossible to get an aéroplane on Sunday.

Sometime during the night, he dreamt the phone was ringing. This was odd, because he was eleven years old and collecting mussels for his mother off the pilings of an abandoned pier at Tréboul, outside Douarnenez. He knew there was no phone on the pier. And, if there had been, the call would not have been for him because he never received any calls when he was eleven. Consequently, he ignored the ringing and continued picking mussels.

He arose next morning at 7 and noticed a message on the answering machine. Philippa had called from London at 4 A.M., GMT. She sounded a little drunk.

"Why aren't you home in bed at this hour? Don't answer the question. Instead, listen to my notices:

" 'Miss Watten elevates Bournonville to a new level of sensuality' — *The London Times.*

" 'Miss Watten's formidable bravura, always within the constraints of the Bournonville style, is nevertheless remarkable in its carnality' — *The Guardian.*

" 'A standing ovation for this latest Gallic dish! Darling Philippa Watten captivates as Teresina' — *The Sun.*

"Not bad, huh? Nicky got most of the kudos, but then he has the best part. At least they didn't ignore me. Actually, I was divine. By the way, Nicky took one look at Stéphane and offered her a job in Copenhagen, but he didn't say as what. Love you. See you Monday."

Alex erased the message, reset the machine, and called Varnas at home to alert him to the Catherine Labouré story. But he hung up after the first ring. Varnas and Madame were undoubtedly at early mass.

25

Varnas

MADAME ROGET stood in the first pew, holding his hand. They had both been to confession the day before. This Sunday was to be their final communion before the marriage.

Varnas was certain that no two people had approached the state of matrimony with more impeccable credentials than he and madame. The fact that he was climbing the wall did not diminish that fact. However, while he floated on a nimbus of virtue, he remained vigilant to anything that might threaten their serenity.

He was therefore mildly discomfited when, during communion at the altar rail, when he was about to receive the body and blood of Christ, his beeper went off. He had the impression, just for a second, that madame pretended she didn't know him. She seemed to have something in her eye. He switched off the pager, swallowed the Host, crossed himself, genuflected, and tiptoed past the sacristy to the sexton's office, where there was a phone.

He called the Maison. The assignment desk gave him a

mobile phone number to call that he recognized as Joëlle's. She was still on stakeout at Pierre-Yves' house in Rue Marbeau.

She said, "A red Ferrari with Swiss plates just went through the gates into the allée next to his house. It had a remote wireless gate-opener. The car's inside now and the gates are locked. I didn't get a good look at the driver."

"Probably Pierre-Yves' sister," Varnas said. "She —" He broke off in mid-phrase. "I call you back, Joëlle. Keep close surveillance."

Alex phoned Gus at home. The male nurse, Arnaud, answered after the third ring.

"Good morning," Varnas said cheerfully. "I have the good news."

Arnaud whispered hoarsely, "Do you know what time it is?"

"Seven-fifty," Varnas replied.

"It's the middle of the fucking night!" Arnaud hissed. "Gus is asleep. I was asleep. Jesus Christ!" Varnas had never heard such swearing in church. "What's the good news?"

"We find Pierre-Yves. He is safe."

"I'll tell Gus."

"Good. But please, for police record, we need phone number of Pierre-Yves' sister in Lausanne."

"Hold on." After a moment, Arnaud supplied the number. "And don't call again before ten."

Varnas dialed the international code and number, and carded the call to the Maison. After a few rings, a professional woman's voice answered.

"Hospice d'Ouchy."

Varnas asked to speak to Mademoiselle Gastin.

"One moment, please." The same voice came back immediately. "I regret, monsieur, but Mademoiselle Gastin has just gone down to chemotherapy. Is there a message?"

"No message," Varnas said. "Thank you."

Rue Marbeau

Without flashing lights or claxons, the Maison closed off Pierre-Yves' street at both Rue Pergolèse and Boulevard de l'Amiral-Bruix. Maison techniciens noiselessly sprang the electronic gate. Varnas and Joëlle, with two men from Special Weapons and Tactics, entered the back of the house from the allée. Varnas wrinkled his nose. He smelled a curious odour of hot butter mixed with lavender water. He walked into the kitchen. There, standing at the stove, frying an egg, was the wardrobe mistress from the Théâtre Bakoledis.

The Maison

Alerted by Varnas's too early call, Gus descended on Rue des Saussaies with a bag of fresh clothes and an order of Chinese takeout food for Pierre-Yves. Assuming that his friend was in custody for some minor infraction for which Gus vaguely expected to post bail, he demanded to see Chef-Inspecteur Grismolet or Inspecteur Varnas. He was told to wait.

While he sat, fuming and purloining bits of egg roll on a bench in the entrance hall, he was greeted by the spectacle of his wardrobe mistress being herded into the premises, shackled to a young policewoman, and escorted by several armed constables. Varnas followed at a distance. Seeing her employer and assuming he was there on her behalf, the woman opened her mouth to speak, but was hurried along to the Duty Officer's desk for booking. Gus, scandalized that not one, but two, of his colleagues were in police custody, leapt to his feet and shouted, "Release that woman at once!"

Varnas came over and touched his arm. "Follow me, Gus," he said gently, and led him outside into the sunshine.

Leaning against the ornate, freshly scrubbed sandstone wall of the Ministry of the Interior, Varnas quietly reprised the story of Pierre-Yves, Angélique, and the death of Virgile de la Pagerie.

At first, out of habit and instinct, Gus challenged, defended, and counterattacked. He refused to believe that Angélique was alive. He had attended her burial. But, when it became clear that no amount of face-shaking outrage would alter the fact that his two closest friends were culpable and would eventually be confined forever for their profligacy, he fell silent. He placed the bag of clothes and Chinese takeout on the sidewalk and turned his face to the wall. Varnas left him that way.

"I hope there is Théâtre Auguste for you some day," Varnas said, and went inside.

As Alex had conducted the interrogation of Pierre-Yves, Varnas, believing the wardrobe woman might be an accomplice, wished to give Alex the opportunity to interview her as well. He called *Le Yacht Club*. Alex was already out. Varnas directed the assignment desk to radio-page him. He called back within five minutes.

Varnas said, "Pierre-Yves' Ferrari is here, but driver is not Pierre-Yves' sister. Driver is wardrobe mistress from Théâtre Bakoledis. She says her name is Véronique."

"Véronique. Is that the Véronique the mayor of Seigneur-sous-Tarn mentioned was Angélique's companion?"

"Probably. She says she is Angèle's dresser for many years now and now works for Gus and Pierre-Yves. Do you wish to interrogate?"

"Can't. I'm trying to rent an aéroplane."

"Where are you going, Alexei? Tomorrow is wedding day."

Alex outlined the Catherine Labouré story and the need to go to Saissac. He promised he'd be back in time for the ceremony whether Catherine Labouré was or was not Angélique.

"How much to rent aéroplane?" Varnas asked.

"Six thousand an hour."

Varnas whistled. "I hope for your sake Catherine Labouré is Angélique." He rang off.

Véronique

To avoid the possibility of another domestic crisis over the lavender water, Varnas requested that the wardrobe mistress undergo a shower and shampoo and be issued fresh cotton prison garb.

This took place under the vigilant eye of Joëlle, now an active candidate in the Sûreté Inspecteur-trainee Program. When the bathing ritual was complete, Joëlle brought Véronique to the holding room where Varnas was waiting.

"We meet again," Varnas said pleasantly. Véronique took a seat across the table. "Do you wish coffee?"

"I only wish to be done with this nightmare and to get out of these convict pajamas."

"Of course."

Joëlle removed the handcuffs and left.

"Before we begin, mademoiselle, please understand that Pierre-Yves already confesses to murder and implicates Angélique Églantine beyond reasonable doubt."

Véronique hesitated. "Has Angélique been arrested?"

"Not yet. It is only question of time."

"I see."

"I tell you this so your testimony does not suffer from the creative hanky-panky. Okeh?"

"Whatever you say."

"Good. Now, during your long association with Angélique as dresser and companion, are you ever aware that she and Pierre-Yves plan to commit this crime?"

She stared at the tabletop.

"Take your time."

"I was never aware of it — until after it was over."

"That is good."

"When I helped the mayor of Seigneur place her body in the coffin and watched him nail the lid shut, I thought I would never see her again." Véronique's eyes glistened. "I wanted to die with her. A short while later, after the mayor left the villa, Pierre-Yves arrived with the mannequin. When he pried open the lid I couldn't imagine what he was doing. But it didn't matter because she opened her eyes and smiled at me. The rest of the afternoon was a blur.

"When we removed her from the box and replaced her with the mannequin and the bricks, I of course knew something was up and that whatever it was, I'd been left out of it. But I didn't ask and I didn't care. I was too happy. Later, Pierre-Yves said something about a project they had in mind, a joke really, which made it essential that certain people believe Angèle was dead."

"But you never suspect that project is murder."

"Not until I read the paper the morning after *Eurydice* opened."

"That is good. However, when we meet in theatre wardrobe room couple nights later, you know already who kills Delap?"

"I suspected, yes."

"That is bad. Because you are withholding the information."

"Inspecteur, I have found that withholding information, like lying, is frequently more beneficial to those you love than telling the truth. I saved my parents' marriage, such as it was, by not telling my mother that my father was sleeping with her best friend. So don't imagine I would betray Angélique by not withholding information if I thought it would help her."

"As long as you understand it doesn't help her now."

She shrugged.

"So. Who is this Angélique you care for so deeply? What sort of person is she?"

"The question is not applicable. Angélique is not exactly a person. She is an acting instrument, with perfect pitch, extraordinary sensibility, superb muscle control and coordination, who functions only when she has a role to play."

"Theatrical role?"

"Usually."

"And when she has no role to play, who is she?"

"Well, she's this great European artist, obsessed with technique, with body and language disciplines. When she's between roles, she enters her training regime. She tunes the instrument, physically and aesthetically. She takes class. She studies. If she will do a play of Racine, she studies the painting, literature, architecture, clothing, music, and politics of the period in which she will perform. It tells her how to breathe, to walk, to turn her head. If she will do a play in translation, she will learn enough of the author's native tongue to read the play in the original, whether it's Turgenev, Tang Xiansu, or Terrence McNally."

"Really? Pierre-Yves attributes her success to spontaneity. All this training doesn't sound very spontaneous."

"Spontaneity only comes with practice. Actually, 'spontaneity' is Pierre-Yves' word for her. I prefer 'versatility.' I once
watched her play Phèdre at a matinée and, an hour later,
convulse her dinner companions with an impression of
Nancy Reagan trying to get Arnold Schwarzenegger high on
pot."

"Yes. But, at some point, after all this, she has to go home,
do laundry, shop for groceries, go to toilet, sleep, get up, and
look in the mirror. When she looks in mirror, who is she?"

"The question is N.A. She is no one."

"Out to lunch?"

"No, no. Never out to lunch. When she looks in the mirror, it is to decide what to do with what she sees. What she
sees is a blank canvas waiting to be filled. Surely, it's better to
start a painting with a blank canvas than with a canvas that
has already something on it. Listen, when you think of a per-
former or entertainer, you press a button and out pops Mi-
chael Jackson or Johnny Hallyday. They're personalities.
She's not. If you passed her on the street, you wouldn't recognize her. Offstage, she's completely inconspicuous, even insignificant. She's the antithesis of personality.

"Actually, personality is a hurdle for most actors. That's
why so many try not to have one. Laurence Olivier, for in-
stance, or Lena Olin, or Isabelle Adjani. Olin says her ambi-
tion, as an actor, is to have no self at all. Adjani claims that
the more she tries to be herself, the lonelier she becomes.

"But to answer your question, I took care of her laundry
and Pierre-Yves took care of her groceries. Until she moved in
with Delap."

"And then?"

"He tried to domesticate her, to mold her to his specifica-
tions, to destroy the qualities in her that attracted him in the

first place. Why do men do that? Would you believe he tried to force her into analysis? Analysis, for Angélique, would have been fatal."

"Why?"

"Because she doesn't want to know who she is, only what she can become. She believes that art and life are indistinguishable. He, on the other hand, believed that if she couldn't distinguish between art and life, and didn't know who she was, she'd never be able to portray a character truthfully. What he never understood was that his truth wasn't her truth. Her truth is stage truth, where any role for her is possible if she understands the circumstances. It doesn't matter who she is. 'It's not *who* I am!' she says, 'but what I *do!* After I get the nose right!' "

Varnas guessed this was getting closer to the reality of Angélique. For if art and life were indistinguishable, so were shadow and substance, fact and fiction. He asked, "What role does she play when she switches inhalers at Barcelona airport?"

Véronique thought for a moment. "A supremely talented character actor up to Molière mischief."

"Does she know it is deadly poison she places in shoulder bag?"

"Again, the question is N.A. The *moment* engaged her. The *performance* received her attention. I'm sure she brought the same intensity to the character of the airport attendant that she brought to Joan or Claire Zachanassian. Whether the inhaler contained cyanide or celery salt was probably a matter of complete indifference to her."

"Then she is monstrous!"

"No. She's not monstrous. She can play monstrous. Or sweet. Or gentle. Whatever the role requires."

Varnas was becoming exasperated with these theoretical

responses. He said, "Mademoiselle Véronique, you tell me everything about Angélique but *why!* Why does she kill Virgile de la Pagerie? And don't say because he gives her bad review."

Véronique sighed and looked away. "Very well." She took a deep breath. "One of her favorite plays is *Intermezzo,* by Jean Giraudoux. And her favorite speech from that play is the second act speech by the character of the Ghost. She says that speech saved her from committing the folly of marrying de la Pagerie. In the scene, the Ghost speaks of young girls." Véronique recited softly.

"Seated at their windows with a book in the lamplight, a pool of radiance between shadow and shadow; like flowers in summer; in winter like thoughts of flowers, they dispose themselves so gracefully in the world of men that we are convinced we see in them not the childhood of humanity, but its supreme expression. Between the world of the young girl and the world of the spirit, the wall seems no more than a gossamer; one would say that at any moment, through the soul of a girl, the infinite could flow into the finite and possess it utterly.

"But all at once, the man appears. The young girls watch him intently. He has found some tricks with which to enhance his worth in their eyes. He stands on his hind legs in order to shed the rain better and to hang medals on his chest. He swells his biceps. They quail before him with hypocritical admiration, trembling with such fear as not even a tiger inspires, not realizing that of all the carnivorous animals, this biped alone has ineffective teeth. And as they gaze at him, the windows of the soul, through which once they saw the myriad colours of the outer world, cloud over, grow opaque, and, in that moment, the story is over . . . and life begins.

"The pleasure of the bed begins. And the pleasure of the table. And the habit of pleasure. And the pleasure of jealousy . . . and the pleasure of cruelty . . . and the pleasure of suffering. And, last of all, the pleasure of indifference. So, little by little, the pearl loses its lustre and long before it dies, it is dead."

Véronique exhaled and turned back to Varnas. "In September of 'eighty-four, after submitting to repeated recrimination and abuse over the direction her career was taking, over *Hedda,* over *Rachel,* she taped the Ghost's speech, left the cassette on Delap's desk with a note, and moved out."

"Where to?"

"To Pierre-Yves'!"

"And?"

"Delap came home late. When he listened to the tape and realized what she was telling him, his ego suffered a stroke. After spending a fortune on renovating the flat, after publicly announcing his intentions, this humiliation at the hands of a woman whom he thought he could control, and plainly considered his intellectual inferior, was more than he could deal with. He went berserk. He drove to Pierre-Yves', broke into the house, and dragged her out of bed. He nearly killed her. If she hadn't been in such superb condition, he would have. He tried to strangle her. He injured her vocal chords, injured the instrument she'd spent half her life perfecting."

"Where is Pierre-Yves during all this?"

"In Lausanne."

"Does Angélique bring charges?"

"No."

"Why not?"

"Well . . . denial. She wanted to pretend it never happened. Ask any battered woman why she attacks the flic that comes to arrest the man who beat her."

"But that's insane! She has no reason to protect him."

"She wasn't protecting him. She was protecting herself; and trying to stay out of the newspapers." Véronique was silent for a moment. She peered off. "Angèle never fully recovered before she undertook *Rachel* weeks later. That was a mistake. She should have postponed. She wasn't up to the part and she knew it, which made matters worse. Then, when *Rachel* opened, and he nearly killed her again, this time in the press —" She didn't finish the sentence.

"Are you saying that it is Angélique's idea to murder him?"

"No. It was Pierre-Yves' idea."

"And what was his reason?"

Véronique hesitated then gazed directly at Varnas. "Reason? He was in love with her."

Varnas stared. "Pierre-Yves in love with Angélique?"

"Yes."

"Nowhere in his testimony does he suggest such thing!"

"That's because he's technically gay. He didn't want to sabotage his credibility in the theatre community, and of course he didn't want Gus to know. I hope Gus never does."

"Dear God! Is Angélique in love with Pierre-Yves?"

"No. Angélique only loves me."

"You? You are lovers?"

"No. I'm her mother."

26

Saissac

A FEW MINUTES after 8 P.M., Alex left Orly airport in a highwing Mitsubishi Marquise turboprop. It was a police aircraft provided by the Senior Terrorist Investigator's office at the last minute. Alex's destination was the small aérodrome at Castelnaudary, on the Canal du Midi, where he'd rented the hire-cruiser *Sirocco* for his and Philippa's not-holiday. Castelnaudary was also the home of Thérèse Chalant, and now of Marie-Rose Fournier and Vercingétorix. The village of Saissac was scarcely twenty kilometres to the north, in the foothills of the Montagne Noir. Alex sat in the right front seat, next to the pilot, with his arms locked tightly across his chest to forestall the temptation to seize the control yoke and fly to the moon.

Before departure, he'd phoned Varnas to hear about Véronique's testimony.

Varnas reviewed the salient points, particularly as they contradicted Pierre-Yves' characterization of events and motives. He added, "Pierre-Yves has big secret, Alex."

"What's that?"

"He is in love with Angélique."

"Well, that's a surprise. Does Gus know?"

"Véronique hopes not. Incidentally, Véronique is Angèle's maman."

That fact, though unexpected, did not seem significant to Alex, until later. He said, "See you in church," and rang off.

The Mitsubishi landed at Castelnaudary a little before 10. An Aérospatiale *Aloutte* helicopter, from Police Air Wing, Marseille, waited on the ramp, its whirling rotor reflecting, stroboscopically, the landing lights of the taxiing turboprop. Alex transferred to the chopper and was airborne in minutes.

A few pinpoints of bright amber moved below, the moon momentarily reflected in the surface of the canal, and Castelnaudary fell behind. They flew six hundred metres above the pale darkness of the vineyards, broken here and there by a light from the odd farmhouse.

After a few minutes, the pilot tapped Alex on the arm and pointed ahead to a rectangle of light on the horizon. Occasionally this bright object appeared to dance, to change in intensity and colour, like a distant television screen. As the chopper drew closer, the expanding light frame took on shape and texture. Spidery ruined towers appeared, suspended above the frame. The frame became a stage, ablaze with light. Splashes of yellow, black, and crimson became costumed chorus figures on several levels in the background. And what started as a solitary speck in the foreground became a female figure, gowned in white, trussed to a stake in Pierre-Yves' tilted clearing.

The entire stage picture abruptly ascended and disappeared behind a stand of evergreen trees as the *Alouette* descended and landed in a pasture at the edge of the village. The landing site was illuminated by the headlights of a police vehicle with a chauffeur and two CRS officers aboard.

Within minutes, they were at the scene of the presentation.

The château ruin and stage faced a semicircular hillside, which formed a natural amphitheatre. The audience sat on seats built into the hillside, while the space between stage and audience was occupied by the orchestra and conductor. At the top of the hillside, a short distance from where the police vehicle had stopped, was a projection booth, which was the control centre for the directeur and his light and sound equipment.

Now, from this booth, a small, furious man, the directeur, appeared. He ran up to the police car and kicked the door.

"Animals!" he hissed. "Why didn't you land on the stage? Instead of ruining the show, you could have killed the actors!"

He reminded Alex of Gus, only smaller. "Idiots!" he cried and rushed back to his booth.

The intrusion didn't seem to have distracted the audience that much. The oratorio, now entering its final moments, received their solemn attention.

The stage was bathed in orange light and smoke. Onto the gray strips of transparent scrim material that now fell between the stage portals and the amphitheatre, a projection of astonishingly realistic flame appeared and grew, crackling and sparkling.

The chorus sang:

> *No one has greater love*
> *Than he who gives his life*
> *For those he loves!*

The orchestra built to full crescendo. Joan, at the stake, her hands unshackled by God's love, her arms raised and crossed at the wrists, appeared to be consumed by flames. The lights behind the scrim slowly faded. As the final notes were sounded, only the flames projected on the front of the scrim were visible. The performance concluded, and the audience roared its approval.

The chauffeur drove the vehicle down an access road and round the back of the château to a wooden staircase that led up to the rear of the stage. He parked next to the ambulance, required by law at all outdoor sports and theatrical events. Alex and the CRS officers exited the vehicle as the cast and conductor, assembled above, began to acknowledge the audience's applause.

Mademoiselle Labouré took a bow with Frère Dominique, took another with Frère Dominique and the conductor, another with the entire company, and, finally, a triumphant solo bow to cheers and applause. But after the solo bow, as she straightened up, she suddenly faltered, teetered, and crumpled to the stage. There was a collective gasp from the audience, followed by a stunned silence.

Members of the cast surrounded her. Someone shouted, "Don't touch her! . . . Stand back! . . . Give her air!"

Alex followed the medical team as they ran up the stairway to where the inert actress lay on her back, eyes staring. The medical technicien knelt beside her. He unfastened the top of her white tunic, spotless except for a makeup stain on the collar. He examined her for a moment, then sat back on his heels.

"Get a stretcher," he said quietly. "She has severe first-degree burns."

They evacuated her in the *Alouette* to the small hospital clinic in Castelnaudary where she was declared in guarded condition. Guarded indeed. Believing her entirely capable of stopping her heart again, or of disappearing before their eyes, Alex stationed a nurse on one side of her bed to monitor her pulse, and a police matron on the other.

He spoke to the much-chastened directeur and a representative of Windows-on-the-Theatre. Both appeared to be in semishock.

They established that Catherine Labouré had been active with Windows and ATP (Association du Théâtre Populaire) since May. She had played small character roles to begin with but displayed such a range of style that, when they planned the Honneger, they were unanimous in their decision to cast her as Joan.

Alex asked if she had been associated with them continuously since May.

"Yes, apart from a two-week period prior to rehearsals for the present production when she went on holiday in Spain. And while she was away, she worked on scenery and costume design."

"She said she designed the scenery and costumes?"

"It was a collaborative effort," the directeur said. "She supplied the elevations and costume plates, and we built the production in our shops here. She is an extraordinary talent."

"Yes," Alex said. "Extraordinary. But she is not Catherine Labouré. I hope you have an understudy, because this Joan of Arc is under arrest."

At midnight, the physician in charge of the clinic stated that he did not have the facilities to care for the patient if her pulse rate and temperature became further elevated. He urged Alex to arrange for her transfer to the Burn Unit in Marseille or to Paris.

Alex contacted the Senior Terrorist Investigator's office once again. At I A.M., an air-conditioned ambulance plane, just out of the shop after a two-thousand-hour overhaul, was flown in from Tarbes. They airlifted Angélique to Paris and transferred her to the Hôpital Americain in Neuilly.

Though blood tests revealed no sign of infection, she received broad-spectrum antibiotics, tetanus toxoid, and intravenous fluids. The prognosis was neither good nor bad.

Indeed, there was no prognosis. They had no idea what was wrong with her.

Alex got back to the Maison at 6 A.M. With the wedding only four hours away, he still had much to do, and all without sleep.

He went directly down to the holding cell facility and ordered the police matron to wake Véronique. After an interval of ten minutes, she shuffled in wearing a prison-issue cotton wrapper and slippers, and smelling of toothpaste and mouthwash.

"Sorry to wake you," he said. "I need your help."

She didn't respond.

"Before we arrested your daughter last night, she collapsed onstage with severe first-degree burns."

Véronique nodded. "She always gets burns when she plays Joan. They usually disappear in time for the next performance."

"There won't be a next performance."

"That may be a problem. Where is she?"

"In a private room in the Hôpital Americain. She's lying on her back in bed. Her eyes are closed. She's placed her hands together on her chest, in prayer, like a stone saint recumbent on a catafalque. The burns have not disappeared, and she's running a temperature of forty-one degrees centigrade."

"I can't help you."

"Why?"

"She's burning. She's burning because she's your prisoner. And she's still playing Joan."

"But it's an act!"

"Of course it's an act! She's an actor!"

27

Orly

WITH TIME RUNNING OUT, Alex reached *Le Yacht Club,* showered and changed. He experienced a near fatal encounter with his bow tie, but after the fourth try, succeeded in creating a reasonable facsimile of the classic butterfly bend.

Now, in bright morning sunlight, utterly exhausted and feeling conspicuous in his midnight-blue tuxedo at 8 A.M., he drove the Bug to the airport to meet the early flight from Heathrow. While the distraction of Angélique's arrest had temporarily diminished his Philippa-Stéphane anxiety, it resurfaced now.

Philippa made her arrival-lounge entrance all in mauve: a short-jacketed mauve Chanel suit, suede pumps, and a wide, flat-brimmed straw hat. She looked like a film star. A red-faced older man in a macintosh carried her mauve makeup case. She demolished him at the gate with a piano keyboard smile, allowed him a peck on the cheek, and sent him away, mumbling.

When she saw Alex, she put down the case, removed her

hat, and waited. At that moment, the exhaustion and tightness around his shoulders loosened and slid down his back like melted butter. He took her in his arms, kissed her hair, her face, her lips, and her face again.

"More, please," she whispered, and clung to him. A tiny, gray-haired Oriental woman took a flash photo of them with her Fuji automatique.

"Who was your distinguished escort?" Alex asked, as he maneuvered the Bug out of the airport.

"Haven't the faintest idea," she said. "He's a commodity trader in cocoa, from Bristol. His wife's name is Gemma and they have six children." She paused as they reached the A6. "Stéphane sends her love and says good-bye."

Alex blinked. "Is she off to Copenhagen then?"

"Alex. If she can't do Brussels with Maurice Béjart, she can't do Copenhagen with Nicky Blixen. No. Yesterday she flew directly from London to Antibes, where she expects to stay for a while." Philippa glanced at Alex's profile. "She's changed. She's subdued . . . and thoughtful. And I don't want to talk about it."

"Okay."

She paused again. "Incidentally, I didn't sleep with Nicky."

"Why not? I thought it was programmed."

"Well, it was expected. Actually, we sort of tried. But I got the hiccups. He was terribly offended."

"I don't want to talk about it."

She smiled and squeezed his arm. "Listen, I meant to tell you when I phoned. Olivia came to the opening."

"Olivia?"

"Rudy's assistant. She said I don't have to be back for *Nutcracker* rehearsals until the fourteenth of October. Which means I have two weeks off. Which means we can still do the Canal du Midi, if you can get off. Can you get off?"

"Depends on Angélique."

Philippa frowned. "Who the hell is Angélique?"

Église St-Charles de Monceau

The wedding took place in a small side chapel of the church.

If there had been a major federal crime committed in Paris that Monday morning, the perpetrators would have had a fair chance of success without detection, since all but a handful of Inspecteur-trainees and assistant section heads were at the wedding, including Isabelle, Joëlle, Alex, Biramoule, Varnas, of course, and the Commissaire, with his wife on one side of him and a striking, young red-headed woman on the other. This woman received Isabelle's undivided attention throughout the ceremony.

Also present was a substantial cross-section of the Paris underworld, petty-crime division, all of whom, at one time or another, had served as informants for Varnas. This lot kept their coats on.

In the first pew, on the bride's side, sat Suzanne, of Chez Suzanne, wearing a bright red dress, a bright silver hat, and all of her jewelry. She resembled a fire engine and beamed proprietorially from the moment she sat down to the moment she left.

Behind her sat a group of tenants from 8, Rue Georges-Berger, whose gift to the bride was the collection and disposal of the building's refuse for one week.

When all were seated, Varnas and Alex appeared at the altar rail with the priest. A violin duo played the wedding march as Philippa, carrying daisies and carnations, entered the tiny chapel followed by the veiled bride, radiant in a fitted, white brocade gown decorated with tiny pearls. She walked on the arm of Chef-Inspecteur Hippolyte Maurice Ludovic du Temple (Hippo), who, due to the absence of a mature male relative, had volunteered to give the bride away.

During the ceremony, Clothilde never took her eyes from Varnas's face, not when she received the priest's challenge, not during prayers, not during the ring exchange, nor when she knelt for the final blessing. When Philippa removed the veil, and Clothilde folded herself, at last, into her new husband's embrace, the assembled congregation, aware that something tangible had occurred in their presence, collectively sighed. Suzanne applauded. The violin duo played Mendelssohn.

The wedding was followed by a sitdown luncheon reception at Chez Suzanne. The café-bar was closed to its regular clientele on Mondays. This was Suzanne's gift to the bride and groom, and she outdid herself: hors d'oeuvres variés, saumon fumé, soupe aux poirots, coq au vin, salade verte-cresson, tartelette aux framboises à la crème fraiche, and fromages variés, with champagne and three kinds of wine.

Isabelle, giddy on champagne, encountered Alex during the interval between the end of lunch and the moment when the bride and groom were scheduled to depart.

"The smashing redhead with the Commissaire?"

"What about her?"

"We had it wrong. She's his wife's daughter by her late first husband. Ex-flower child, estranged from her mother until Demonet undertook her rehab. When I gave two to one he had a trick, I lost six hundred francs. But my wager that she was under thirty-five got me back two hundred twelve. And the eight to five he'd never shag her got me back five hundred two. So I'm one hundred fourteen francs ahead." She drained her champagne glass as people began to throw rice. "Where are the Varnases going on their honeymoon?"

"Home to bed."

The Maison

Philippa returned to London on the mid-afternoon flight. She'd be back in Paris on Thursday. If Angélique's condition somehow improved and she were arraigned by then, Alex and Philippa could fly south and pick up *Sirocco* in time to get under way by the weekend. At the moment, it seemed unlikely.

Earlier the tabloids had sniffed out the Angélique story. There were photographs of the famous gold statue of Joan of Arc in the cathedral at Reims, lithographs of the actress Rachel as Joan, photos of Ingrid Bergman as Joan, of Siobhan McKenna, Julie Harris, and Angélique as Joan. Joan was suddenly back in fashion. Soon there would be T-shirts and tote bags. Heretofore unknown archivists of the Hundred Years War were interviewed on television for their arcane insight into the phenomenon of the Maid, executed for heresy in 1431, exonerated in 1456, declared venerable in 1904, and canonized a saint in 1920.

Alex, however, was convinced that Angélique's comatose condition was a stunt, and that when she finally understood the circumstances of her situation, she would drop the pretense and yield.

He was therefore not prepared for the call he received from the Hôpital Americain when he returned to the Maison at 3:30. The hospital said that Angélique's cardiac status had been continuously monitored electronically since her admission to hospital.

Here it comes, Alex thought. She's stopped her heart again.

"This afternoon," the hospital spokesperson said, "Mademoiselle Églantine's pulse increased to one hundred forty, at which time the cardiac monitor showed a sharp elevation of the ST segment. At 3:04 P.M., the entire QRS wave complex collapsed. The cause of death is now characterized as radical pyrexia of unknown origin, with symptoms of fatal heat stroke."

Alex didn't believe a word of it. He drove immediately to the hospital and took the elevator to Angélique's floor. As there was no one at the nurse's station, he went to her room. The bed had been stripped and the room was being ventilated. The window was open. The electrocardiograph had been removed but the IV still stood by the bed, the inert tubing swaying slightly in a maverick breeze that ruffled the gauze curtains at the window.

The floor matron appeared. Alex learned that Angélique was already in the morgue, but, due to a mixup by a student nurse, the wrong identification had accompanied the body downstairs. The student nurse heatedly denied the error and face-saving charges and counter-charges followed. As a consequence, the coroner insisted on a positive identification before he would sign the death certificate.

Angélique's identification had somehow got attached to the corpse of an elderly Asian woman named Charan Pornthip, while Charan Pornthip's identification tag had got attached to a middle-aged Caucasian woman. Alex viewed both corpses. Although he had never seen Angélique except as the airline flight attendant and as Joan of Arc, he was certain that neither of these women was she. He sent for Véronique to make a positive identification.

Véronique arrived from the Maison, accompanied by Joëlle. She seemed remarkably detached. Nevertheless, she requested a sedative, and was given ten milligrams of Valium.

Alex stood next to her for the viewing. Véronique said that neither the Asian woman wearing Angélique's identification nor the Caucasian woman wearing Charan Pornthip's identification was Angélique. So far so good. She was then shown three other recently deceased females. They were identified as Françoise Crusson, Madeleine Durant, and Nicole Zeller. When the morgue attendant drew back the sheet from the face of Nicole Zeller, Véronique closed her eyes and quietly wept. The identification had been made. Alex said nothing and sent Véronique back to the Maison with Joëlle.

Thus, for the moment, Nicole Zeller became Angélique, the middle-aged Caucasian woman became Nicole Zeller, and the elderly Asian resumed her identity as Charan Pornthip. Everyone seemed satisfied except Alex. He asked to see the student nurse.

This young woman was in seclusion in the student nurses' residence near the hospital. She was sent for. After a few minutes, red-eyed and defiant, she appeared in the main lobby. Alex took her aside. They sat in upholstered stainless steel chairs next to a palmetto plant.

Alex said, "Mademoiselle, walk me through what happened after you were instructed to wheel Mademoiselle Églantine down to the morgue."

"I didn't wheel her, monsieur. We are not permitted to do that. After Doctor Doyle removed the EC and IV, a gurney was ordered, and two male attendants transferred her onto it and covered her. I cut off her admissions bracelet, made out the identification tag, attached it to the gurney, and accompanied the body to the morgue."

"You accompanied the body down the hall from her former room, into the elevator —"

"Into the elevator and down to the sub-basement, where the morgue is located."

"At no time while you were in attendance was there the opportunity for anyone to tamper with her identification?"

"No, monsieur."

"What happened when you reached the morgue?"

"We placed her in the corridor adjacent to the morgue. The attendants departed. I went inside, presented the decedent form, waited for a receipt, and returned to my floor."

"You placed her in the corridor?"

"Yes."

"Outside the morgue itself, unattended?"

"Yes. That's an altogether normal procedure."

"How long do you estimate she was in the corridor?"

"Perhaps a half hour. There were two ahead of her."

Alex stood. "Show me."

As it was now the visiting hour and the elevators were jammed, they took the stairs to the sub-basement. Predictably, the long corridor was white-walled, black-floored, and brightly lit. There were presently no corpses waiting outside the automatic double doors to the morgue.

Alex peered down the corridor. "Is there an exit from this sub-basement?"

"I don't know, monsieur. I always use the elevator."

There were several doors in both walls farther down the corridor. "Are those doors part of the morgue?"

"I don't know. I've never been down there."

"Let's have a look."

They walked down the corridor. The first door to the right was marked "Maintenance." Alex opened it. There were buckets, mops, a rotary waxing machine, a Peg-Board with assorted pliers, hacksaws, et cetera. He closed the door and continued down the corridor.

The student nurse asked, "What are we looking for, monsieur?"

"Angélique's gurney."

She stopped in her tracks.

"Mademoiselle, if Angélique Églantine is alive, as I believe she is, and she transferred her identification to Charan Pornthip, and transferred Charan Pornthip's to the Caucasian woman before leaving the hospital, we should find her discarded gurney down here somewhere, and, possibly, the identification tag of the Caucasian woman. If we do, you will be automatically exonerated of all responsibility for the so-called mixup."

The student nurse followed at a safe distance as Alex proceeded down the corridor, opening doors to a laundry room, a small gymnasium, an empty men's WC, and an empty ladies'. The corridor terminated in a ninety-degree turn to the right. Ahead, after the turn, was a staircase to street level marked "Exit," and, opposite, a steel door marked "Boiler Room."

Alex opened the boiler room door. The room was dark. He found a light switch and flicked it on. Just inside the door hung three white, cotton coveralls on brass coat hooks. A fourth coat hook was unoccupied. The missing gurney was parked next to the hot-air draft control of the heating system. On it was a rumpled sheet and a paper tag on which appeared the name Faïence Krumwiede.

Alex handed the tag to the student nurse. "Inform the coroner that the body recently identified as Angélique Églantine is Nicole Zeller after all, and that the deceased identified as Nicole Zeller is actually Faïence Krumwiede. I will inform the hospital that you are blameless and that Mademoiselle Églantine discharged herself this afternoon at approximately the same time they reported her death to me by telephone."

The Maison

Alex put out an APB to include Customs and Immigration, Passport, Interpol, all airlines, and SCNF. The APB was accompanied by photographs of Angélique as she appeared in her last four roles, plus a notation that she might be wearing white, cotton coveralls.

As Angélique might not be aware that both Pierre-Yves and Véronique were in custody, Alex took the additional precaution of placing a stake at Pierre-Yves' residence and at Véronique's flat. He then went down to the cell block to confront Véronique. She was still groggy from the Valium.

"Your performance at the hospital promoted you from a misdemeanor to a felony."

She shrugged. "I do what I can to help."

"You could help yourself back to a misdemeanor if you'd cooperate."

"Cooperate how? Tell you where she is? I don't know where she is." Véronique leaned forward and shouted, "Listen to me! I don't want to see her in prison! If she's in prison, she'll die! Really die! Do you understand what I'm saying? Acting is her life! Not acting will be her death!" She leaned closer and her eyes shone. "Great actors beguile by deception," she cried. "Pity we're not at war! She'd make a superb spy!"

Alex returned to his office. Still on his feet after thirty-six sleepless hours, he gingerly pecked out his latest report on the office word processor, made a copy, and rang for an Inspecteur-trainee to carry it down to File. Joëlle answered the ring. Without a trace of condescension, she explained to Alex that he no longer needed to make hard copies for File. She said that the Maison's new computer system was designed to network. That is, all the computers could interface, could access files and run programs.

Alex peered at the bright, trusting, healthy young face and seriously contemplated early retirement.

"Interface," he muttered. "Where did you learn 'interface'?"

"At the école normale."

"Can you do long division, for God's sake?"

She grinned. "With a calculator."

"I expect you want my job."

"Eventually."

"You can have it now. Meanwhile, run this hard copy down to File just in case my bloody PC WP doesn't IF. And take my calls."

Joëlle left. Alex put his feet on his desk and leaned back. Before she reached the first floor, he was asleep. The time was 6:20 P.M.

Joëlle didn't wake Alex for the fax that came in from the Ministry of the Interior at 7:02. It stated:

Persons accessible to the government witness program confirm that when Charles Fannois learned he was no longer a suspect in the de la Pagerie murder, the staff of the psychiatric hospital in Toulouse noticed a marked change in his behavior. He has stopped painting compassionate faces on old TV sets and now spends his time in the hospital library reading the newspaper and law books. He has been reevaluated and approved for weekend passes.

At 8:15, however, Joëlle came upstairs and shook Alex. He snorted, opened his eyes, and said, " 'Blue Turning Gray over You,' Fats Waller, b flat." He then blinked and added, "Whatsit?"

"Phone for you, Chef," Joëlle replied, and shook him again.

"Whosit?"

"Gus."

Alex was instantly awake. He pushed the blinking button on his desk phone and picked up. "Yes?"

The deep, resonant voice was barely audible. "Chef-Inspecteur Grismolet?"

"Speaking."

"She's here."

Rue Pirandello

Appropriate to his vocation, Gus lived in the north central section of the Thirteenth Arrondissement on the street named after the noted playwright.

Joëlle's three years as Motor Scooter (female) No. 2 now paid off. With a veteran taxi driver's knowledge of the streets of Paris, she unerringly directed the three unmarked police cars along the boulevards and avenues of the Eighth and Seventh, and across back streets and allées in the Sixth and Thirteenth that Alex had never heard of, let alone seen. They reached Rue Pirandello in less than ten minutes. The local Commissariat of Police had already closed off the street by the time they arrived. A crowd had gathered behind the barricades.

Alex ordered the basement, the fire escapes, and all entrances to the old residential building covered. He and Joëlle started up the stairs to Gus's third-floor flat. There was no elevator.

At the second-floor landing, Alex whispered instructions to Joëlle and had her ring Gus's number on her mobile phone. Gus answered.

Joëlle said, "Sûreté, monsieur. Your pizza is here."

"Send it up," Gus replied and rang off.

They climbed the remaining flight and found the flat. The door was slightly open. Gus was stretched out on a chaise longue with a bottle of Chartreuse in one hand and a 5.5-millimetre Mauser automatic in the other. He was drunk.

"She's in the bathroom," he said. "She appeared on my doorstep, seeking sanctuary, innocent as a fucking lamb. Can you beat that for chutzpah? I mean, donnez-moi a break!" He handed Alex the gun. "I wanted to be sure she didn't leave before you got here. Let me know if you want a drink."

Alex walked through the bedroom and opened the door to the bath. Angélique had just stepped out of the shower when Gus shot her. She lay half in and half out of the shower stall under an enormous beach towel emblazoned with purple letters advertising *The Visit*, St-Jean-de-Luz. Apart from the tiny hole in the centre of her forehead, she had the scrubbed face of a child, unremarkable but inquisitive, and expressive, especially around the eyes, which were dark brown. At the moment, her expression seemed — Alex could think of no other phrase — one of relief.

Before they took him away, Gus made a statement. "I cannot forgive her for what she has done. She was utterly without remorse and deserved to die." His statement was widely misinterpreted, both at the time of his arrest and later.

28

Le Yacht Club

IN SPITE OF HIS FATIGUE, Alex could not get to sleep.

He found he'd developed a nagging respect for Angélique. That was not an unusual sentiment in the hunter for his quarry. But this one had eluded him. She was brought down, not by him, but because she was at the apex of an emotional triangle not of her making. The passion had not been hers. The passion had been Pierre-Yves'. And Gus's, when he found out.

Her passion was to pretend. She would not have understood this ending at all.

He turned over in his bunk for the tenth time, put on his Walkman phones, listened to a few minutes of the Lully opera *Atys,* and slept.

He slept until mid-morning. When he groggily climbed the companion ladder onto the bridge deck, he found a large, flat wooden crate in the cockpit. His name and address were stenciled on the front and back. There was no return address.

He fetched a claw hammer from below, carried the crate

ashore, and pried it open on the quai. He carefully removed a slim, paper-wrapped frame. When he tore away the wrapping, he was stunned. The frame contained a dazzling watercolor portrait of *Le Yacht Club* as she might appear if she were floating in a clear, amethyst Caribbean cove, surrounded by lush jungle vegetation and exotic tropical birds. The painting was signed DGB.

There was a note.

Monday

Cher Alex:

Please accept this as a memento of our gratitude and affection.

I fly my son home tomorrow. Honoré follows in a few days, after a brief — probably his last — visit to Perpignan, where he was born. God bless.

Délice Géronte Bloch

Without hesitation, Alex hung the painting in Philippa's cabin, where the morning sun would illuminate but not fade the vivid colours.

He admired the work for a few moments, locked up the barge, then walked to Mariette's for a fresh croissant, and caught the No. 7. Emerging from the Opéra métro, he dawdled across the Madeleine and along Rue St-Honoré, pretending to be a normal Parisien for whom homicide was as alien as the tropopause.

Délice's portrait of *Le Yacht Club* in a lagoon had given him the wanderlust. He was revisited by a youthful urge to emulate those great French sailors Gerbault, Moitessier, Colas, and Lacombe, complex men who, singlehanded, ventured across the world's vast oceans in search of simplicity. Then he remembered the Canal du Midi and Philippa.

The Commissaire greeted him warmly. "Aren't you entitled to a few days off?"

"The Maison owes me six weeks, Commissaire."

"I can't spare you for six weeks. And I can't spare you and Varnas at the same time. You don't want me to disturb Varnas on his honeymoon, do you?"

"No."

"Take two weeks."

29

Le Canal du Midi

SIROCCO was waiting for them at the Grand Bassin. While Philippa shopped for ship's stores at the local super-marché, Alex refamiliarized himself with the vessel's operation, saw to the fuel and water tanks, and studied the *Waterway Guide,* which contained descriptions of the canal, the locks, and general items of interest. At some point, he climbed into the cockpit to check the propane tank and came face-to-face with Thérèse, holding the carton of galley stores she'd saved from his aborted first cruise.

"So, you are going at last, Monsieur Alex?"

"If the phone doesn't ring."

She laughed and blushed at the same time. "Marie-Rose is out with Vercingétorix. Otherwise she would be here to thank you herself for your part in her deliverance."

"Mine was a very small part."

"I wish to thank you as well," she said. She stood self-consciously for a moment, then impulsively seized his hand and fled.

Philippa returned soon after with a taxi full of groceries,

wine, bread, and cheese. They spent an hour stowing, after which Alex fired up the diesel to let it warm. As they prepared to cast off, the manager of the boat-hire firm waved from the office door, shouted, and pointed to his ear and mouth. Phone. Alex groaned. Philippa held the vessel alongside as he ran to the office.

Joëlle was on the phone from the Maison assignment desk. She said, "This is just in, Chef. Charles Fannois was found this morning floating facedown in the Tet River under the Pont Joffre in Perpignan. Do you want to handle it?"

The saintly face of Honoré Bloch flashed across the screen of Alex's mind and disappeared. "No, thank you," he said. "Perpignan is not on our itinerary."

Now, at last, in late afternoon, with an orange sun stationary in the clear western sky, and sycamores casting their long shadows across the bassin, they eased *Sirocco* away from the quai and moved slowly toward the first gates of the four-stage St-Roch lock. The gates were already open.

They entered, looped their lines around bollards fore and aft, and lay against the curving lock wall on the left. The gates closed behind them. The water level dropped. They eased their lines as *Sirocco* slowly descended to the next level. The lower gate now opened and they moved into the second lock.

This procedure was repeated four times. Philippa underwent a moment of dry mouth while first performing the locking exercise, but, by the fourth lock, she was exhilarated. The beauty and simplicity of the seventeenth century was upon her. She felt time-warped and transformed.

As they left the fourth lock and entered the magnificent tunnel of trees opening ahead, she stood on the cabin top and, out of pure joy, opened her arms and went up on half toe. The day seemed warmer, the air sweeter, and life more delicious than at any time in recent memory. She felt blessed.

Suddenly, clothed in sunlight, she reached for the sky and performed a grande arabesque. At the same instant, she noticed a huge-eyed young girl and a dog watching from the canal towpath. The dog barked and wagged. Philippa smiled and waved.

Later, alone in the kitchen with her aunt and Vercingétorix, the child said, "Guess what, Aunt Thérèse?"

"What, chérie?"

"We saw Our Lady again. This time she smiled and waved."